A Dragon To Agincourt

A Dragon
to Agincourt

Malcolm Pryce

Cover Illustration: Dylan Williams

ISBN: 0 86243 684 2

Dinas is an imprint of Y Lolfa

Published and printed in Wales
by Y Lolfa Cyf., Talybont, Ceredigion SY24 5AP
e-mail ylolfa@ylolfa.com
website ylolfa.com
tel (01970) 832 304
fax 832 782

PROLOGUE

IT IS SPRING-TIME, in the year of Our Lord, 1401. These are troubled times in Wales, where the people resent the growing power of the Marcher barons. In the previous autumn, a Welsh nobleman was crowned Prince of Wales and his followers had ravaged lands held by the English, until they were defeated outside Welshpool, since when, their leader, Owain Glyndŵr, seemed to have vanished into the mountain mists.

In Powys, a young man yearned to follow the family tradition and travel to Europe to serve as a mercenary bowman. On the Continent there was always a demand for men who could handle the Welsh long-bow, for its effect on the field of battle was devastating. Now, however, many of these men were making their way home, eager to serve a fellow countryman, and young Huw Gethin had not much longer to wait before his daydreams became reality.

Chapter 1

The autumnal wind howled over the bleak Welsh hillside, buffeting the large house which stood in a shallow hollow. Inside, a group of men sat around the hearth. John Leggatt was one of them and he drew back when a cloud of smoke billowed down the open chimney, then, with a curse, settled himself once more. The rickety chair on which he sat groaned under his weight and Leggatt made a wry grin, thinking it likely that at any moment he could be sprawling on the floor amongst its splintered frame. He studied the man who sat opposite him, the handsome Welsh Prince, Owain Glyndŵr, and wondered if such a spectacle would force a laugh or even a smile, to lift his air of dejection.

John continued to watch for a while, aware that Glyndŵr's mind was far away from this isolated farm. His face wore a blank look and the normally twinkling eyes scarcely blinked when more smoke belched into the room. The strained silence, which had gripped everyone after they had eaten supper, was getting on John's nerves. He stood up and faced his companions but addressed his words to Glyndŵr.

"Come now, my lord," he said, raising his voice above the roar in the chimney, "all is not lost. There are many stout hearts that will rally to your call, come spring."

His companions mumbled their agreement and,

sorrowfully, Owain let his eyes travel over the group.

Leggatt continued to speak. "You have lost much this past winter, possibly more than anyone else, yet do not give up the struggle, I beseech you."

Owain stared at him for a while then said, "You have never spoken truer, my friend. I have lost a great deal. My estates, my sources of income and, worst of all, my beloved home at Sycharth, all were taken from me, or destroyed, in a few short weeks. I was called a prince one month, a pauper the next." Glyndŵr got to his feet and placed a hand on Leggatt's shoulder. "Yet, all these losses are of no account to me tonight. My thoughts are full of Margaret and our children," he said gruffly. "Not knowing where they are and whether they are safe and well weighs heavily on me."

Desperate to distract Glyndŵr's thoughts, John sought for a new topic. There was little point in continuing in this present vein, for they had had no news of Owain's family for several weeks. Glyndŵr's wife, Margaret, had taken their children and gone to seek safety with her family, near Flint, and no-one knew whether or not she had reached her goal. Messengers sent secretly by Owain had been unable to discover her whereabouts.

"Do you honestly believe that any man would answer another call to arms from Owain of Glyndŵr?" he asked. "The shambles outside Welshpool must surely have made them lose confidence in me."

"The men were confused by the appearance of the King's standard from an unexpected quarter," John Leggatt replied. "They were suddenly fighting to their front and to their rear. Men do not act well in those circumstances. You did the sensible thing when you ordered them to scatter." He tossed a log onto the fire, sending a shower of sparks flying upwards. "I have heard that they did well enough against Grey of Ruthin."

His mention of the name had the effect he desired. Owain moved away from the fire and began to pace angrily up and down the room.

"By all the saints in Heaven," he said through gritted teeth, "could I lay my hands around that schemer's throat, he would never again connive to enrich himself at another man's expense. He is the root cause of this sorry business. I had no quarrel with the King, yet for reasons of his own, Henry chose to aid Grey of Ruthin, the villain of the piece."

"It is my guess that the King had little choice," one of the others commented. "His hold on the English throne is far from secure. He needs the support of the Marcher Lords and, had he refused to aid Grey, he would have damaged his standing with them."

"We know that now, brother," Owain snapped, halting in front of the spokesman. "It was a likelihood that should have been foreseen; by myself more than anyone, and I would probably repeat the error in the same circumstance. To have allowed Grey to march in and steal my lands is not in my nature. I will swear to you that some day I shall extract full payment and more from our neighbour."

He returned to his seat and let his eyes roam across the faces around him. Apart from his brother, who was a younger image of himself, they were a hard-bitten lot. Their shaven features were weathered brown by the southern sun, their clothing and weapons worn by much use. One of them had a scar which ran the length of his cheekbone, the old wound showing white against the tanned skin. Though their dress varied in colour and design, all wore one item in common: the leather jerkin, the sleeves of which were cut short above the elbow, favoured by those who served as bowmen. Owain glanced across at the unstrung bows stacked neatly in a corner.

"What of you and your men, John?" he asked Leggatt. "You know how little I possess and it would be wrong of me to make you promises of payment which I may never be able to keep." He saw several of the bowmen shift uneasily at his words and wondered if raising this subject had been a mistake. Still, it was a matter which had best be settled now.

"We have talked the matter through, my lord," Leggatt answered. "Not one of them owes his allegiance to me. They are free to leave whenever they please, most of them, though, including myself, wish to serve you, no matter that there are no terms between us. The others are prepared to stay throughout this coming summer. All they ask is that they be provided with food and ale. "For myself," he said firmly, "it is a welcome change to serve a man whom I hold in high regard. I believe that you have a future to look forward to and am content to wait for better days."

Leggatt gestured towards Tudor, younger brother of Owain Glyndŵr, and smiled down at the nobleman, who had been sitting quietly. "The message your brother brought today may hold a ray of hope for all of us," he said, turning his smile on Glyndŵr.

Owain looked into Leggat's grey eyes. He felt a surge of affection toward the mercenary and he smiled back.

"I thank you, John," he said warmly. "I shall remember this moment." He fell silent for a while, thoughts churning in his mind, then he spoke to Tudor.

"Are you sure that it was Henry Don who met up with

you, brother?" he asked. "It could be that we walk into a trap set by Grey. He is well able to think up such a scheme."

"I can not be positive, Owain," Tudor answered. "You know that I have never met the man before, but he knew so much about your days at the Inns of Court, and his tales of the wild evenings you spent together at the *White Hart* tavern led me to believe that he was genuine."

"So be it," Owain said after a pause. "We shall leave in the morning. It will be a difficult journey, we must travel with caution. Let us get some sleep."

While John Leggatt lay on the straw pallet which served as his bed, he thought back over the past few years. Bored with garrison life in one castle or another, he had taken service with Henry Bolingbroke, son of the famous John of Gaunt, Duke of Lancaster, with whom he had travelled through much of Europe, on the road to Jerusalem. They had been joined by men of many nations *en route* and when they came to the shores of the Aegean, Henry's force was swallowed up in the multitude. This was as close to the Holy Land as John came. Within days, the nobles began to quarrel amongst themselves about the structure of command, and Bolingbroke, short of money, became disenchanted with his fellow knights. He endured the petty arguments and the indecision for two more weeks, then led his men on their long march home.

While travelling homeward through Bavaria, a score of bowmen, including John Leggatt, had taken their leave of Bolingbroke, who was only too pleased at having fewer mouths to feed, and had readily agreed to their wish to serve a local baron, himself a mercenary. Following his banner, the bowmen plied their trade in Spain, France and Italy. They were marching north towards the Baltic, when news of an uprising in Wales, led by Owain Glyndŵr himself, reached them. More than half of the bowmen were of Welsh blood and they had decided to head for their homeland, with John Leggatt as their leader.

It proved difficult to meet up with Glyndŵr, Prince of Wales. However, they finally found him and a handful of his followers on the banks of the upper Dee. When Leggatt and Glyndŵr discovered that both had served under Henry Bolingbroke, they had much to talk about that formed a bond of mutual respect between them. Glyndŵr remarked that fate was indeed a strange force. Henry Bolingbroke now sat on the throne of England, as King Henry IV, and numbered his past esquire as one of his enemies.

Settling himself more comfortably on the rustling straw mattress, John smiled into the darkness. What the future held for him he did not know, but he had not felt so contented for a long time. It really was good to be back in Wales.

Chapter 2

The buzzard wheeled in the sky, then plunged downwards after prey. Huw Gethin watched the bird disappear and he stretched his lanky frame. It was a blessing to be alive on a day such as this. The winds had finally died away, leaving the skies cloudless.

To the north of where he stood, he could see the far off peaks of Cader Idris, the wild range of Aran Fawddwy lay to his right. He walked to the crest of the hill and looked down on the familiar scene. The infant Hafren ran eastwards, dividing the broad meadow land, and it was joined here by the waters of Cwmdu. The cwm itself ran southwards, a huge gash in the earth's surface, some four miles in length, and came to a dead end several hundred feet high. A streak of white indicated where the waters from the high ground plunged into the cwm in a sheer drop. Hundreds of years ago, men had cut a path diagonally into the rock face, to shorten their way south, a route he avoided when possible.

The sun was setting and Huw felt the air grow cool. He gave an ear-piercing whistle and an answering whistle came from somewhere out of sight. Suddenly, he saw a hound appear on the sky line and come bounding towards him. He grinned, bracing himself as the gap narrowed rapidly and, with an enormous leap, the hound struck him in the chest, knocking the lad to the ground, and thrust a wet muzzle against his face.

"Off, Pero, off!" he shouted through his laughter. "Seek Hywel. Away with you and seek him out."

The hound stood over him for a few moments, tail swishing, then, at Huw's repeated command, it loped off. The hound was still quite close when Huw saw the first of his father's flock come into view, followed by the slight figure of his younger brother, Hywel Gethin.

"Has your day gone well?" he asked, when Hywel reached him.

"Well enough," his brother answered, gesturing toward the sheep. "They found some spring grass on the south slope and did not wander far. I've spent much of the day working on a new poem. It's not finished yet, so you will have to be patient."

The two lads laughed at his words. Although they were brothers, they were as unlike in tastes as in looks. Huw did not share Hywel's love of poetry and Hywel knew that Huw would listen only out of politeness.

"What of yours?" Hywel asked in turn. "Has anything happened to cause your blood to race?"

"Only the usual movement amongst the holdings," Huw said. "Even old Griffith Lloyd has had a quiet day."

They looked across the meadows to the large stone and timber mansion which stood some distance from the Hafren, their humour dying. The past few weeks had seen a great deal of activity around Plas Hirnant, home of their neighbour, Griffith Lloyd. An ancient ditch, which formed a circle around the building and stables, had been cleared of undergrowth and post holes had been dug along the inner perimeter.

"Griffith seems to be preparing for trouble," Hywel

remarked. "I pray that he is not going to start it with us again."

"He would be a fool to do so," Huw said. "The men of Cwmdu have pledged their support to father. We would be more than a match for the old rascal and his retainers."

The trouble of which Hywel spoke had occurred three years back, when Griffith Lloyd purchased the property. A man who had acquired his wealth by a combination of marriage and ruthless trading practices in distant Shrewsbury, Griffith Lloyd had attempted to take over all the meadow land. The rich pasture which lay on the south bank of the Hafren had, for generations, belonged to Argoed, ancestral home of the Gethins, and Griffith had been served formal notice of this fact. The temptation to take the land and hold it by force had been too strong for their neighbour, however.

One morning, Morgan Gethin drove his small herd down to the meadow and discovered three of Griffith's retainers there, guarding their master's cattle. A man of few words, Morgan Gethin asked them to leave and, when he was ignored, he grabbed the nearest fellow and heaved him into the stream. The bigger of the remaining two then made the error of attacking Morgan. A mighty blow knocked the man senseless, and his comrade fled. Morgan had knelt beside the man he had felled, whereupon, the man recovered enough to strike Morgan Gethin with a dagger. The blade passed through the muscle of his upper arm, its blade slicing against his ribs.

Roaring with pain and rage, Morgan kicked the dagger clear, dragged the struggling man to the bank and booted him into the Hafren. He was desperately trying to stem the flow of blood from his wound, when Griffith Lloyd galloped across the meadow and savagely reined his horse to a stop on the further bank. From here, he screamed abuse at the bloodied figure opposite but made no attempt to cross the stream.

Morgan's wound, thanks to his wife's ministrations, had healed well, though the use of his left arm was now limited. Griffith had let the matter rest, though on numerous occasions the Gethins had seen him at a distance, his gaze intent on their land. The Gethins remained ever vigilant, for they felt certain that the man would try again to trespass there.

"Come on, little brother," Huw said. "My belly tells me that it wants its supper."

Between them, they began to drive the sheep along a well used path for several hundred yards. Reaching the place where the path led down to the Hafren, Huw took the lead, following its zigzag route onto the meadow. The sound of a high-pitched voice came to them through the gathering gloom and, with a deep, baying call, Pero ran ahead.

"I hope the hound shows more respect for father than he did for you," Hywel chuckled.

They came to the wide track which led up to the mouth of the cwm, and smelled wood smoke before the holding's long shape came into view. They coaxed the sheep into the pens and waited for their father to bring in the cattle, eight blacks and two whites. The blacks were put into their byre and the two white cattle were led into some stalls which made up one end of the house. Here, with the ponies, they were as safe for the night as possible. Hiding their smiles, the brothers watched Morgan inspect each animal in turn, fondling their distinctive reddish ears as he spoke softly to them.

"Not much longer now, my lovely," the big man cooed,

stroking the swollen flanks of one of the beasts. "Let us pray that all goes well for you. You also, my handsome one," he added touching the larger of the two. "The good Lord knows that you have cost me a pretty penny. It would be a blessing to get some of it back."

It was plain to everyone that the two white cows were Morgan's pride and joy. He had travelled to Pembroke to buy them and they had, indeed, cost him nearly all his savings.

"See to the hound, will you, Hywel," he ordered. "Something tells me that the brute is hungry."

Hywel dutifully picked up the dog's bowl and called a greeting to his mother, who was in the kitchen. Satisfied that all was well in the stables, the others followed him.

"I take it that you have had a quiet day, Huw," Morgan said, coming to a stop. "Nothing out of the ordinary to tell of?"

"Not a thing," Huw replied. "My day would have been better spent working down here."

Morgan shrugged his broad shoulders and stared up into the night sky for a few moments.

"The chances of danger are slim, I grant you," he said eventually. "Yet we cannot afford to take any risks. Should any body of men appear, it is vital that we in the cwm receive sufficient warning. I wonder what has taken place in the north?" he mused. "Since that fight near Welshpool, there has been little news. Glyndŵr has not been slain or taken captive yet, and he is not a man who would give in easily. It could well be that, with the weather improving, he will begin another campaign."

He lowered his gaze and looked at Huw's slender shape, noticing that the lad now stood almost as tall as himself. During the past year it seemed as if his son had grown by the day. When he finally filled out, Morgan told himself, Huw would have the right build to handle a long-bow. He sighed as a complex series of thoughts entered his head.

The tantalising smell of cooking meat wafted through the doorway as Hywel hurried past with the hound's bowl.

"Come on, lad," Morgan said. "Let's not keep your mother waiting."

Emma Gethin ladled a steaming stew into individual bowls and she smiled a greeting as the two seated themselves at the table, where they were shortly joined by Hywel. As usual, they ate with relish, their conversation limited to small talk. Later, as Emma moved about the room, Morgan sat by the hearth, sipping a tankard of weak ale and watching her. At thirty-six, his wife was still a striking woman, taller than average and slim of figure. You could not call her beautiful but, with her raven hair and dark skin, Emma made many men look twice at her.

Morgan considered his two sons; Huw had Emma's colouring and build, Hywel was shorter and of fair countenance. They differed in temperament and manner also. The eldest lad was quiet by nature, but would have finished a task while others yet talked about it. During the long winter evenings, Huw loved to listen to Morgan's tales of his years serving as an archer under the banner of John of Gaunt. It had been during this service that Morgan had met his wife to be. He was one of the garrison of Monmouth castle and, when the two were married, they set up their first home within its walls. On the death of his father, Morgan had given up his chosen life and returned to Argoed. As the eldest son, he inherited the better half of the land, while his brother, Iolo, received the remainder. There had been good and bad in those days of soldiering, and the likelihood was that Huw would soon have a taste of the same.

When Emma completed her chores, she joined her family at the hearth and asked Hywel to play for her. He was happy to oblige, running his young fingers over the strings of an old harp, its gentle notes adding to the restful scene. Morgan watched Huw out of the corner of his eye and was not surprised when the youth stood up and walked to the far end of the room. He reached up into the rafters and brought down the six-foot-long staff which Morgan had bought him the previous summer. Then he went to Emma's work box, picked out a handful of sheep's wool and began methodically to rub it along the bow's length. His fingers, Morgan observed, seemed to caress the wood as Hywel's did the harp strings. He had long suspected that Huw harboured thoughts that he himself had held at the age of seventeen, and he glanced uneasily at his wife.

Huw was examining the bow's horned tip when Emma spoke, her tone causing Hywel to stop playing. "Is that all you can find to do?" she asked sharply. "I swear you care more for that bow than you do for anything else. I expect you have spent the day filling your head with dreams of soldiering in far off places."

Unable to meet his mother's gaze, Huw stared down at the flagged floor, his mind in a state of confusion.

"Oh, Huw, put such thoughts from your mind, I beg you," she said, in a softer tone. "What with the trouble in the north and Griffith Lloyd up to no good, you are needed here."

Morgan stared at her, scarcely hiding his astonishment. Not once had Emma given a hint that she shared his own suspicions. "Now, Emma, calm yourself," he said apprehensively. "There is nothing wrong in Huw learning to use a bow, and show me one lad of his age that does not wonder what lies beyond the mountains. I know that I did, at his age."

"Do you want our son to follow in your footsteps?" Emma snapped, her eyes flashing at him.

Recognising the danger signals, Morgan thought desperately how to find a way out of the trap he had landed himself in. "I'm glad I did what I did, Emma," he said, suddenly inspired. "Otherwise, I would never have met you."

Emma opened her mouth as though to speak, thought better of it, and gave him a look which said more than words. She gave a deep sigh and returned her attention to Huw. "Keep in mind what I have said. You are needed here at Argoed. Now, play on, Hywel."

Once more the music filled the room, and Huw gave his father a look of gratitude. The big man winked in return, glad to let the matter rest.

Later, in the small room that he shared with his brother, Huw lay awake in the darkness. It had surprised him that Emma had known his innermost thoughts.

Chapter 3

Once again, Owain Glyndŵr sat amongst a group of trusted friends and relations. One of these men was his brother-in-law, Robert Puleston, who had brought news that Margaret and the children were safe, not at the home of her parents, the Hanmers, as had been planned, but with the Pulestons.

"You have my everlasting gratitude, Robert," Glyndŵr said, in a voice thickened with emotion. "Your news has taken a great weight from my shoulders. I must admit that my thoughts lately have been more with my family than on our present predicament. The need to keep them hidden from the world has not helped me, I can tell you. These past weeks without news of them have been endless."

"I can assure you, Owain, the secrecy was necessary," Robert Puleston replied. "The Hanmers' home was being watched by Grey's men. Your lady almost rode into their trap. It seemed wise to offer her my home and not send word of it to anyone. I believed that the risk of trying to contact you was too great. However, they are in fine spirits, though missing you. Also, as you can see, Henry Don and I have not been idle."

All those present knew Henry Don, by reputation, if not by sight. He was one of the top men in the country, having recently been appointed as one of the stewards of the Lordship of Kidwelly. The other newly appointed steward was William Gwyn ap Rhys.

Some of the men gathered at the long table Glyndŵr knew well, some brought back vague memories, while the remainder were unknown to him. His gaze came to rest on a dark, thick-set man who sat at the far end of the table.

"Greetings, cousin, I trust all goes well with you and Rhys?" he asked.

"That it does, my lord," William Tudor answered. "Rhys wishes to renew his pledge of support to you, although he decided to remain with our men. They are full of fight and need a restraining hand. The ease with which we took Conwy castle has made many a man restless and eager to be rid of the English crown but I must confess that we were both at a loss as to what our future actions should be. The news of this meeting, with your presence likely, has given us a sense of purpose once more."

Glyndŵr knew that his two cousins, with their fiercely independent men of Gwynedd, were his staunchest allies. Between them, the two had caused panic amongst the castles dotted around northern Wales. He looked now at the young man seated next to William Tudor. Despite his rather unkempt appearance, the fellow had an air that commanded attention. He was Iolo Goch, the famous bard, whose paeans of praise for the great and the good had kept him in bread and ale and given him a soft couch by a warm fire for years. He knew how to be pleasant, how to flatter and how to wheedle his way into the good graces of the upper class families. He was also a source of trustworthy information, gathered during his travels round the various noble houses of Wales. He probably knew more of the pedigrees of the top families than they themselves knew.

"I am glad that God has protected you, Iolo," Glyndŵr said respectfully. "You have been much in my prayers. I feared that you may have been taken prisoner, or worse." He stared into the man's startling blue eyes and smiled warmly. "It does my heart good to see you, old friend. Have you been busily engaged in keeping the spark of freedom alive?"

"That I have, my lord, though not alone, I can assure you," Iolo Goch answered in his rich voice. "We bards have been forced to practise our calling by use of subterfuge over the past century. We are well-trained in the skill of evading the English, as you well know."

Fanatically opposed to foreign rule, since the death of the last native Princes, the bards had led lives fraught with danger but, between them, had kept alive the dream of a free Wales in the minds of many men. Banned by successive kings of England, not once, over a period of a hundred years, had a bard been betrayed or brought to trial. A polite cough brought Glyndŵr out of his brief reverie and he turned toward Henry Don.

"Forgive me, Henry," he said. "I realise the need for haste. Please begin."

"Your desire to speak with those who have served you so well is understandable," Henry Don replied. "However, we should not linger here too long." He pushed back his chair and strode over to the room's only window, where he peered through the opaque glass. "The reason that we are here is simple. Our setback at Welshpool must not be allowed to deflect us from our aims. Every man in this room is here to pledge his support, be it with money or fighting men. I have spoken to each in turn and we are of one mind. You have been hailed as the true Prince of

Wales and, therefore, the conflict must be widened throughout the whole land."

He walked back to his seat and looked earnestly at Glyndŵr. "Some of these men are from the south. They assure me that their people are as restless as our own, all they need is leadership. Think on it, Owain, we are not strong enough on our own. With their added numbers, we would be a force strong enough to deter any Marcher lord; even the King himself."

Glyndŵr sat in silence for a while, turning Henry's proposal over in his mind. At the mention of the title bestowed on him, he shifted uneasily in his chair, a movement noticed by the others. Yet despite this, he felt a stir of excitement course through him.

"You seem sure that the men in the south will accept my leadership," he said. "Why should *they* acknowledge me as their Prince?"

"Do you need ask such a question?" Iolo Goch cried out. "Shall I remind you yet again of your blood line?"

He got to his feet and, placing his hands on the table, leaned forward to lend weight to his words. "You are a descendant of the great Lord Rhys who ruled the lands in the south so nobly. His name is still revered in those parts. Here in the north, you alone can lay claim to the title. Should you doubt me, then ask your cousin William. The Tudors have always paid great attention to matters like this." He drew himself up to his full height so suddenly, that his cloak fell open, showing a flash of red lining. "Our people are yearning to have a Welsh Prince again. They care not a jot for Henry Bolingbroke's son, even though he was born in Monmouth. Do not deny them this chance, I beseech you."

He sat down, though he continued to stare intently along

the length of the table. What he had said was true enough and Owain already knew it.

"There is more news besides," Henry Don added quickly. "Hotspur has withdrawn his support from the King's son. He has left the lad at Chester and returned to Northumberland. Rumour has it that he and the rest of the Percy family are disenchanted with the King. They could easily become friendly to our cause."

These words caused a ripple of excited conversation to go through the men, as Don knew it would. This was news indeed, Glyndŵr thought. Should this powerful family become his ally and challenge the King, then Wales could be his for the taking. Strong though he was, Henry Bolingbroke would be stretched to breaking point, were he faced by two armies. The outcome could only be his downfall.

"You must reach a decision today," Henry Don urged. "There is much to be done, should you agree to move south."

"The omens could not be better, cousin," William added. "Rhys and I will keep the English busy here in the north. We shall not face them in battle but we can lead them in a merry dance through our mountains."

Glyndŵr rose to his feet and looked around at the expectant faces. He felt strongly the need to think the situation through on his own. The responsibility of leadership was a heavy burden, when so many lives might be at stake and the outcome uncertain. "I beg you to be patient, my friends," he said. "I must have a short while to myself. Have no fears, for you shall have my decision the moment it has been taken."

Leaving the room, he strode down a wide hall and let himself out into the sunshine. A short distance away, he saw John Leggatt standing guard amongst a windbreak of pines and walked over to him.

"Does all go well with you?" Glyndŵr asked, noting the bow strung at the ready.

"Well enough, my lord," the mercenary answered, "though this is not the safest of places. The land around us is too thickly wooded for my peace of mind. I have stationed the others further afield, yet we could not cover every foot track."

Owain nodded his understanding and began to move away.

"What of the meeting, my lord?" John Leggatt asked tentatively. "Has the outcome been all that you wished?"

"Far more than I had expected," came the answer. "I need to think on it for a while."

Directly in front of him lay a small clearing, which led to a stream, and Glyndŵr walked down to the water's edge. John's voice called out, warning him to go no further, so he seated himself on an old tree stump and began to review the words spoken. All of what had been said was true enough, he thought. With the men of both south and north under one leader, they would be a force to be reckoned with. Also, the possibility of an alliance with the Percy family was an opportunity too great to be missed. What he could be sure of was sweet vengeance on the hated Grey of Ruthin, who had dared lay an ambush for Glyndŵr's dear wife and children.

His thoughts then turned to Margaret. Their separation had already lasted over the winter months and he had had enough of it. To be together once more would mean that he must make the move, whatever the risks. He had everything to gain and nothing more to lose, he decided. Getting to his feet, he walked briskly back toward the watching bowman.

"Your pondering did not take long, my lord," John said, as he approached.

"I really do not have any choice, my friend," Glyndŵr said. He did not slow his stride as he passed, and John walked beside him for a few paces. "We shall be marching south," he added. "Tell your men that their Prince will have a need of them shortly."

Chapter 4

Morgan Gethin and Huw were out on the meadow and the older man was instructing his son in the use of the longbow. Huw was already tiring.

"Now, hold it there until I give the word," Morgan commanded. "Hold it steady, lad. Your arms are trembling like an old woman's."

Huw gritted his teeth and willed his limbs to steady themselves but the strain of holding the bowstring taut was unbearable. He began to think that his father would never give the order to let the arrow fly. To draw the goose feathers back to his ear had taken all his strength and to hold the bow in this position was almost beyond him.

"Loose." his tormentor finally snapped out.

With relief, Huw relaxed his three fingers and the arrow sped through the air. His target was an ancient sycamore at the far end of the meadow, and the lad watched the white flight climb and then fall to earth, about fifty paces short of the tree and some way to the right. Expecting a scornful comment, he faced his father and was surprised to see him smile.

"Not too far off," Morgan remarked. "A little different from handling a hunting bow, though, would you not agree?"

Huw nodded, then plucked another arrow from the bundle at his feet.

"Holding a drawn string is a good test of a man's

strength." Morgan told him. "You would do well to practise that as much as possible, to build the muscles needed to control the bow's power. Remember that your bow is made from elm; a tough wood but not as strong as yew. Now, shoot again, and release as soon as the feathers touch your cheek."

Huw did as he was told and the arrow sped straight, but again fell short. When all twenty arrows had been loosed, he placed one end of the bow against his heel and unstrung it. From where he stood, the flights looked like a cluster of white flowers, except for the first one, which stood alone.

"Here endeth the first lesson," Morgan said with a chuckle. "You did well, Huw. They have all travelled more than two hundred paces, your shooting is fair and straight, all you need now is more distance, which will come with more practice, I'm sure."

The fletcher who had sold Morgan the bow and arrows, for the sum of three shillings, had been an honest fellow. He had assured Morgan that, even with regular use, the bow would give good service for at least a year, and the big man had no doubts of that now. No longer able to draw back a bow string himself, since the injury to his arm, he'd had no choice but to take the fletcher's word.

With the arrows collected and tied in a bundle, the two made their way home across the meadow. It was a fine, early summer's evening, scented with new grass and wild flowers. Overhead, martins swept low, seeking insects.

"What of your daydreams, Huw?" Morgan asked. "Do you think that they will ever become a reality?"

His son remained silent for a while then stopped to face him. "I don't know what to think," he answered. "All

I do know is that I am unhappy when I think of my future."

"Then you must speak about what troubles you," Morgan said kindly. "There is nothing wrong in wanting to leave home, I can assure you. Is that what you want to do? Most men of your age feel the same urge. It's only natural that you wish to see other places and meet different people. I felt the same and took my leave."

"You were free to do so," Huw replied. "With me, it is different. You know how mother feels about me using this bow. You saw the look she gave me this evening. I'm no scholar or tradesman, Hywel is the farmer of the family, so a soldier's life is the only one open to me, or so it seems."

Morgan put his good arm around his son's shoulders and was about to speak when Huw added, "Don't misunderstand me; I love you and mother greatly. I like my life here, if it does seem rather dull sometimes. It's simply that I have a wish to see more of the world before I settle down."

"Then a bowman you must be," Morgan said. "I must warn you that it can be as dull as a rainy day in Cwmdu. You would have to contend with long periods of boredom, then, possibly, moments of fear when you are called on to fight. Ask any man who has seen military service, and he'll tell you the same. Few men will call you friend and, of those that do, some will be quick to forget this when danger threatens. Life as an archer is very different from what you imagine."

He stopped briefly and gave his high pitched call. The cattle raised their heads and slowly began to approach. Huw and Morgan drove the animals up the track towards Argoed.

"You do not have to make a decision now," Morgan

said, as the house came into view. "Give the matter some more thought during this summer. Besides, you will have to improve your archery before any nobleman would hire you. As for your mother, let me worry on her account. I have had problems with her before and, somehow, have succeeded in having my way. It's not always easy, though." he added with a smile.

When the cattle were safely penned indoors for the night, father and son entered the house. Hywel was already eating, although, as Huw noted with pleasure, he was not alone at the table. Seated beside him were his Uncle Iolo, brother to Morgan Gethin, and his Aunt Morwen.

"You two had best hurry," Morwen called out laughingly. "The way this youngster is eating, there will only be scrapings left over for you. I tell you, Emma, your skills with the cook pot will be the ruin of your menfolk."

Huw leaned over and fondly kissed his aunt's upturned face. "A good evening to you, Aunt Morwen," he said. "I see that you are as lovely as ever."

"Your brother has already paid me that compliment," Morwen replied. "Now, sit you down and eat."

Huw ate while keeping one ear on the conversation around him. His Uncle Iolo and Aunt Morwen were Huw's favourite visitors. A childless couple, they doted on their nephews, spoiling the lads at every opportunity.

"Iolo has brought you more ale, Morgan," Emma said. "I've given Morwen a cut of cloth in exchange."

"It should be a good brew. The fine weather aids the fermenting. Best take care when you are supping, lads," Iolo warned.

When the meal was over, the two women cleared the table while Iolo and Morgan went outside, where their talk was chiefly about the low price of wool. Over the past two years, demand for this commodity had lessened, making life difficult for the smallholders who depended on sheep for a living. In an attempt to earn money, the men of Cwmdu were following Morgan's example and turning to cattle, even though this was a long term policy. Iolo extracted a promise that he would have the first chance to buy Morgan's expected white calf, and then they changed the subject.

"What do you make of all that?" Iolo asked, pointing towards Plas Hirnant. "It would seem that your neighbour is expecting troubles of the worst kind. My hope is that the fighting in the north has ended. Life is hard enough as it is these days."

There had been a flurry of activity around the mansion lately. A few days previously, several great drays had brought a load of stout posts and these were now being set into the earth to form a formidable defence.

"I've no idea what the old devil is up to," Morgan replied. "The fact that he seems to be expecting trouble at Hirnant could mean that he is not planning to cause any for the rest of us."

Iolo looked at his brother affectionately, and said, "Lay your fears at rest; there are enough good men in Cwmdu to put a stop to any scheme that rascal dreams up."

"I pray that you are right," Morgan said softly.

"Well, now, we must be off," Iolo said, looking at the lengthening shadows. "It will be dark before we get home as it is. The saints watch over you and yours, brother."

The Gethins of Argoed watched their kinsfolk walk up the cwm, until they passed out of sight, then, settled themselves around the hearth, at the end of another day of routine.

The following morning the brothers spent working on the fallen sycamore, under the watchful eyes of Pero. Their father had set off early for Machynlleth, a twelve-mile ride away, while Emma busied herself around the house. The brothers used a long, double-handled saw to cut across a thick branch, using the minimum exertion, allowing the blade to do the work. Even so, when the sun was higher, they were both sweating profusely and had sawed some half dozen logs.

"Enough for now." Hywel gasped. "Let's rest a while. I swear my arms are going to drop off at any moment." He pulled his jerkin over his head and made for the stream. "Are you coming in?" he asked. "The water looks so inviting that I can't resist the urge."

"Then, you had best get undressed. No need to rouse mother's ire," Huw shouted after him.

He heard Hywel's cry of delight as his brother slid into the stream, and he flung off his own clothing, ran to the edge and jumped in, with the hound close at his heels. Laughing and shouting, the two lads played in the stream until the cold water finally drove them back to land. Making no move to dress themselves, they resumed their labours on the tree and were soon warm and dry. The sun felt good on their naked bodies and when they judged it to be noon, they sat down against the sycamore and shared a light meal of bread and cheese, prepared by their mother. Huw was about to throw a scrap of cheese rind down for Pero, when the hound raised its head and turned toward the stream, giving a deep throated growl.

For a few moments the two lads sat still, then, cautiously peered over the tree trunk. Huw grabbed Pero by the scruff of his neck. Almost opposite to where they lay, and on the far bank of the stream, a lone rider sat on his pony and stared toward their place of concealment. With his eyes on the fallen tree, the man urged his mount into the water and allowed it to pick its way across. The pony heaved itself up onto the other bank and its rider dismounted.

"A good day to you both," the man called. "I was sure that somebody was watching me, other than that fellow up on the hill top." Leading his pony by the reins, he walked over to the tree. "You seem to be expecting trouble in these parts. Your friends across the stream are building quite a fortress for themselves."

Both brothers suddenly became aware of the fact that they were stark naked. "Griffith Lloyd is no friend of ours," Huw told him, as they hurriedly dressed. "Indeed, he is the reason for much of our fears."

The man shrugged his broad shoulders and gave a deep sigh. "It's a shame we Welsh are always at each other's throats. These days, there is a need for us to stay together."

"He's not one of us," Hywel snorted. "He acts as though he were a Marcher nobleman. Given a chance, he would take our land by force."

"Not the best of neighbours, then," the man said. "Now tell me, lads, what else do you fear?"

"The fighting that happened late last year," Huw answered. "Father reckons that we should be prepared for any trouble, even though the chances of it reaching here are unlikely."

The stranger grunted, then swung himself up into the saddle. "I'm looking for Cwmdu. Would yonder gap be the entrance?" When Hywel answered that this was so, he smiled his thanks. "Would some kind person offer me food and drink?" he asked. "I would pay with good coin for my meal."

"Mother would gladly see to your needs," Hywel answered. "You can come home with us. We shall have a good reason then to leave this chore until another day."

The man laughed and turned his mount, to ride beside Hywel; Huw followed, carrying the saw. While Hywel conversed with the stranger, Huw studied him. His weathered features had an open, honest look about them, while his manner was one of quiet confidence. The staff of a long-bow was looped over one shoulder, and a quiver packed with arrows hung from his other. At his side, he carried a short sword, the scabbard showing signs of much use. He wore a leather jerkin, opened to the warm air, and Huw noticed a leather band tied about his left wrist. There was no doubting what trade this fellow followed.

There was something about the arrows that caught Huw's attention and he moved closer, to see the better. His eyes were not playing tricks in the sunlight, as he'd first thought, for each arrow had one flight dyed black. Becoming aware of his close scrutiny, the rider turned in his saddle to see what held the lad's attention.

"Have you not seen their like before today?" he asked. "These are arrows for use in battle." He plucked one from the quiver and handed it to Huw. "They are heavier than normal and, at a short range, can unseat an armoured foe with ease. I dye the one flight for speed, then, notching my arrow into the bow's string, like this, you see that the two other flights are set close to this one, leaving a space. This gap allows the arrow to pass smoothly over the bow staff. The trick gives you a sure shot." He showed them what he meant.

They were close to Argoed by now and Hywel ran ahead, calling out to warn his mother that she had a visitor. In the yard, the man dismounted and handed the reins to Huw.

"Will you take care of him for me?" he asked. "I'm no horseman and my backside is letting me know that fact. I would welcome the chance to stretch the aches out of my body."

He was about to say more, when Emma stepped out of the house and into the sunshine. She had been kneading dough for baking and now stood before them, her arms white with flour, a wisp of hair hanging loose down one cheek. The stranger stood for a few moments as though frozen to the spot, his mouth slightly agape. Then, with an effort, he gave a strangled cough.

"I bid you a good day, mistress. Your sons tell me that you may be kind enough to offer me food and drink."

Emma looked him up and down and satisfied with what she saw, invited the man into her home. "Do you have business here in Cwmdu?" she asked, offering him a pot of ale. "You must pardon my curiosity, but you are plainly no tinker or drover."

"My business is elsewhere," her visitor replied, before drinking deeply. "I am journeying to Carmarthen, to deliver a letter of some importance. My name is John Leggatt, and I serve a nobleman who has lands in the north."

Emma placed a plate of cold meat and cheese before him, her brow creasing in a frown. "I trust he is not the same noble who caused the troubles in those parts," she said.

Her guest looked keenly at her, his eating knife poised above the meal. "Rest assured mistress, he is not the one who was the cause," he replied, emphasising his last word.

Emma returned to her baking, and John Leggatt talked

with her sons while he ate. Both boys observed that Leggatt's eyes followed their mother as she moved about the room. His meal eventually finished, their visitor made ready to leave. Emma refused his offer of payment.

"Then, a small gift for you, Hywel," John said, pressing a penny into the lad's hand. "And for you, the arrow which you still hold," he told Huw. "Practise well in its use, for it may save your life some day."

Standing together in the yard, the three watched him mount up, give a farewell wave and ride on up the cwm. When he had passed from sight, the two lads moved off and began to attend to various tasks. Their mother remained near the doorway, a thoughtful look on her face.

Night had fallen when Morgan returned and, despite the lateness, the brothers were waiting for him. Hywel excitedly told him of their visitor. His father, however, was weary and hungry, and merely grunted occasionally as he ate. Only later, when all were abed, Emma spoke softly to her husband about the man.

"By all that is holy," she said, "he reminded me of you as you were in the past; he had much the same dress and manner. I would say that he is one who has seen and done much in his lifetime. He was quite open about why he was passing through Cwmdu, yet he left me with an uneasy feeling. I pray that he does not spell trouble for us."

Morgan turned towards her and placed an arm around her. "You worry yourself too much, my love," he told her gently. "His reason for passing through the cwm is probably quite innocent. You must not see danger where none exists."

He was soon in a deep sleep but Emma remained awake for a long while, staring sadly into the darkness.

Chapter 5

For a day or two after the visit of John Leggatt to the cwm, he was the subject of speculation amongst the people but was soon forgotten. Every evening, his work for the day finished, Huw went down to the meadow, determined to master the elm bow and, with practice, he became able to hold the bow steady when fully drawn.

This evening, as usual, the arrows stood planted into the earth at his feet, a few goose feathers now showing signs of wear. Bracing one end of the staff against his heel, he drew the top toward him, sliding the string along the wood until it slid into the grooved horn. He selected an arrow, notched it and drew back, releasing the string as the flight kissed his cheek. He knew the moment he'd loosed it, that this shot was going to be his best yet, and he watched the flight expectantly and saw his arrow fall behind the sycamore, some three hundred paces distant.

He clearly heard a startled cry come from its direction. Apprehensively, Huw stood rooted to the spot. A figure suddenly burst into the open and he glimpsed a white face turn to look along the meadow. For a worrying moment, he thought that his arrow had struck the person; his fear was quickly dispelled when the figure began to approach him. Resisting an urge to run for it, Huw waited as a very angry young man came near.

"Hell's fire," the man shouted. "Have you left your

brains at home? You came close to killing me."

Despite his own jangled nerves, Huw could not fail to notice the young man's rich clothing, and, with growing alarm, wondered if he was related to Griffith Lloyd. His only comfort, at that moment, was the fact that he stood more than a head taller than his likely assailant.

"I'm sorry," he said. "Truly, I am. I had no idea that anyone was behind the tree."

"You would be a damned sight sorrier had your arrow struck me, I can tell you," the other retorted. "I don't carry this for show." He touched the hilt of his sword. "My blade and I have seen off a few rascals in our day."

Huw could feel his own temper begin to rise within him. "How was I to know that you were skulking down there?" he asked heatedly. "You had no rights to be there. That tree is on Argoed land and belongs to me."

The two glared at each other for some moments, then, to Huw's surprise and relief, the young man's face split into a wide grin. "My God, you did give me a fright, you know," he said. "There was I, dreaming of the old Cymric warriors, when there was Old Death himself, less than an arm's length away." He suddenly threw back his head and laughed. "I've not moved so fast in an age. Your arrow didn't do my bowels much good either. Praise be my belly is empty." He choked back his mirth and thrust out a hand.

"My name is David Mostyn, late of the College of Oxford. I'm travelling to Harlech, where my family live. It was my intention to bed down for the night by yonder tree. Would you object to my doing so, when you have done with your practice?"

Relieved that the young man had no connection with Plas Hirnant, Huw gripped the proffered hand. "I can offer you a better bed than that," he said. "You will be welcome at Argoed. It's a fine night, I grant you, but you will sleep the easier with a roof over your head. Come on, we will go now. I've had enough of the bow for today."

David's boyish face lit up in another smile and he thanked Huw for his invitation. Together, they walked over to the sycamore, where Huw retrieved the offending arrow and David collected a satchel bag which lay by the tree trunk.

"Have you heard of a man named Glyndŵr?" David asked, as they set out for Argoed. "To be honest with you, he is the reason I am returning home."

Huw told him that he knew of the name, as did everyone in these parts, then asked if David knew the nobleman.

"Only of him, unfortunately," came the answer. "Though I aim to meet up with him. It is my earnest wish to serve under his banner. What of you? Would you join him in his struggle?"

Huw let the questions go unanswered for as long as possible, aware of the youth's intent gaze. "I have not given the matter any thought," he explained, coming to a halt. "Look here, I'd best warn you now. Do not talk about such things at Argoed. My mother gets upset when people speak of war. Yet, have no worries as to your welcome there. Simply keep your conversation away from that subject."

David was, indeed, welcomed warmly at Argoed. Emma prepared a meal for him and, when he had eaten, he joined the Gethins around the hearth. At their urging, he spoke about himself. He had spent the past three years at Oxford, studying law and learning as much English and French as possible. It was his wish to become a secretary to some nobleman, or rich merchant. This year, however, his life and those of his fellow Welsh students had been forcibly changed.

"We had always got on well enough with our English colleagues," he told them. "Then, one day, they began hurling abuse at us and calling us traitors to the King. Whenever we ventured outside the college, there would generally be a fist fight." He saw Huw shift in his seat and took the hint. "I decided to end my studies and return home, before seeking employment," he added lamely. The fact that there had been a number of sword fights and that he had fled for his life after one such incident, the ex-student kept to himself.

The following morning, when he left his makeshift bed, David Mostyn found Emma holding his shirt at arms length.

"When did this last see clean water?" she asked, wrinkling her nose. "You cannot leave my home wearing a garment in that state. Break your fast, young man. There's food on the table."

She opened the lid of a chest, selected a homespun shirt and tossed it toward him. "Wear this for now. It's one of Huw's. You must wait at Argoed until I have washed yours." Her manner brooked no argument. "You could go with the boys, after you have eaten," Emma suggested. "It's Huw's turn to keep watch today. He will be glad of your company."

Later, when he went outside, David found his shirt draped over a chair, drying in the sun. Huw and his brother were preparing to take the flock up to the high ground and he asked if he could accompany them. In single file, they followed the sheep up the zig zag path to the top, where Hywel moved on, taking Pero for company.

As usual, Huw settled himself on the rock ledge, though his companion walked some way along the rim of the cwm before joining him.

"I am on watch for trouble. With the stirring news that comes our way, the local men take it in turns to see who comes to the cwm and pass on a warning, if it becomes necessary," Huw explained, before David had a chance to ask why Hywel had gone away alone with the flock.

"You should think yourself fortunate to live in surroundings such as these, Huw. It is truly a magnificent view," he remarked. "Though, tell me, what goes on at the big house across the stream? Whoever lives there cares a great deal for their safety."

Huw told him of the past trouble with Griffith Lloyd and of the recent activity around the Plas.

"I wonder whom he fears," David said thoughtfully. "Does he protect himself from the English or from Glyndŵr?"

Huw had to admit that nobody in Cwmdu knew for certain, as no man had spoken to Griffith since the incident with Morgan and the cattle. "We suspect that he would support the King. He makes his money in England, so that is probably where his loyalties lie."

The morning passed by companionably and it was around noon when the student eventually made a move. "I'd best be on my way," he said. "My shirt will be dry by now and I can cover a few more miles before night falls. I hope that we shall meet again some day, Huw."

They shook hands and said their farewells. Huw was sorry to see the other leave. Although their meeting had been brief, he had taken a liking to the student and suspected that his feelings were reciprocated. It was as

David turned to leave, that both young men stood still, their eyes fixed on the far end of the meadow. From the cover of the woodlands, a number of men marched into the open and, although some distance away, the youths saw the bold flash of colour which came from amongst them.

Huw felt his pulse begin to race with excitement as more men emerged and, once out onto the pasture, formed into a column. In the open, they came to a halt and several of their number broke rank and began walking towards Argoed. Ignoring David Mostyn, Huw turned to look down the cwm and gave three long whistles. An answering call came from below. He saw his father run into sight, pause briefly to wave up at him, and make for the house. Following a plan worked out long ago, Huw now ran along the rim until he came to the adjoining holding, where he repeated his warning. It was Morwen who appeared first. She raised an arm in acknowledgement before scurrying over to one of the farm buildings.

Satisfied that all of the Gethins were now alerted, Huw ran on, giving the alarm signal at each holding as he came to it. He was halfway along the length of the cwm when he came to a panting halt, whistled and heard a similar reply. In a remarkably short space, the fellow from the holding below began to gallop further up the cwm, on an unsaddled pony. Pausing to regain his breath, Huw watched him ride on to the next holding, carrying the warning further afield, then, his breathing easier, he picked his way down.

As he set off for home, he forced himself to keep his pace down to a steady trot. There would be no sense in arriving at the arranged rendezvous in a state of exhaustion, he reasoned. The other men from Cwmdu would be converging at the meeting place, a stone bridge which crossed a deep drainage ditch that ran the width of the cwm. Both bridge and ditch had been constructed by Morgan's father and now marked the boundary of Iolo's land. On his arrival, Huw found his father and uncle already there, in the company of four other smallholders, all of whom carried some form of weapon. There was no sign of David, however, and he wondered if the student was still on the hilltop.

"What caused your signal?" Morgan asked, thrusting Huw's bow into the lad's hand. "Is Griffith Lloyd making a move against us?"

"Unlikely, father." Huw answered. "There are more than a hundred men down on the meadow and they came from downstream."

"We had best pray that you are right about Griffith Lloyd," someone remarked. "It would be madness to stand against so many. We would be wiser to get our families up to the falls."

"I do not believe that Griffith could hire so many men," Morgan told him. "They could be from the north but are more likely a force of English. We have no quarrel with either, so I say that we go to meet them."

Morgan walked across the bridge towards Argoed, the other men following, though somewhat reluctantly. From behind them came the thud of approaching hooves, and Morgan slowed his pace until they were joined by the remaining men of Cwmdu. Now a dozen or so in number, he led them down the cwm, passing Iolo's home, where Morwen and Emma stood, ready to take flight.

From ahead there came a cry of relief and, to his surprise, Huw saw David running towards them, waving both arms in excitement.

"It's Glyndŵr. It's the Prince himself," the student cried out. "I met some of his men in the meadow and they told me to seek you out. They assured me that they mean you no harm. Glyndŵr is merely passing through on his way south." Drawing close, he grabbed Huw's arm and beamed at his new friend. "They have the dragon standard with them," he exclaimed. "It's a sight to stir any man's blood."

"I hope he has his own food supplies, also," Morgan growled. "A hundred empty bellies would empty our larders."

Morgan lengthened his stride and David was compelled to break into a trot to keep up with him. Despite the situation, Huw smiled as the student hopped and skipped along. His own reaction to David's message had been to offer a silent prayer of thanks; he was curious to see this nobleman for himself. Any fears the men of Cwmdu had were quickly dispelled when they arrived at Argoed, where Glyndŵr's men were resting, the majority seated on the ground between the farm buildings, a few eating the food they carried in their satchel bags. They seemed friendly enough, and the local men were soon mingling amongst them, talking and joking.

Huw followed his father to where a small group sat slightly apart, their backs against the sheep pen wall. There was no mistaking the man named Owain Glyndŵr, who sat on the earth as the others did, for there was no disguising his magnetism.

"I am Morgan Gethin, owner of this property," the big man said politely. "You are welcome to rest here awhile, although my invitation is rather late."

Glyndŵr scrambled to his feet, a warm smile on his handsome face. "We thank you for that, my friend," he replied. "The place was deserted, so we invited ourselves in. The young man over there was the first person we encountered," he added, pointing out David. "I asked him to seek you out and assure you that we mean no harm to any man here. In fact, we need men such as you to fight for our cause. Our aim is to rid Wales of English rule."

Morgan stared at him in astonishment for a few moments, then cleared his throat. "A bold aim, my lord," he said finally. "Your cause will appeal to many men. I cannot speak for the others in Cwmdu, but circumstance forces me to stay close to my home."

He then told Glyndŵr of his need to keep watch on his neighbour across the stream, the nobleman listening and asking an occasional question. While they talked, Huw switched his attention to some of the men who sat close by. They were a hard bitten lot, he thought, reminding him of the man who called himself John Leggatt.

"Do you fancy your skill with that bow of yours, lad?" one of them asked. "Let me take a look at it." Huw handed his bow to the man, who had an unsightly scar down one side of his face. The fellow ran a hand along the length of the staff, before effortlessly bending it into shape. "Elm, I'd wager," he chuckled. "Good enough for a child to play with."

Huw felt himself blush as the man's companions laughed. He tried to think of some retort to make, though nothing suitable came to mind.

"Take no heed of Idwal," one of the others told him. "The day when he says a pleasant word to anyone, that will be the day that pigs grow wings."

Idwal thrust the staff back at Huw and eyed him up and down. "Reckon he's right. Come a year or two and you could possibly handle a yew bow." His face twisted into a hideous leer as he attempted a smile. "When you master this, you can always join our company. You would be made welcome."

Huw mumbled his thanks, and, hearing Glyndŵr give the order to make ready, he rejoined his father. The local men now grouped together and Glyndŵr spoke earnestly to them.

"We are making for a place called Hyddgen, which lies at the foot of Plynlimon," he said. "I am going to raise my standard there and call on the people of Wales to join our struggle. Our nation has had enough of these Marcher lords and we must be free of them, once and for all. Should the King choose to support them, then so be it." He paused to look at the men, who were hanging on his every word. "Our ancestors fought and died in the cause of freedom. Now, it is our turn to pick up the sword. Think on my words, men of Cwmdu."

A bowman stood close, holding Owain's horse, and he helped the Prince to mount. Glyndŵr leaned down from the saddle and spoke to Morgan.

"I understand your present worries. Who knows, I may soon have the opportunity to rid you of them. Until then, my friend, support me in any way that you can."

Glyndŵr rode to the centre of the column and gave the command to march on. As the men moved away, the watchers saw the huge, golden dragon standard rise and unfurl above the bobbing heads.

"Hell's fire, who can resist such a sight?" David cried out emotionally. "I must join them, Huw. My search has ended sooner than I'd hoped. I owe you much, for had it not been for our chance meeting, I would have missed Glyndŵr. I hope we meet again and soon. It is a shame you are not free to come with me. Give my thanks to your mother. You are fortunate to have the like of her."

He punched Huw playfully in the ribs and abruptly turned away, to walk quickly after the column. Later, when the Gethins were alone, Huw found the student's shirt still draped over the chair. He folded it carefully and placed it in the wooden chest. Drifting into sleep that night, he had the picture of the dragon standard in his mind.

Chapter 6

The days passed by, the people of Cwmdu busy with their lives. Yet now there was an air of excitement amongst the holdings. Each day brought more armed men, seeking the path up the falls. In twos and threes, they passed, taking food and drink whenever it was offered. Some were men from Gwynedd, carrying their fifteen-foot-long spears, others were from Glyndŵr's lands, and, more recently, the travellers hailed from the Severn valley. Their presence unsettled Huw. He became even more withdrawn, scarcely speaking to anyone and avoiding Emma whenever possible. He would snap irritably at Hywel, who would lapse into silence, when their work brought them together.

Late one afternoon, something forced Huw to come to a decision. He had spent much of the day working on the sycamore, when two more travellers stopped and asked their way. One was a man of some forty years, while the other was a lad of about Huw's age. Both were delighted to learn that Glyndŵr had passed by some days ago and had rested at Argoed. Innocently, the older man asked if Huw was going to answer the call to arms, and shrugged when Huw stammered some excuse. The lad, though, gave Huw a look which said more than words.

When the pair had gone on their way, he returned to his task and swung the axe in a savage frenzy. That look had really hurt him. Thunk, thunk went the axe, at an ever increasing speed, sending splinters flying through the air until, exhausted, Huw flung it away. His chest heaving, limbs shaking, he stood there for a long while, then, suddenly picked up the axe and made for Argoed.

The instant that she saw him, Emma knew what would follow. She had been only too aware of his mood over the past few days and instinctively knew that what she dreaded most was about to happen.

"I'm going," he told her bluntly. "Now or next year, what is the difference? Yet, go I must."

He had expected an outburst and was surprised when Emma remained silent, looking up at him, her eyes filling with tears. "I'd best get things ready for you, then," she finally whispered. "You will not leave until the morrow, will you?"

He shook his head and, unable to endure her look of anguish, he stumbled out of the house.

From afar, he heard his father's high pitched call and he started toward the top end of the pasture, walking slowly. The cattle were already making their way up the track when he reached it, and he stood aside, as they plodded slowly by. He waited until his father drew level, then walked beside him.

"I'm leaving in the morning," he told Morgan. "I know we thought to wait another year, but so much is happening, that I simply cannot stand back and watch."

Morgan saw the look of determination in his son's face and gave a reluctant nod of his head. As with Emma, he had been expecting the news.

"I have told mother, she took it better than I'd hoped."

The Gethins ate supper that night, almost entirely in silence; only Hywel attempted to make conversation.

Emma retired early to her bed, to be followed after a while by Hywel, who sensed that the other two wished to be alone. When the younger son had taken his leave, Morgan took up a candle and told Huw to follow him. He led the way to the gable end of the house and entered the cattle byre. Here, he passed the candle to Huw and opened a chest in which he kept a number of tools. He extracted a roll of cloth, gave it to Huw and took back the candle.

"I want you to have this," he said. "It has been with us Gethins for more than fifty years. My father brought it home from France; he used it at a place called Crécy. I carried it during my service as a bowman and was going to pass it on to you when the day came. That day has come, sooner than wished, perhaps. Take good care of it, Huw, it could save your life."

Huw unwrapped the cloth and found that he was holding a short, heavy sword in its scabbard.

"Hide it from your mother's sight," Morgan told him. "Keep it under your jerkin, where it will be safe."

When he was in bed, Huw soon fell into a deep sleep. Despite the thoughts of what the morrow would bring, he felt emotionally drained to the point of exhaustion. He was up and about shortly after dawn, the sword tied onto a length of twine and looped around his neck. There was scarcely any need for this precaution, though, for he was the only one astir. With the thought of a painful farewell uppermost in his mind, he took a drink of milk, then gathered his satchel and the bow with its bundle of arrows. Hurriedly, he crossed to the door, pausing to take a last look around the familiar room. He became very aware that his next step was probably going to be the biggest one in his life. Taking a deep breath, he walked out into the early morning, firmly closing the door behind him.

In her bed, Emma heard him leave. From the cattle byre, Pero whined and gave one deep howl. Emma turned onto her side, toward Morgan, who she thought still slept, and murmured a prayer of gratitude when he held her close.

Huw strode up the cwm towards the falls. He had thought to use the sheep path, but had put this route from his mind. Now that he was on his way, he could not reach his goal quickly enough and the way up the falls was by far the shorter, saving him several miles. Reaching the head of the cwm, he came to the path and began to climb. The path had been cut diagonally across the sheer face and he soon lost sight of the tumbling water, though he could plainly hear its roar. The higher he climbed, the narrower the path became, and he kept as close to the cliff face as possible. Nearing the top, the empty void to his right seemed to beckon and he felt a sickening dread in the pit of his stomach. With laboured breath and gritted teeth, Huw forced himself onward until, at long last, he reached the point where the waters spewed out into space at the top of the rise. The ground levelled out and his way turned sharply to his left. With relief, he began walking away from the sheer drop.

The path followed the stream, and Huw could clearly see the imprints of many feet in its peat surface. Thus far, he was on familiar territory. He came to the small lake which fed the stream, and he was soon deafened by the calls of hundreds of gulls which wheeled around him. Huw strode on, and when he came to a fork in the path, he turned right. The peat under this new path was full of water and it gave him a strange sensation of weightlessness as he walked along, and his pace quickened without effort. Ahead of him, the path swung around a low hill and, as he drew near, he stepped off the path, onto long, yellowish grass, and climbed to the top. The long ridge of Plynlimon stood before him. From the south, he heard someone call and saw a group of men on another hilltop, some distance away. One of them waved and Huw waved back, watching until they dropped out of sight. He was soon climbing steadily up a moderate slope, which led to the summit. The ground became more broken, the higher he climbed, coarse heather taking the place of grass. In places, he had to skirt around great pits of evil black ooze. When he was close to the summit, he found firm ground littered with boulders and stones.

"Welcome Longshanks."

Huw's feet almost left the ground with shock. He looked wildly around him, seeing no-one, until, from behind a rock, Idwal, with the scarred face, stepped into the open.

"Seeking my company so soon," he chuckled. "I've not known my charm to work so speedily before." He walked over to a flat stone and sat down. "Come, rest yourself for a while. I've been watching you, lad. You can cover the ground quickly with those long legs of yours."

Huw made to sit beside him but the sword's scabbard dug into his flesh. Pulling the looped twine over his head, he took the sword from under his jerkin and placed it on the stone. Idwal looked at it for a moment, before giving a soft whistle of appreciation.

"Now, how did a lad like you come by that?" he asked. "I've only seen its like once before, and that was years ago. Huw repeated his father's tale and handed the heavy weapon to the bowman, who drew the blade free. "By God, I'd give much to have one like this," he said, hefting its weight. "Treasure it and, whatever you do, trust no man with its keeping."

He gave the sword back to Huw, then began to gnaw on a bone, which he took from his pouch. Only then did Huw realise that he was ravenous and, seating himself, he began to eat some bread and cold mutton. Becoming conscious of Idwal's eyes on him, he offered food from his satchel but the bowman declined.

"My thanks for your kindness," he said. "But your need is greater than mine. There's food enough down at Hyddgen and I will eat my fill tonight."

While he ate, Huw studied the sword. Short sword or long knife, it was difficult to say. The blade and handle were fashioned from the same length of steel, the blade widening at its centre, then narrowing to a sharp point. The handle was plainly bound with cord, while a loose metal ring served as a hilt. It was a weapon which could be used to stab or hack an enemy. Huw thrust the blade into its wooden scabbard, with a grimace of distaste, then slipped the loop over one shoulder. Finishing his meal, he put the remains of the bread into his satchel, and his hand touched something soft. Taking out a roll of linen, he found that he was holding David's shirt. He replaced the garment and got to his feet.

"You will find our camp easily enough," Idwal told him. "There's a stream on the other side of the ridge. Simply follow it down. You will find Glyndŵr but a short distance away. I take it that he is the one you wish to meet up with, not me." Huw grinned and nodded his agreement.

"Then, we shall meet later, Longshanks," Idwal said. "Seek out a man named John Leggatt. Tell him that I command that you serve with him."

Reaching the top of the ridge, Huw found the stream

and began to descend. The slope on this side of the mountain was much steeper, and he followed the water's course with care until he reached level ground. Here, the stream was joined by another and, walking with the flow, he soon came to an encampment which was spread on either side of the water. Most of the shelters comprised pieces of timber, covered with bracken, and placed close to the stream. On a low rise in the valley floor, he saw the dragon standard flapping idly and, guessing that this would be the camp's centre, he walked toward it.

Several pavilions had been set up around the standard and a number of carts stood in a line close by. Two bowmen stood at their ease outside one of the pavilions, and Huw went to talk with them. Before he could speak, however, a familiar figure appeared in the open entrance.

"I do not believe what I'm seeing," David Mostyn called out. "Is it really you, Huw Gethin? By all that's holy, the sight of you does me a power of good." He rushed over to Huw and led him to one of the carts. The pair climbed inside it. "In truth, I'm in need of company. These fellows are friendly enough, but they will not take me seriously. They know that I have travelled from Oxford to join them, yet, whenever I offer my services, they tell me to wait and see."

He gestured toward the pavilion, a scowl on his normally cheerful features. "I've just seen Glyndŵr himself and he has told me the same. Their attitude is beginning to make me disenchanted with the whole business, I can tell you. You are going to stay, I hope?" he added anxiously.

Huw fumbled in his satchel and brought out David's shirt. "No, I've simply brought you your shirt. It's too short in the arm for me."

He saw his friend's expression change to that of dismay, and laughed, placing an arm around his shoulders. "Forgive me, I'm only teasing. I am here to stay, right enough," he said.

"Then, welcome to my new home. It's not much but it keeps the night air off me. I'm also as close to those that matter as can be. There has been much coming and going earlier, I fancy that there is something in the wind, Huw."

Even as he spoke, a horseman drew rein outside Glyndŵr's pavilion, hurriedly dismounted and rushed inside.

"That fellow must be bringing news of great importance, judging from the condition of his horse," the student observed, looking at the lathered animal. "I'm convinced that something has happened that Glyndŵr did not expect." He clambered down from the cart, keeping an eye on the pavilion. "I think we had best find a captain who will take you under his command, Huw."

"I was told to seek out a man named John Leggatt," Huw replied. "It's a name that I have heard before today, though cannot put a face to it. Perhaps he can find a use for our services."

"Not much chance of that," David joked. "He and I have already met. He told me, as did the others, that I was of no use to him at present. However, follow me. I will take you to where his men are camped."

He led the way through the scattered shelters, passing groups of men who were standing talking amongst themselves. At one such group, he stopped and motioned Huw forward. The men looked at the newcomers and, with a start, Huw recognised one as the bowman who had eaten at Argoed.

"A good day to you, Master Gethin," the man said. "I was not expecting your presence." He looked Huw up and down, his eyes resting on the short sword, then, apparently satisfied, he led him away from the others. "Did your mother agree to you coming here?" he asked. "I trust that you have her blessing."

"She said no word to deter me." Huw answered. "I met one of the bowmen on the mountain top, a man named Idwal, the man with a scar," he went on, anxious to change the subject. "You are John Leggatt?"

"I am indeed, and told your mother so. It is no secret," came the answer.

"Idwal commands that you and I shall serve together," Huw told him.

John looked up at the mountain top for some moments, not saying a word, then, with the corners of his mouth twitching with mirth, he turned his gaze back to Huw.

"Then we had better do as the old rogue says. Now, listen well to what I am going to say. Should there be a fight, stay close to your comrades and do what you are ordered to do. Do not attempt to win any battle on your own. Should you do so, you will not see the sun set, I can assure you. Come now, let's join the others."

Leggatt saw David watching them and a frown creased his brow. "What is it you want now?" he asked, a note of impatience creeping into his voice. "I've already told you that I have no need of your services."

Huw saw his friend's face redden with anger, and stepped to his side. "We are friends of long standing and wish to be together," Huw said. "David will fight as well as the next man, should he have to."

John glared at the lanky recruit who stood determinedly before him, then shrugged his broad shoulders. "So be it," he said resignedly. "Though, mark me well, scholar. You will not find the glory you seek in this company. Stick your neck out too far and you will find yourself alone."

David stammered his thanks and the two friends turned away and began to walk back to the cart. They had scarcely moved off, however, when a messenger ran past, calling John's name. "Glyndŵr bids you attend him speedily," he shouted. "He wishes you to hear some news from the south." Leggatt led the way into the pavilion, the messenger at his heels.

"I tell you, something is amiss, Huw," David hissed, coming to a halt. "There is an air of urgency about those bringing news." The two waited until John had passed, then carried on walking. "I think that I shall vacate my palace," David said, when they reached the cart. "We had best be with the others in the event of something happening." They collected their satchels and began to retrace their steps.

"Why would Glyndŵr speak with John Leggatt?" Huw asked. "I thought that he was just a simple bowman."

"A bowman he is, indeed," his friend answered, "though no ordinary one. He is Glyndŵr's captain of archers."

Huw muttered a curse and looked up at Plynlimon. The scar-faced bowman up there had much to answer for, he thought.

John Leggatt looked around at the thoughtful faces inside the pavilion. A man did not have to be a magician to see that something was wrong, for gone was the mood of optimism which had prevailed until now.

"You had best hear this for yourself, John," Glyndŵr

said. "This scout has confirmed what we believed to have been merely rumour. The King has raised a strong force and they are already marching against us. Tell my captain what you have seen," he told the scout.

"They are Flemish settlers from Pembroke," the man said. "We counted them as best we could, when they forded the river Rheidol, on their way to Aberystwyth castle, and they number about fifteen hundred men. They have English captains in command, who seem to know their business. When I left, they were resting and eating outside the castle walls. We feel sure that they mean to move on today."

"Our thanks for your warning," Glyndŵr said. "Refresh yourself, then take a fresh mount and rejoin your comrades. Be sure to send me news on our foes' progress. For now, tell no man outside this pavilion."

When the scout had departed, Glyndŵr sat deep in thought for a long while before looking at John. "I had hoped that we could have had longer here at Hyddgen," he said grimly. "We number scarcely more than five hundred: unfavourable odds. It is plain that our precautions over the past months were not wasted, for the English must have spies everywhere. How else could Henry Bolingbroke have moved so fast?" He rose to his feet and crossed over to the open flap, where he looked up at the surrounding mountains.

"I have no choice other than to give battle. No choice at all," he said, as though speaking to himself. Turning to face the others, he looked at each man in turn. "Were I to take the sensible course and wait until we are stronger, our cause could well vanish into the air. We have two things in our favour, my friends. The first is, that the Flemish are more skilled in trade than war; the second, that we have bowmen and they do not. The scout was sure of this, when I asked him. The outcome of the fight would rest with your men, John."

"I feel sure that they can be counted on, my lord," the captain replied. "Most of them are experienced soldiers. The remainder are of good stock and will learn quickly. We should not offer to fight on level ground, though. We must find a place more suited to a bowman's skills."

"My thoughts are the same," Glyndŵr agreed. "We need to find a suitable mountain slope. Our spearmen at the fore, your bowmen behind and above them, able to shoot over their heads. Such tactics worked well for our forefathers. No reason why they should not succeed ." He smiled at those about him and drew his sword, testing its edge with his finger. "Whatever the outcome, we will give them a fight they will not forget. Go now and find us such a place. Remember, though, not a word to any man as yet. We need to keep the men together while we can."

When they had left him alone, Glyndŵr went down on his knees and began to pray. He prayed for victory, for the safety of Margaret and their children, and for Tudor, and the men who had answered his call to arms. Finally, he commended his soul to God.

When John rejoined his men, he called Huw over to him. "Go, string your bow and bring some arrows with you. I want to see how well you shoot," he said, ignoring the enquiring glances from several of the mercenaries.

Not waiting for the lad, he set off up the stream, looking intently about him. Huw hastily strung his bow and, accompanied by David, ran after him. They had not walked far when John came to a halt, pointing a finger ahead of him. "Do you see that white rock yonder?" he asked. "Drop your arrows as close to it as you can."

Some two hundred paces from where they stood, a large quartz boulder stood out clearly in the coarse grass, and Huw began to aim at it, his arrows falling around the gleaming target. He had only loosed six, however, when John told him to stop and began walking towards the rock.

"Now shoot for distance," he told Huw, as the lad picked up his arrows, "Let's see if you can cover three hundred paces with every shot."

Loosing each arrow as soon as its feathers touched his cheek, Huw shot up the valley until all were gone. He knew that he had done well and unstrung the bow, waiting for some word of approval. The captain's verdict was disappointing, for he merely grunted, his eyes fixed on a slope to their right.

"Go and gather your arrows," he said. "I need to take a look around and will meet you back here."

"John Leggatt would seem to have other matters on his mind than your archery," David remarked, as they made for the distant arrows. "He scarcely looked at where your shots were landing. What do you suppose he finds so interesting on yonder hillside? It appears no different from the others, to me."

Aided by the white flights, Huw had no difficulty in retrieving his arrows, which he tied in a bundle at his waist. This done, the two walked back down the valley, watching the captain. John Leggatt had climbed some three hundred feet up the slope and, as they came directly below him, he moved out of sight.

"The slope must level off a little way," Huw said, looking closely at the hillside. We cannot see it from down here because of the length of the cotton grass."

John reappeared and stood looking towards the

encampment, before he made his way down. He gave no reason for his interest in the hillside but looked at Huw's bundled arrows. "I see you still have the arrow I gave you," he said. "Let's see you make a flat shot down the valley."

Huw re-strung his bow, notched the heavy arrow and loosed, and was pleased to see it flash away, straight and true.

"You shoot well enough," the captain told him. "Keep in mind to save that arrow for some desperate moment, in the event of a battle."

Returning to where the mercenaries were camped, they were greeted by the smell of roasting meat.

"There's plenty for all," one of the men called, as he basted the joint with fat. "Tonight, we dine on venison. A meat fit for men of our standing."

"Then, save some for me and that joker, Idwal, on the mountain," John told him. "He's probably on his way down by now, if I know him."

David watched the captain of archers make his way to Glyndŵr's pavilion and enter. He was still puzzling over the man's interest in the hillside, when Idwal arrived. Despite the cook's warning, the mercenary squatted down beside the roasting joint and cut himself a slice, eating the partly cooked meat ravenously. It was as Idwal joked with the cook, that David saw four horsemen gallop towards the camp, from a southerly direction. The riders drew rein outside Glyndŵr's quarters, where they dismounted and hurried inside.

"I fancy it would be wise to eat now," the student said to Huw. "Something tells me that it could be our last opportunity for some while."

The mercenaries were of the same mind, and the two

had to wait their turn to cut a slice of rare venison. They were still chewing on this, when the rapid beat of a drum sounded over the encampment. Glyndŵr appeared outside his pavilion, talking earnestly with his brother, Tudor, and several others, and it was then that David had the answer to what puzzled him. He saw the Prince and John Leggatt step clear of the group and look up the valley, the captain pointing at the hill up which he had climbed. Within moments, John was hurrying back to his men. The drum stopped, leaving an uneasy silence and, with mounting excitement, David saw Glyndŵr don a coat of chain mail.

Chapter 7

"Up you go, lads," John Leggatt urged his bowmen. "The slope levels part way up. Form a line when you get to it. Hurry now, it will soon be dark."

He watched the two hundred and sixteen bowmen file past him, seasoned veterans, such as Idwal, and others whose first taste of battle this would be. There were far more than he had ever commanded before, yet he felt confident. Taking a last look down the valley, he followed the men up the hill, where he joined Glyndŵr and his brother, who stood in front of a line of men armed with a variety of weapons. From below, the spearmen of Gwynedd began to arrive. Forming a line to the fore, they laid down their spears and sat to wait for whatever was to come. John stayed with Glyndŵr for a while before making his way along the line of bowmen. Coming to where his old comrades stood, he took Idwal aside and spoke softly to him. He wanted Idwal to keep a special watch over Huw. Then, taking his place in the centre of the line, he seated himself, forced to wait in patience, which he, like all military men, loathed.

With the coming of night, the moon rose above the great ridge of Plynlimon, casting deep shadows wherever there was a fold in the earth. Many of the men watched its passage through the night sky, talking quietly with their companions. Some men fidgeted, some dozed, a few slept as though at home in their beds. Seated next to the sleeping Idwal, Huw looked enviously at him. He felt deeply tired, yet his mind would not allow him any rest. He was thinking too much about the coming day and how he would behave in battle. On the other side of Idwal, David sat with his chin resting on his drawn up knees. Huw desperately wanted to say something to the student but was at a loss for the right words.

A man scrambled up to the shelf and, panting heavily from the climb, spoke to Glyndŵr. The Prince listened and then moved along the waiting lines, murmuring words of encouragement to the troops. When he came to John, he knelt down.

"They are here," he whispered. "They have halted at our encampment. Our scout says that they seem undecided as to their next move. We must be patient, my friend. May God watch over you."

As the night passed, the moon dipped behind the opposite hills and the Welshmen were once more in darkness. To Huw, the night seemed endless and, eventually, he stood to stretch his limbs and ease the tension within. Slowly, he pushed his arms out to their full extent, then froze, when he heard the unmistakable clink of metal and the sounds of men rising to their feet. He peered down into the darkness. The captains moved amongst the men, bidding them be silent.

Huw shook Idwal awake and the mercenary got to his feet, fumbling instinctively for his bow and bundle of arrows. A few moments later, Huw heard him begin to chew on what he assumed was Idwal's interrupted supper. Again, they waited, until the sky began to lighten. Moving through the ranks of men, Glyndŵr stood with the lightening sky behind him, and looked down into the valley. The sight that met his gaze he found incredible. Below him, their backs to the slope, his enemy stood in disarray, ignorant of the danger above. Their straggling column was far fewer than the reported fifteen hundred, and he guessed that the Flemish had split their force, to seek him out.

He moved away from the skyline and called softly for his brother, Tudor, and John Leggatt. "We will not wait for them to come to us," he told them. "It changes our plan of battle, yet this is an opportunity too good to miss. Tell your men to string their bows and make ready, John. We shall rush down on them now."

With a rustle of movement, his men made ready to charge. At John's low-voiced command, Huw pulled the heavy battle arrow from his bundle and slipped it into his belt. Checking that the short sword was secure, he stood ready, nervous yet glad that the waiting was over. Glyndŵr returning to his place in front of the pikemen, raised his sword and began to walk down the slope. The bowmen followed until they could see the Flemish column, where they came to a halt. With a ringing shout, the pikemen broke into a run. The English and Flemish troops down in the valley turned towards the oncoming spears, their pale faces clearly visible to the bowmen.

"Loose," John Leggatt roared.

Two hundred and more bowstrings twanged in unison and sent their deadly missiles screaming through the air. With trembling fingers, Huw notched another arrow, aware that Idwal had already sent his second shot away. He drew the string back and loosed again, losing sight of his arrow amongst the constant shower which fell on the Flemish. From below, the sound of men screaming in pain rose above the growing din. Twice more Huw shot before

John cried out to cease. Moving to the fore, the captain led his bowmen down towards their foe, keeping a steady pace. Only now did Huw look at the conflict below. His throat turned dry when he saw men hacking savagely at each other. A hand grabbed his shoulder and, risking a glance, he saw Idwal point to the short sword. Somehow, he drew the blade without breaking his stride. Nearing the valley floor, John began to run faster, making for a group of Flemish who were trying desperately to fight their way clear. At full tilt, the bowmen struck, sending men reeling.

Tradesmen they may have been, cowards they were not, for the Flemish fought back bravely, trapping some of the bowmen when they closed ranks. Caught in the sudden crush, Huw felt real fear and, with panic taking hold, he tried to squirm his way out of the pack of men. Bow in one hand, sword in the other, he found it impossible to defend himself with either weapon. Suddenly, he went down under the trampling feet. Frantically, he attempted to crawl clear, with men tripping over him. For one blessed moment, he found himself unimpeded and began to get to his feet. A booted foot kicked him flat and directly above him stood a mailed figure, sword raised in both hands, ready to stab downward. As though in a terrible dream, Huw watched motionless as the blade's point plunged.

The sword failed to reach its target; a bow staff struck it aside and its point dug deep into the earth, inches from his head. At the same moment, an arm shot into his view, and he cringed away as warm blood splashed his face. The mailed figure swayed, staggered forward, then fell, trapping Huw's legs. He felt a hand grab his shirt, he was pulled free and hauled to his feet. Idwal's face loomed close to his.

Punching and elbowing through friends and foes alike, the mercenary forced his way through the melee, Huw holding on to his jerkin. Once clear, the two stood side by side, gulping air into their burning lungs. From the hill, Tudor's men charged into the fray, cheering loudly and adding to the confusion. At this stage, a number of the Flemish broke ranks and began to run wildly down the valley.

"Are you hurt, lad?" Idwal asked. Huw shook his head, scarcely believing that he was still in one piece. "Then, back to it. Stay close, now."

Idwal did not return to the action, however, but ran off to their right. Anxious not to lose the mercenary, Huw followed. He was so intent on watching Idwal that he failed to see what caused the stinging blow which caught him on the side of his face. The pain was excruciating, causing him to drop his bow and he put a hand to his cheek. Through eyes filling with tears, he saw someone rush toward him, swinging a pole, and he heard Idwal's cry of warning. In some strange way, his pain triggered anger, and he launched himself furiously at the attacker. With all his strength, he swung the short sword from side to side until he felt its blade connect with a solid object. His foe stood open-mouthed for a brief moment, then flung the stump of his pole away, turned and fled.

Huw wiped the tears from his eyes and looked wildly about him. No other enemy appeared about to challenge him, so he rejoined Idwal, who was keeping a close eye on the battle. Handing Huw his bow, the mercenary's face creased in a smile.

"A living demon, you are," he shouted above the noise. "You put the fear of God into that fellow." He placed a restraining hand on Huw's arm as the lad made to move towards the fighting men. "Stay yourself, the worst is over. No need to take further risks."

Now able to look further afield, Huw could see the sense in what Idwal said. All along the line the Flemish were breaking away, throwing armour and weapons aside as they ran. Only the group from which Idwal had helped him escape still stood firm. In awed fascination, he watched as the attention of nearly every Welshman focused onto this defiant band. A growl, which grew into an animal-like roar, came from hundreds of throats, as the Welshmen surged over their foe, stabbing and hacking like mad men. In what seemed like moments, the fighting was over and a strange silence, broken only by the groans of the wounded, fell over the place.

The first voice to be heard was Glyndŵr's, who called the men to rally to his side. In haste, they formed two lines behind the dragon standard and advanced down the valley, eager to get to grips with the retreating Flemish. Nearing their abandoned encampment, they saw another large body of men off to their right, and the Welsh turned towards it. These were the other part of the enemy force, that had been seeking Glyndŵr. Until now, they had not witnessed the outcome of the first fight.

John Leggatt's bowmen loosed several volleys into their packed ranks before Glyndŵr ordered his men to charge. Their morale shaken by the arrows and sight of their fleeing comrades, these Flemish also took to their heels, adding to the general panic. Their main route of escape was a narrow gap between two hills and this rapidly became choked with men, who pushed each other aside in their haste. At John's command, the bowmen loosed again and again at this easy target. Unable to avoid the stinging arrows, some of the Flemish sought to escape amongst the water courses which scarred the hillside. It was then that Huw caught sight of his friend, David Mostyn.

Sword held high, the student was chasing a man, who bounded through the long grass like a hunted deer. David's experiences of the battle were very similar to Huw's. He had advanced down the slope with the bowmen, been buffeted and bruised in the crush and been unable to strike a blow in return. Now, he had his chance and, forcing his short legs to move faster, he slowly began to overtake the Flemish soldier. His foe risked a frightened backward glance. When he came to a water course, he swerved into it. David followed, sprinting recklessly over the spongy earth. Ahead of them, a huge rock barred the way and he saw his foe's pace slow as he neared it. Wild with excitement, David hurled himself forward, swinging his sword at the bobbing head. At the same moment, he saw the pool of black ooze which lay around the rock's base. He felt his feet slide away from him and, thrown off balance by his sword, he fell heavily.

The air was forced from his lungs and, before he could recover his breath, his intended victim turned about and flung himself atop the helpless student. Strong hands grasped his hair, forcing his face down into the stinking slime. Twisting and kicking to no avail, David tasted the foul liquid and his head began to pound violently. He knew that he was going to die and searched for a prayer but found none in the turmoil of his mind. Suddenly, unbelievably, the powerful hands were snatched away. The crushing weight went from his shoulders and he flopped over onto his back, dragging air into his lungs. Desperately trying to wipe the slime from his eyes, he began to push himself clear of the pool. Hands touched his face and he lashed out blindly, his fists finding no target. He cried out. The hands withdrew and he faintly heard his name through his blocked ears. When his sight cleared, he looked up into Huw's anxious face. He tried to speak, but a rush of bile filled his mouth and he rolled onto his side and began to vomit. Once he had recovered, Huw helped him to his feet.

"Were I you, I'd be rid of this," Huw said, picking up the student's sword. "If I had not seen you leave the fight and followed you, it would be you lying here in place of that one yonder."

David looked to where his friend was pointing. "By the saints," he croaked. "Is that your doing?"

Huw nodded and they moved closer to the still figure, which stared at the sky with unseeing eyes. It was not the sight of the dead face which caused David to gasp aloud, but the shock of seeing an arrow protruding obscenely from the gaping mouth.

"A lucky shot," Huw remarked softly. "You have John Leggatt to thank for this. It was the arrow he gave me that found the mark. It must have been providence that made me keep it in my belt."

"Providence or whatever, you saved my life. I shall always be in your debt, Huw," David replied.

They heard someone running towards them and saw Idwal coming up the water course.

"Praise be, you're safe, Longshanks," the mercenary gasped. "I'd have John Leggatt to answer to, had you been hurt, or worse. The thought of his wrath gave strength to my legs, though not enough to catch up with you. Like I told you, you can cover the ground with those legs of yours." Reaching out, he held David gently by his shoulders. "A word of warning to you, scholar. Say not a word of this to any man. Should our captain hear of it, there's no telling what he may do. Though I'm sure that it would not be pleasant."

He knelt beside the dead man and began to search through the soiled clothing. "You will have to buy yourself a new arrow, lad, there's no way I can free this one," he said.

Huw winced at the thought of pulling the arrow out of the dead man's throat and using it again. Until this day, death had not come within the youth's experience, and he found it unpleasant.

Idwal gave a satisfied grunt and tossed a small, leather pouch to Huw. "There you are. That should pay for some more arrows." Huw instinctively put out a hand to catch the purse, then snatched it back, recoiling with horror. The purse struck the earth with a tinkle of coins. "Take it, lad, it's yours now," Idwal urged. "It won't do this fellow any good. Take it, I say. It's the spoils of war. You'll soon learn the rules."

Huw reluctantly picked up the purse and pushed it to the bottom of his satchel. An overwhelming feeling of guilt swept over him and he glanced at the dead face from lowered eyes. He knew that no matter how long he lived, this ghastly picture would always be with him, burned into his memory. He heard Idwal call him. He tore his gaze away and followed the other two back down the water course.

On the banks of the Hyddgen, the fighting had almost stopped. The remaining Flemish forces were on the run, making for the safety of far off Aberystwyth castle. Here and there along the valley, small groups of them, who had become trapped against the hillsides, fought to the death.

"I'm for the pickings," Idwal announced. "Come on, you two, let's beat the others to it."

He headed for the scene of their first charge. The only living beings there were three other mercenaries, who were moving amongst the dead, searching for booty. The two friends watched Idwal join in the search, his hands busily fumbling through the dead men's clothing. His callousness increased Huw's feeling of guilt. He wanted to call out, tell the mercenaries to stop, all the time knowing that they would pay him no heed. From close by, a man moaned, and Huw and David walked towards the sound.

It was as though all of the horrors that they had experienced that morning had been condensed into this one dreadful sight. Lying in the long grass, a Flemish soldier writhed in lone agony. His hands plucked feebly at the broken shaft of a spear, which was firmly embedded in his stomach. It was obvious that the man was beyond aid, and the two friends stood rooted helplessly to the spot, willing the wretch to die. It was Idwal who put an end to his torment. He bent over the moaning figure and swiftly drew his knife across the exposed throat.

"For the love of God," David cried out. "Have you no feelings at all? Is it ice that runs through your veins?"

Idwal wiped the bloody knife on a handful of grass and glared at the student. "You think it better to have let him linger in such pain?" he snarled. "Were it me with a spear in my belly, I'd thank the man who ended it for me." He turned away from them and resumed his search amongst the dead.

"He's right," Huw remarked quietly. "His action was, indeed, a kindness. "Come on, let's go away from here. Back up the hill will do for me. There will be no smell of blood up there."

David placed a restraining hand on Huw's shoulder. "A drink first, my friend. My throat is parched. You would smell sweeter if you were to wash that jerkin of yours. It looks as though you have been dragged through a slaughterhouse."

Huw grimaced when he glanced down at his blood-stained homespun. He pulled the garment over his head and made for the stream. In the cool, clear water, he washed his face and torso, before rinsing the jerkin. David, meanwhile, drank his fill, and washed away the worst of the now dried black mud. Refreshed by the water, the two climbed the hill to where they had awaited the Flemish. The only signs that some five hundred men had spent a long night on this narrow strip of land were the flattened grass and some scattered arrows. Huw collected a handful of these arrows, then sat beside his friend, who was gazing towards Plynlimon.

"Do you realise that the sun is only now beginning to show?" he asked incredulously. "I find it hard to believe that so much has happened in such a short while." He lay back on the grass and turned to look at Huw. "I shall be forever in your debt. Some day, I may be able to repay you for saving my life."

Settling himself comfortably, he closed his eyes and lay quietly, his breathing steady. Huw sat for a while, feeling his bruised body begin to ache. He had made an early start the day before, completed the journey to Hyddgen, missed a night's sleep and fought a battle. Now, he felt utterly drained, yet, strangely, wide awake. Spreading his shirt to dry on the grass, he lay down beside the now sleeping David. In his mind, he relived the fighting. The face of the man he'd killed kept returning, no matter how hard he tried to shut it out. He had given up all thought of sleep when, without a hint of drowsiness, he slipped into oblivion.

He awoke with a start, feeling hands shaking him, and hearing David's voice calling his name. As he rose to his feet, he saw that the sun was now high. He felt a painful stiffness down one side of his face.

"That's an ugly welt you have there, Huw," David said, as he gingerly touched his cheek. "I'm loath to say this, but you look like friend Idwal. Praise be, yours will not be a permanent scar." He picked up Huw's jerkin and handed it to him, before gesturing down the slope. "I think we should make for the encampment. The others are bound to be wondering where we are."

At the bottom of the hill, they found a number of men digging pits, while others were laying out the dead in rows. The two friends skirted the area and walked quickly towards the encampment. Much to their surprise, they found that the Flemish had not destroyed any of the shelters, even the carts stood in their neat line, just as they had been left. They found the mercenaries grouped around their cooking fire, scarcely a man showing any sign that they had fought a bloody battle earlier that day.

"Where in God's name have you been?" Idwal asked, when the two joined them. "I had a hard task getting John to believe that you were safe. Do me a kindness and go to see him. You will find him in Glyndŵr's pavilion."

Before they could set off, however, they caught sight of John Leggatt striding toward them. "You are safe, then," John called out, as he drew near. "Forgive me, Idwal, for my doubts." He cupped Huw's face in one hand and examined the raw welt. "Safe, though not unmarked, I see. I trust you gave a blow in return?"

"The lad did well," Idwal answered. "I would be content to have him by my side in any scrape."

Later, when they had eaten, Idwal spoke privately with the captain. "I've got to ask, John. We have been together for many years, yet I have never known you fret over anyone as you do about that lad. Will you tell me your reason?"

"I will not. Not to you or any man," John answered bluntly, then, seeing the hurt in Idwal's face, softened his tone. "I don't wish to give offence, but I'd rather not speak on this matter. My thanks for watching over him as you did, old friend. I shall not forget it."

From down the valley a drum began to beat and Huw and David joined their comrades, who were preparing to move off. There was a general movement in answer to the drum's summons, and the mercenaries mingled with the flow which was headed for the dragon standard. When all were gathered, Glyndŵr appeared, still wearing his coat of chain mail. He spoke to the crowd, congratulating them on their victory and praising their courage. He told them that they would make merry that night, to celebrate. The carts would leave shortly for Taliesin, their drivers and escorts taking money to purchase ale and mead. When darkness fell over the Hyddgen, the remote valley echoed with sounds of revelry. News of the victory had spread quickly and people from the lands below made the journey to join in Glyndŵr's triumph. The Prince welcomed them, urging Tudor and the others to do likewise, for amongst the visitors were men who had preferred to await the outcome of the fight before committing themselves to his standard. His brother found this injunction difficult to comprehend. However, he concealed his contempt, and forced a smile. Bonfires blazed, barrels were tapped, and people danced to the sounds of pipes and drums.

Huw drank some ale but refused offers of the sweet mead. The ale only served to make him drowsy, so he was soon seated alone by the mercenaries' camp fire. Coaxing the flames into life, he lay back and, despite the loud voices and laughter, he was soon asleep. David remained close to the carts. He was determined to blot out the terror of the morning, though it meant drinking himself into a state of oblivion. Idwal and his fellow bowmen drank steadily, eyeing the women who had made the journey up to the battlefield. Glyndŵr sat with John Leggatt, talking over the day, his mind already busy with plans for the future. Hyddgen had been a small affair, in terms of numbers, yet the consequences would be very far-reaching.

Chapter 8

On the day after the battle, abandoned weapons and armour were gathered in, examined and distributed. A search was made for more of the dead, who were buried where they lay. The carts were dispatched to the low land in search of food. Riders came and went with messages. Men who had been hurt in the fight were tended to, some returning to their homes.

Huw and David had been looking for the dead, and when they returned to camp, found John Leggatt waiting for them.

"'Well now, my learned friend, your moment has arrived," he told David Mostyn, "Glyndŵr commands that you attend to him in his pavilion. He needs the services of one who can write letters."

Huw was about to look for something useful to do when Leggatt said, "Stay a moment, lad. I wish to speak with you. Idwal tells me that you showed spirit yesterday and he says you have the makings of a bowman. I must ask if you would join our company? Glyndŵr will need every man he can get, for the King will not take his defeat here lightly."

Huw stared in silence at the captain. To be invited into John's elite band of men was more than he'd dared hope for, yet he hesitated

"You would be paid for your services, the same as the

other men. The Prince is not short of money," John added, a little harshly.

"It's not the money," Huw stammered. "I would dearly wish to serve with men such as Idwal but I'd be uneasy away from Argoed. Should Griffith Lloyd move against father, I would never forgive myself if I were absent. Yesterday, I was certain that I was right to leave home. Now, faced with this decision, I'm not so sure."

John recalled the man who had caused trouble for the Gethins, and he softened his tone. "Oh yes, your unfriendly neighbour," he said. "The one who thinks and acts like a Marcher Baron. What if this Griffith did not pose a threat? Would you then become one of us?"

"Indeed I would," Huw answered fervently.

The captain thought deeply for a while, then came to a decision. "Go find Idwal and the others. Tell them that we are going on a short journey and they are to meet me here as soon as they are ready. We shall pay a visit to Cwmdu and call on your neighbour."

When Huw had sped away, his heart beating rapidly, the captain went to Glyndŵr's pavilion. The Prince was dictating a letter to David, and broke off when John entered. He listened to what the captain had to say, asked one or two questions and gave his consent.

"Go if you wish," he said, "but understand that we cannot linger at Hyddgen for another day. It is difficult feeding the men up here and my purse will soon need replenishing." He gave John a searching look. "This young bowman must have special qualities for you to take all this trouble. Whatever your reason, the Gethins struck me as the type of people we shall need in our struggle. So, bide a while, John. You shall deliver a letter to this troublesome neighbour."

He started dictate to David, whose quill was soon scratching furiously on the parchment. The letter was brief and to the point. It carried a dire warning, that any move against the people of Cwmdu would be taken as personal attack on Glyndŵr. He signed and sealed the letter, appending the title Prince of Wales after his name.

He handed the letter to Leggatt and warned, "We shall be away from here by early morning. Rejoin me as soon as possible, for who knows when I shall need your bowmen. Our road lies to the south, towards Carmarthen."

John found the mercenaries ready to march and they set off at once for Cwmdu. Despite the need for speed, he did not rush the pace. Once over Plynlimon, his men swung into the easy, loping stride they had used on their marches through Europe. Huw found the journey easy enough but as the day wore on, he guessed that John had no intention of calling a halt. It was only when they came to the head of the falls that the bowmen broke step. Making sure that he was the last, Huw followed the others down. He knew them well enough now to know that, should they even suspect his fear, he would suffer their wicked humour for many days to come.

As they came to each of the holdings, they were greeted joyously. High up on their left, a look-out whistled and began to scramble down, eager for news. The people joined their ranks, offering food, which was taken with eager hands and eaten on the march. At last, Argoed came into view and Huw ran on ahead.

Warned by the look-out, his family stood waiting in front of the house and, as he drew near, Emma ran toward him.

"Thank God you are safe," she cried, as they held each

other close. "We had news of the battle and I have been praying for your safety every moment since." She stepped back a pace and looked up at him. "Look at you though. Let me tend that bruise on your cheek."

Despite Huw's protests, she led him toward the house, ignoring his embarrassed glances at the arriving mercenaries. John Leggatt watched them enter, his expression inscrutable. He looked away when his eyes met Huw's.

After Emma had bathed Huw's wound with melted butter, he went back outside and discovered his father in conversation with John.

"Your captain tells me that you are taking a letter from Glyndŵr to Plas Hirnant," Morgan said, embracing him briefly. "Its contents warn Griffith Lloyd that we in Cwmdu are under the prince's protection. We thank him for this, although our neighbour has been quiet enough of late. He is even entertaining a few visitors at present."

The big man studied his son from head to toe and gently touched the bruised cheek. "Your captain also tells me that you are hesitating about joining his men. I would say that you would be a fool not to, Huw. These bowmen know their trade better than most, I'd wager. Serve with them and learn all you can. That way you will stay alive and come home again to us one day."

Anxious to deliver the letter, John gave the order to move off. With the peoples' enthusiastic cries ringing in their ears, his men followed him down to the meadow. Hywel had slipped away from Argoed and appeared at Huw's elbow when the mercenaries were fording the Hafren. The lad seemed unaware of the seriousness of their mission and skipped merrily along, questioning his brother about the battle. Not until Idwal growled a threat did he fall silent. Drawing closer to Plas Hirnant, they saw that the gates had been closed; a number of heads showed over the palisade. Coming to a halt, John glared up at the anxious faces and demanded entry.

"Inform your master that I have a letter from my master, the Prince of Wales. Make haste, now, or you shall feel my wrath." The heads bobbed down out of sight and John winked broadly at his men. "I think that I'm going to enjoy this business," he chuckled. "When they open the gates, follow me in. Look as though you are ready to knock a few heads together."

Within moments the gates swung open and he led the way in, looking around for any signs of treachery. All seemed well, and he drew the mercenaries into a line in the centre of the courtyard. Griffith's retainers stood grouped about the doorway of the mansion and John beckoned to one of them.

"Your master seems reluctant to show himself," he said. "My men are impatient and can be hard to restrain. Go and bring him to me."

The man was staring transfixed at Idwal, who was smiling his frightening leer, and gladly he turned away and entered the mansion. While they waited, Huw took a good look at Plas Hirnant. To his left stood a large barn and a byre, on his right, a row of stables formed the other wing of the courtyard. Through a gap between these and the mansion, he could see that the land had been turned into a garden. The house itself, constructed of stone and timber, was a two-storey affair and told of wealth, for all the apertures had been covered with glass. He was staring intently at these when a young girl came out of the mansion and walked boldly up to the bowmen, stopping directly in front of him.

"My uncle will attend you shortly," she announced, speaking slowly. "He is not of good health and begs you to be patient."

Huw could not take his eyes off the girl. He guessed that she would be about fifteen years of age, pretty in a boyish kind of way, with startling blue eyes. It was the colour of her hair, however, that held his attention, for he had never seen a head so fair; ash blonde, almost white. Becoming aware of his scrutiny, the girl stared back and defiantly tossed her head.

"Are you Griffith Lloyd?" John's voice barked out, as an elderly man limped out of the building.

Huw observed that two men had appeared and now stood side by side in the courtyard; the older of the two leaned heavily on a stick, a look of apprehension on his ruddy features, and, instinctively, Huw knew that this was the master of Plas Hirnant.

"Where is this letter?" Griffith asked, limping closer. "I have no quarrel with Owain Glyndŵr."

"I am pleased to hear you say that," John replied sternly, handing over the parchment. "However, the Prince wishes you to read this and has commanded me to make sure that you understand its content."

Griffith broke the seal, squinted at the writing, then passed the letter to his companion. "Please read it for me, Richard," he said. "My sight is not as clear as it was."

The young man took it from him and glanced briefly at it. "I cannot read that, Uncle," he said, speaking in English. "My grasp of Welsh is limited." He gave the letter to John, a smirk on his face. "It would seem that you must read the message for us," he said.

The captain gave him a hard look, held the letter at arm's length and, in a loud voice, he repeated in English

Owain's warning against any attack on the people of Cwmdu.

Meanwhile, Huw studied the arrogant younger man. There was no doubting that he was closely related to the girl; he had the same colour of hair, and there was no doubting, also, his obvious hostility to Leggatt. He seemed surprised that John could read and translate, and stood listening intently.

"I trust that this is plain to all of you," John cried, when the message was ended. "Remember it well, for I have no wish to return here." Rolling up the parchment, he secured it in his belt and forthwith led his bowmen out into the meadow.

They were nearing the stream when Idwal called out, "I didn't know that you could read, John."

"I can't," came the reply, "but I was not going to let that high-nosed Englishman know that."

Griffith Lloyd watched the bowmen until they passed from sight. The relief at their departure was overwhelming, causing his limbs to tremble. He had reason enough to fear the worst, for he had sent a warning to Aberystwyth, when Glyndŵr had passed through Cwmdu. The thought that this action had been discovered had thrown him into a state of panic and, with Richard's help, he'd hastily buried his money in the garden, at the first glimpse of the delegation from Glyndŵr.

"You will understand now why I have stayed my hand against the Gethins, Richard," he said, limping toward the doorway. "I have not dared to make a move while this rebel Glyndŵr is free. We now know for certain that he will aid those in Cwmdu and I could well lose everything."

He led the way into the dining hall, calling the blonde girl, Elinor, to join them. Lowering himself carefully into a chair, he poured three glasses of wine, offering one to the girl and another to Richard, her brother.

"Drink slowly and enjoy the taste, Elinor. We have earned a treat today. I still find it hard to believe that your parents are no longer with us. You should be proud of your sister, Richard; she is growing up to be quite the lady."

"Life can be dull, Uncle. I see little enough of my brother. I have only my maid for company most of the time," the girl said.

"I must be about Uncle's business, little sister," Richard said. "I must say, Uncle, that, I am not happy with this Welsh maid of hers. She influences Elinor in all matters. Were it my choice, I would send her packing."

"It was your father's wish that she remain in your service and I shall honour his request," Griffith told him. "Would you leave us now, Elinor. Your brother and I must speak of money matters, which will only bore you."

He waited until the girl had gone and then poured more wine. "What you have told me about the business is quite disturbing. I had hoped that the wool trade would improve, though this is not the case. We are the main source of dyes in the Marches, yet there is little demand for them. If we are to hold onto our wealth, we must buy and breed more cattle, and for that I need more pasture." He drained the last of his wine and stared moodily into space for a while.

"This cursed revolt has ruined my plans to drive out the smallholders in Cwmdu, which is our only chance of increasing our land holding. It would seem that we have to play a waiting game. The situation is not to my liking, yet there is no choice left to me."

"I have to agree with you," Richard replied. "Yet we cannot wait for long. We must pray that the King will take the field himself and crush these peasants. I feel that it would benefit our aims to let our loyalty to the Crown be known. Are you agreeable to me seeking an audience with his son? The Prince is at Chester acting for his father."

The young Prince Henry, son of Henry IV, known as Bolingbroke, was taking an active role in the affairs of his father and was presently in Chester, in charge of the north-west.

"Go to Chester, by all means, Richard, but what of your scheme to hire a band of cut-throats?" Griffith asked. "Have you found out how much they would cost? Such men would not come cheaply, of that I'm sure."

"I spoke to a man who once served as a soldier and now lives by his wits. He told me that, for six pennies a day, he could hire any number of men to do the work we would demand. It would be money well spent. With twenty men the likes of him and your own retainers, we would soon have yonder valley for ourselves, Uncle."

Later that evening, Griffith Lloyd stood alone in the gateway, looking out over the meadow. The scene was idyllic but he saw nothing of the beauty around him. The picture that he held in his mind was of a large herd of cattle, grazing on both sides of the Hafren and down into the cwm. Each animal carried a mark of ownership, and he was determined that the mark they bore would be his.

Chapter 9

Huw leaned against a wall of the tiny church at Pilleth, and looked around him at the carnage. The battle of Hyddgen, which had taken place about a year earlier, had been a bloody affair yet seemed as naught compared to what he saw now. His eyes swept up the body-strewn hill called Bryn Glas to the crest, where earlier Welsh bowmen had rained death on those below. Today however, they numbered more than a thousand and had created equivalent havoc amongst their foes.

The English had marched into the wild hills of Radnor, proud and confident, their ranks ablaze with colourful banners. It was mid summer, in the year 1402, and the Welsh were in the ascendancy. Now, the symbols of the Marcher knights lay broken, scattered amongst the dead and dying. The nature of the ground had forced the English to attack up the steep hill; many had died before they had even began to climb. Many more perished when Rhys Gethin unleashed his hidden horde of spearmen from behind the crest. Caught completely by surprise, the English paid a dreadful price. Swept from the hill, they had crowded into the narrow valley, still within range of the bowmen, who loosed until every arrow was spent.

The clash of steel rang out from nearby and Huw moved away from the wall, his short sword ready for use. Cautiously turning a corner of the church, he saw that a handful of Welsh had trapped one of their foe and were slowly moving in for the kill. Their intended victim, an armoured knight, stumbled backward until he reached the church wall, where he wearily raised his sword. The visor of his helmet had been tilted open and Huw could see a trickle of blood on the knight's face. He wanted no part in what was about to happen, and was turning away when John Leggatt brushed past him.

"Stay lad, I may need you," the captain growled.

"Take an arrow Huw and make ready to shoot," Idwal muttered in his ear.

Huw took the proffered arrow, notched it but did not draw back on the string. "We can't kill our own men."

"Is that a fact," Idwal chuckled. "Glyndŵr needs prisoners of rank for ransom. Remember who is paying you, lad. The Prince expects you to have a care for his interests."

By now, John had pushed through the encircling men and stood facing them, his back to the knight. "Enough of this, my friends," he cried. "We need this one alive. The Prince wishes to question him and would be greatly displeased to learn that you have killed him. If it is more blood you crave, there is plenty to be had down in the valley."

The men hesitated, glancing uncertainly at each other; John seized his opportunity to say, "You could also spill your own blood, if you so wish," and pointed to Idwal and Huw.

The sight of the two bowmen standing behind them startled the men who were intent on killing the knight and when Huw drew back on his bowstring, they quickly moved off towards the sounds of fighting. The next moment, the knight gave a loud groan and slumped to his knees. He would have toppled over, but John rushed to his side and put out a hand to steady him.

"Hold fast, sir knight," he said in English. "We wish you no further harm. Do you surrender your sword?" The knight nodded and handed over the weapon.

"I thank you for saving my life," he gasped. "I must ask now who holds my sword? The rules of chivalry demand it," he added, giving a brief smile.

"John Leggatt, captain of bowmen," John answered.

"Then, captain, I must ask a favour of you. Help me out of this armour, else it will be the end of me."

Between them, the three bowmen released the knight from the heavy suit of burnished steel. His fine linen shirt was soaked with sweat. Huw picked up the discarded helmet and went in search of water. A well stood by one corner of the church and, after quenching his own thirst, he filled the helmet. The knight drank deeply, draining every drop, then smiled his thanks.

"Well, sir, it would seem that you will survive," John said, as the Englishman got to his feet. "May I ask your name?"

The knight had regained his composure and he looked calmly at John for a few moments. "I am Edmund Mortimer," he answered simply.

John's brow creased in thought, then his expression changed to surprise as it dawned on him how important this knight was. "You are the same Mortimer who was once in line for the English throne?" he asked incredulously.

"The very same," Edmund answered.

John placed a hand on his shoulder. "We had best get you to Glyndŵr quickly," he said. "I would not wish to face him, should anything happen to you now that the battle is almost won."

John, Idwal, Huw and the knight left the shelter of the church and followed a track which led away from the receding fighting, avoiding the bodies which lay along much of its length. Edmund's face paled at their number and he had to force himself to keep moving. He knew that he would have to live with the knowledge that it was he who was responsible for the day's disaster. With the King suspicious of him and his family, he had been eager to command this force of Marcher men and thus vindicate the Mortimers.

From the crest of the hill, they saw the dragon standard begin to move down the slope. Glyndŵr followed, in the company of several of his captains, changing direction when he saw John.

"A great victory, John," he cried out, as he drew near. "Your bowmen were truly frightening to behold. Nowhere did the English reach our pikemen." He placed an arm around a short, fiery soldier who came to a stop beside him. "Wales owes you much for today, Rhys," he enthused. "Your entrapment was a complete success. I must confess that I thought our numbers were too great to be kept secret. It pleases me to have been proved wrong."

His eyes came to rest on Edmund and he gave the knight a slight bow, noting that he was unarmed. "Who have we here?" he asked. "You would appear to have had the worst of the encounter."

"My lord, this is Edmund Mortimer," John answered. "He has surrendered his sword, though I believe he would be the happier were it now held by another of his own rank."

He gave the weapon to Glyndŵr, who managed to hide his feeling of delight. "By all that's holy," he exclaimed in

English. "Should this be true, it would be a fitting end to an incredible day."

"It is true enough, my lord," Edmund told him. "My armour is by yonder church, while my banner lies on the hill."

Glyndŵr could scarcely believe the good fortune which had delivered such a high ranking noble into his hands. The ransom for Edward's freedom should bring a fortune to his coffers.

"Your armour and your banner shall be returned to you, sir knight, Give me your word that you will make no attempt to escape and you may have your sword now."

Edmund gave his word and took the proffered sword. "I will tell you that this blade shall never again be used in anger or war. Today has sickened me of killing and I am not ashamed to say so." He looked once more over the hillside, then bowed his head. "It will be hard for me to live with the memories of this dreadful place."

"You must not blame yourself, sir," Rhys Gethin told him. "You had no choice other than to seek to shift us from the hill."

The little captain looked down the narrow valley and turned to Glyndŵr. "I must leave you and follow the fight, my lord. There may be others of rank to save."

Glyndŵr nodded at Rhys, the man who commanded his soldiers. "Take my brother Tudor and the others with you," he said. "You may be in need of their swords. I shall take care of our new guest."

Glyndŵr waited until Rhys and his party had moved on down the valley, then spoke to John Leggatt. "Have your men bring the knight's armour and banner to the hill top. You had best accompany us, although there is little chance now of any threat to his safety."

Nightfall found the Welsh camped on the flat, dry ground atop Bryn Glas, which the English knew as Pilleth. Unlike Hyddgen, there were few sounds of revelry after this battle, for all were very aware of the countless dead which still lay unburied. Seated by a fire with Idwal and the others, Huw reflected on the twelve months which had passed since he joined the bowmen on Plynlimon. He had seen and learned much. After Hyddgen, Glyndŵr had marched south to the Vale of Carmarthen, where he had been warmly welcomed. His small force quickly grew into an army, as men joined him, eager to fight. With the purse taken from the dead Flemish soldier, Huw had bought a bow of yew. He still had a few coins left over and with a small sum borrowed from John, he had also purchased a leather jerkin.

Satisfied that he had the support of the Carmarthen people, Owain had turned his attention back to the north. For six frustrating weeks his men had besieged Caernarfon castle, making no impression on its mighty walls. The fine summer of 1401 came to an end, to be followed by a period of heavy rain. It was a relief when the order to abandon the siege was given. Throughout the following winter and spring, Huw was one of the small company of bowmen who escorted Glyndŵr on his travels. They had been forever on the move, and had to evade English patrols on several occasions. He had learned much from his fellow mercenaries, though was conscious by now that, whenever danger threatened, either John or Idwal was at his side.

His reverie was broken by the sound of women's laughter, which came from the battle field. He rose to his feet and walked over to the crest of Bryn Glas. The moon shone through broken cloud, bathing the slope with its pale light, showing shadowy figures flitting amongst the dead. With rising anger, he saw the shapes of women, bent over bodies, stripping the dead. He ran back to the fire, snatched up a blazing log and returned to the crest. Bracing himself, Huw whirled the length of wood around his head before flinging it out into space. The log soared through the air, trailing a shower of sparks, then fell to earth. He knew that his gesture was futile, yet drew some satisfaction from it, when the laughter ceased momentarily.

Seated outside his pavilion with Tudor, who had returned, Glyndŵr marvelled at the good fortune which had delivered Edmund Mortimer into his hands.

"Think on it, brother," Glyndŵr said, in a low voice. "We hold a nobleman who could one day be King of England. Yet, strangely, I am not sure what should be done with him. Do we demand his ransom, as I'd first thought, or do we hold onto him?"

Tudor turned the options over in his mind, then shrugged his shoulder. "I wish that I had the gift to foretell the future, Owain," he replied eventually. "It would depend on Henry Bolingbroke's ability to hold on to the throne. Should he lose it, Mortimer's claim could well be honoured. It would be to our advantage to treat him kindly and offer our aid, in the hope that this opportunity might one day arise. As for the payment of ransom, we shall soon have enough money, anyway, to support our cause for another two years. Now that we hold Grey of Ruthin prisoner, there is no urgency for us to do anything about Mortimer. Grey's ransom will suffice for our needs."

The two brothers chuckled at the thought of the hated Marcher Lord now lingering in his lonely prison. In the spring, they had set a trap for their neighbour, Grey had taken the bait and ridden headlong into an ambush. Owain had set a high price for his release and the King, knowing that his nobles would judge his actions, had been forced to agree to the demands. It was sweet revenge for Glyndŵr. The man who had been the prime instigator of his own losses was now about to be made bankrupt and would remain so for the rest of his days.

Owain could see a great deal of sense in what his brother Tudor had said. It was no secret that the king was insecure on his throne and that he was also hard pressed for money. A few weeks after Hyddgen, he had gathered three armies, numbering thirty thousand men in total, and had marched them into Wales. Not a single Welshman had contested his grand parade and, in the end, he had marched home, frustrated angry and with empty coffers.

"What you say makes good sense," Owain told Tudor. "I shall inform King Henry that we hold Edmund. It will be of interest to me to see how he reacts to the news. I'm away to my bed," he said stifling a yawn. "This day has been a great one for us, Tudor. It will be a long while before the English make another move against us. Wales is ours for the taking and we must make the most of the chance."

He bade his brother sleep well and entered his pavilion. He looked down at the bed of freshly cut fern on which Edmund Mortimer tossed in restless sleep. Owain felt a rush of sympathy for the young man. Before settling himself, he gave thanks to God for giving him another victory. His last thoughts were of the successes his cause had achieved over the past year and whether his good fortune would continue.

Chapter 10

David drank the last of his ale, placed his empty tankard on the rough-hewn table and debated whether to order another. He decided against it and went over to the low doorway and peered out. The rain fell in torrents, turning the road to Chester into a quagmire. With a muffled curse, he fastened his soaked cloak around his shoulders and glanced enviously at those seated around the hearth. He met Idwal's gaze.

"I'll have a drink for you, master secretary," the bowman called out, giving his terrible grin. "Were it a fine evening, I would accompany you down the road but I have not dried myself from my last outing."

David, unable to find a merry quip in response, stepped out into the downpour, where the deeply rutted road resembled a fast running stream. He began to walk by its side, squelching through the mud. Since Hyddgen, he had been at the centre of events, acting as secretary to Glyndŵr and present when the Prince met with his more powerful supporters. He had, therefore, been present when the ransom for Grey was set at ten thousand ducats, a sum that came as a shock to nearly every man at the meeting, including himself, though the method of payment was a greater surprise. Glyndŵr had been content to allow David to oversee receipt of the ransom for the release of the prisoner, Grey of Ruthin, which was the reason he was out in the deluge and headed for the river Dee

He followed the road for some distance, until he came to a low rise, where John Leggatt and a group of bowmen vainly sought shelter under an oak. From here, there was a good view of the river and, despite the low hanging clouds, he could see the roofs of Chester in the distance. The road dipped gently down to the water's edge, to where a ferry boat plied its trade. David saw the barge moored on the far bank.

"I'm uneasy about this meeting," John growled at him. "You place a great deal of trust in a knight's code of honour. We could easily finish up having our necks stretched, should they so decide."

David was about to reassure him when one of the bowmen shouted a warning and pointed towards the river. He had seen five horsemen, coming from the direction of the town, who rode for the ferry, where they dismounted. The ferryman emerged from a nearby hut, held a brief discussion and led the party aboard his barge.

"Five men, as instructed in my letter," David said. "None the less, John, it might be wise to leave your men here. Tell them to keep watch and send us a warning should anything suspicious happen across the river. Place somebody else in command; I'd like you and Huw to be present at the meeting."

John turned quickly away, to hide his surprise. Until now, David had always kept his distance, treating the captain warily when in his company. For his part, John had watched the secretary working closely with Glyndŵr and had grudgingly come to admire his astute mind. David might be a danger to friend as well as foe on the field of battle but with his pen he was a different person altogether. Feeling somewhat flattered, John told one of his men to take command. He went to stand by the secretary's side.

The barge crossed the turbulent river and its passengers were soon plodding up to where the Welshmen waited. All wore cloaks, the hoods pulled up to protect their heads, and it was only when they drew close that David was able to recognise their leader, one of Grey's men-at-arms, who had been captured with his master and whom Grey had chosen to deliver the ransom payment.

"I have done as you told me," the spokesman said sullenly. "These knights have the authority of the King to negotiate on his behalf. Now, keep your word and set me free."

David told him that he could go. The man went to arrange another crossing of the Dee, to collect his horse from the far bank. No-one bothered to see where he went afterwards. There were matters to be discussed and the rain was as relentless as ever.

"We may as well conduct our business in some degree of comfort," David Mostyn told them. "Let us go into the inn and deal with one another like gentlemen."

On entering the inn, he motioned them to a table and called for ale to be served. The Englishmen pulled back their hoods, three of them sitting silently, their eyes fixed on the table. The fourth crossed over to the hearth and held his hands to the flames. David could now see that he was a youth of some fifteen years, slightly built, with a pleasant, open countenance. Despite being in a room full of his enemies, the lad gave no sign of unease and stood for a while by the fire, before returning to the table.

"Well now, my lords, let us get our business settled," David said. "You will understand that we do not wish to tarry here a moment longer than needs be. Do you have the first payment?"

The three knights looked immediately at their young companion, who gave a slight nod.

"We have," one of them said, placing a heavy pouch on the table. "Two thousand ducats, as you directed. The remainder will follow within six months. May we suggest that this inn be used to make that payment? The place suits us well."

David smiled at the noble and shook his head. "I think not," he replied. "When it is nearer the day, I will send you another messenger. He will tell you where and when to bring the money."

The three looked again at the youth, and a suspicion began to grow in David's mind.

"My lord Glyndŵr, Prince of Wales, wishes me to say that, had the King acted more justly, this war would never have begun," David said, emphasising the title.

The youth had appeared to be more interested in the bowmen seated around him than in the transaction being made but, at David's words, his eyes switched sharply to the secretary's face.

"Your lord assumes much," he said, in an even tone. "It is my belief that Wales already has one Prince. There cannot be two."

His suspicion as to the identity of this confident youth now confirmed, David decided to let the matter rest. He was not here to argue the rights of who held the title Prince of Wales, it was enough that he knew for certain that the King's son was seated opposite him.

"Another matter, my lords," he said. "It concerns Edmund Mortimer, who, as you know, is held by us. We are prepared to release him, in the future, for a reasonable ransom." A long silence greeted his statement, during which the nobles failed to hide their embarrassment.

"The King sends his love to Edmund," the young Henry finally replied. "However, he must be patient. There are many demands on the royal purse at present. We shall inform you when we are in a position to negotiate his release."

David nodded his understanding. The youth had made it perfectly clear that his father was content to leave Mortimer in captivity. No mention had been made of selling any of the nobleman's possessions to raise a ransom. David could only wonder whether the King intended to use Edmund's wealth for himself.

With the business completed, David expected the Englishmen to take their leave and was surprised when Prince Henry ordered more ale. When this had been served, he asked the secretary about Glyndŵr, expressing the wish that the Welsh leader would seek a pardon. He seemed content, after this, to sip his ale and resume his study of the men seated around the room. His attention became fixed on a young man who sat quietly in a corner. This Welshman was only a few years older than himself but Henry sensed that he had seen and done a great deal. Indeed, when the young man met his searching look, Henry could see this vast experience of life reflected in the dark eyes.

From his corner seat, Huw had watched the proceedings with little interest, not understanding a word of what was being said, for it was managed with English, but he knew that David would tell him all later. For some reason, the young lad sitting with the Englishmen irritated him. Maybe it was the air of confidence that he carried, something unusual in one of his years. When Prince Henry gave Huw a smile and a slight bow of his head, Huw did not respond. Instead, he shifted his gaze to

David, who stood up.

"I would suggest that you make your departure," he said. "It will soon be dark and you may be unable to cross the Dee; the river is bound to flood soon with all this rain."

When the four Englishmen had gone, David Mostyn gave the heavy purse to John to guard and moved his seat closer to the fire. The identity of the youth he kept to himself. While the young man was in the room full of mercenaries, it seemed the wisest thing to do, and there was no need to say anything after the prince had gone.

Seated on the barge, Prince Henry thought about the men left behind in the inn. He was convinced that the King, his father, was mistaken in not pursuing this war in Wales with greater vigour, even if it meant borrowing more money. The men that he had met tonight were not those who could be easily subdued; they would have to be beaten decisively on the battlefield, and that was going to be a very difficult task.

Chapter 11

Two months after the meeting on the banks of the Dee, Huw walked east along the road from Machynlleth, his pace quickening at the thought of home. Ascending the short, steep pass which was the watershed of the streams which ran east or west, he soon came to the Church of Our Lady, which served a wide area, including Cwmdu, and as he passed, Huw made the sign of the cross and said a prayer of thanks for his safe return. It was a long while since he had seen his family and then he had spent only one night at Argoed. In the past two years, Glyndŵr's bowmen seemed to have been always on the march, and Huw guessed that there was little of Wales which had not seen the Dragon standard. Now, he had the next six weeks in which to do as he pleased, and when John had told him this, Huw had had no hesitation in deciding to sleep in his own bed, and the thought of eating Emma's cooking was irresistible.

The road home seemed endless, until, at last, Argoed stood before him and he shouted a greeting and ran for the door. His hand was on the latch when the door swung open and his father's bulky figure barred his entry. The two stared at each other until, with a roar of delight, Morgan flung his arms around Huw and held him in a bone-crushing hug.

"Is it really you, lad?" he bellowed. "We had almost

given up hope of seeing you here this winter. Look who is here, Emma, my love. Our wanderer has returned."

He led Huw into the room where Emma stood, her face showing her emotions. Crossing to her, Huw held her tight, kissed her cheek and stood back at arm's length.

"My prayers are answered," she said softly. Her eyes searched his face anxiously, looking for signs of injury. "You are not hurt?" she asked.

"No mother, I am well enough," he answered. "A little tired, maybe, and certainly hungry. I could eat something now, to tide me over until supper."

In a matter of moments, he was seated at the table, a plate of cold mutton and a tankard of Iolo's ale before him. While he ate, Morgan sat opposite him, a smile of sheer pleasure on his face. Emma noted the changes in her son, the gangling, somewhat awkward lad who had left home to join Glyndŵr was now a young man, his limbs and shoulders thickening with muscle. He was, as she had foreseen, quite handsome in his dark way, though a hardness around his eyes made him seem older than his nineteen years. He could turn many a girl's head, Emma decided with pride.

"Now, tell me all," Morgan demanded, as soon as Huw had finished eating. "From what we hear, Glyndŵr holds much of the country, only a few castles still defy him. Is this how it really is?"

"It is true enough," Huw answered. "We have strong support in the north and as far south as Carmarthen, while the people further on to the south-east, in Morgannwg, are friendly enough, yet not all of the men wish to fight for our cause. David told me that Glyndŵr is determined to win them over during this coming summer."

"I wish him well in that," Morgan remarked. "This

suspicion that our people in the south have for those from the north has always been a curse on our nation. Even the great Llewelyn failed to completely unite us."

He poured himself some ale and drank deeply, before speaking again. "Have you taken a part in laying siege to a castle yet?" he asked.

"That I have and it's a task I hate," Huw answered. "With a stout-walled castle to hold, sixty defenders can defy a thousand. Glyndŵr is having siege engines built, in readiness for our next campaign, then we will have a greater chance of getting over the walls."

Morgan sat in silence for a while, then leaned his elbows on the table, an earnest look on his face. "Promise me that you will not attempt to be the first man over those walls. Leave that to others," he said.

"No need for you to fear on that account," Huw replied, with a broad grin. "The very thought of scaling a fifty-foot ladder makes my belly turn. I shall be content to stand off and use my bow."

His father smiled back at him and stood up, peering through one of the partly open shutters. "It will soon be dark, so I'd best get the cattle in," he said. "Will you keep me company? Your brother should be home when we return."

Down in the meadow, a fine mist had begun to form, its white strands reaching to their waists. "We shall have a frost tonight," Morgan commented, before giving his call.

From the far end of the pasture his cattle began to move towards them, seeming to float over the whiteness as though they were ships at sea. There were now three of the white cattle, the two cows and a heifer, and these led the rest of the herd.

"I shall be selling the heifer shortly," Morgan said, as the cattle filed by. "I've had a few men calling here to have a look at her already but probably your Uncle Iolo will end up with her."

When the herd had passed by, Huw looked over at Plas Hirnant. "What of Griffith Lloyd? Is he leaving Cwmdu well alone these days?" he asked.

"He has, until now," Morgan answered. "We see very little of him. The talk is that he is a sick man; his niece and her maid have been living there for a long while, taking care of him." He shivered as the cold air began to bite, and the two men followed the herd. "Come on, lad, let's get home. It is hot food and a seat by the hearth for us tonight," he said.

In the byre, Huw helped his father with the milking, slipping easily back into the once familiar chore. The soft, heavy breathing of the animals and the warmth that they generated provided a pleasing sensation which he had almost forgotten. When their task was finished, the two went into the house, where they were shortly joined by Hywel and Pero. The hound, breaking the rules for once, rushed indoors when it picked up Huw's scent, causing havoc as it leapt excitedly at him. Only when Emma picked up a birch broom did the hound beat a retreat. Later that evening, their supper eaten, Huw had to speak of his adventures to his eager brother. Their parents, seated side by side, listened as Huw answered Hywel's many questions, though both parents guessed that he was omitting much. He scarcely mentioned the fighting, speaking mostly of the antics and wicked humour of his fellow bowmen and, finally, he told them of the meeting with the King's son.

"What did he look like?" Emma asked, in

astonishment. "I hope you showed him some respect."

"He was in no position to demand that," Huw answered. "For all I knew he could have been the son of a money lender. As for how he looked, he was much the same as Hywel, only probably not as gifted." He got to his feet and stretched his tall frame. "I'm for my bed," he announced. "It is one of the things I have been looking forward to."

He kissed his mother fondly on her cheek, touched Morgan's shoulder and made for his room, followed by Hywel. For a while he answered more of his brother's questions, before blowing out the candle and settling down to sleep.

The following few days passed by quickly. Huw helped out around the holding whenever he felt like it, or went hunting in the woods lower down the Hafren. There were no demands made of him and he enjoyed every moment, doing just as he pleased. He spent one whole day at Iolo's, quietly relishing the fuss and attention his uncle and aunt lavished on him. Then, one night, after the grey clouds had given warning, snow fell heavily and left a one-foot-deep layer on the ground, not enough to prevent movement but it made life difficult. It was now that the people of Cwmdu helped one another and, when all was tended to at Argoed, the Gethins gave aid to their neighbours. The snow made it difficult for the look-out to climb up to the usual post, and it was agreed that he would patrol along the Hafren instead.

It was he who called to Huw, early one morning, and asked him to take a look at something he'd found. From the top end of the meadow, what appeared to be the tracks of a large hound led toward Argoed. Where the man was standing, the snow was stained yellow, and he knelt down to take a closer look at the paw marks.

"A hound after a bitch?" Huw suggested.

"No hound made these marks," the man replied. "I'd wager you have had a visit from a wolf and a big brute at that."

Huw grunted his thanks for the warning and trudged quickly back to the holding but there was no sign of Morgan or Hywel, so he told his mother of the wolf, collected his bow and selected several arrows. Returning outdoors, he went over to the stable, where he picked up a length of rope, before going to the byre to fetch the hound. Pero raised himself from his bed of straw as he entered and, for once, stood quietly as Huw slipped a knotted loop over his head. It was as though the hound sensed that something was amiss, for he followed Huw placidly to where the wolf had urinated. In a flash, the hound's mood changed and he began to strain on his makeshift leash.

Huw gave the hound its head and they were soon bounding over the snow, heading towards the lower end of the meadow; the wolf's tracks were easy to follow until they came to the first trees, where Huw slowed their pace as they entered the woods. A well-used path ran beside the stream, occasionally twisting its way to avoid some obstruction, and Pero followed this, his nose close to the ground. The hound now began to strain on his leash with even more eagerness, testing Huw's strength to the limit. At a steady trot, they carried on for about half a mile, until they came on a scene which confirmed that they were drawing close to the wolf. Lying on its back in a pool of blood and shredded wool, an old ewe coughed its last. Kneeling beside the animal, Huw saw a gaping hole in its throat and he was about to release Pero when a scream split the still air.

Slipping the leash, he began to sprint along the track, losing sight of Pero, who gave his deep baying cry. From ahead came the sound of thudding hooves and Huw slowed his pace, but he had not acted soon enough, for a horse and rider suddenly appeared around a bend. He had a brief glimpse of the horse's rolling eyes and of teeth bared in fright, before he flung himself sideways. The horse shied at the same moment and he felt rather than heard a thud, as its rider was flung to the ground. He saw the horse disappear into the trees and he scrambled to his feet and rushed over to its rider, who lay face down in the snow. As Huw dropped to his knees, Pero bayed close by. Huw looked up and had a glimpse of a large, grey shape speeding up the tree-clad slope.

The running wolf made an impossible target for an arrow, so Huw turned his attention back to the prone figure. The rider wore a long cloak, its hood pulled up and, as he gently turned the person over, the hood fell open to reveal a head of ash blonde hair and the unforgettable face of Elinor, niece to Griffith of Plas Hirnant. The girl's eyes fluttered open, then, seeing him, she attempted to sit up.

"Stay yourself. I mean you no harm," Huw said, grasping her shoulders "You may have broken a bone in your fall."

He ran his hands down the girl's arms, then, as they seemed to be unharmed, he unthinkingly shifted his attention to her legs. The girl sat bolt upright at his touch.

"There is nothing wrong with me, I assure you," she said hastily. "My limbs feel perfectly normal."

Realising that he still held her legs, Huw snatched his hands away, feeling his face warm in a blush. "I'm sorry,

I should not have done that," he stammered.

The girl watched his discomfort for a few moments, then she smiled. "You are forgiven," she said, trying vainly to sound stern. "Now, would you please help me to my feet."

Huw took hold of her outstretched hands and carefully pulled her upright, noting that the blonde head reached up to his chin.

"There, you see. I am still in one piece," she told him. She brushed snow from her cloak and smoothed her hair from her face. "Was that your hound that came after the wolf?" she asked.

"It was indeed. There was no chance of me holding Pero back, so close to his quarry," he answered.

"He was a very welcome sight," the girl said, with a shudder. "I've not seen a wolf before and did not realise how large they are. The brute came down the path at speed, as though he were going to attack. My horse took fright and simply bolted."

They heard Pero call from far away and a look of concern swept over her face. "What of your hound?" she asked. "Will he be all right?"

"He can take care of himself, should the wolf turn on him," Huw assured her. "Come, I had best see you part of the way home. It is a long walk to Plas Hirnant."

He collected his bow from where he had dropped it, and, assuring himself that the girl was steady on her feet, led off along the path.

"How do you know where I live?" the girl asked, after a while. "We have never met before."

"But we have, though briefly and almost two years ago," Huw replied, though he said nothing about the circumstances of their meeting.

"What is your name?" she asked.

He told her and turned to face her when she came to a sudden halt.

"You are one of the Gethins of Argoed," she exclaimed.

"Indeed I am," he said, "I am Huw, one of your uncle's friendly neighbours."

"I was not aware that you and he were friends," she exclaimed. "He never mentions your family. I have heard the retainers speak of you, though. They say that one of you fights for the rebel Owain Glyndŵr. Would that be you?"

Huw ignored the question and began walking on along the path.

"Were I you, I would not pay any heed to what people say about me, or about my family," he told her. There was no point in telling her that he was on the opposite side of the political divide from her uncle.

They walked on in silence until they came to the meadow, where the girl stopped once more.

"I have the feeling that you do not care for my uncle. Would you like to tell me why?"

He told her briefly of the incident on the Argoed land, and the dispute between his father and her uncle's men. He took this opportunity to study the girl's face more closely. The blonde hair set off her blue eyes, which looked intently up at him as he spoke. She had a firmly moulded chin that hinted of determination but it was her mouth that held Huw's gaze longest. The wide and generous lips conveyed a strong sensuality and he had a sudden urge to kiss them.

"You men can be so stupid," she said, bringing him down to earth. "Always wanting that which belongs to others and never content with what you already have. I shall tell my uncle exactly what I think of him."

"It would be wiser not to do that," Huw advised. "There has been no trouble between our families since Glyndŵr's men paid your uncle a visit. You could stir up a hornet's nest by speaking rashly."

He led her past the fallen trunk of the dead sycamore, to the place where the Hafren became shallow. The girl's horse had bolted across the river here and now stood on the far bank; it whinnied a welcome when it saw them.

"He seems none the worse," Huw observed. "And now, my lady, we must cross the stream and send you on your way home. There is no sense in both of us having a wetting. Will you trust my two legs as much as you trust your horse's four?"

"I have little choice, gallant sir," she answered with a smile. "Though you must bend your knee to allow me to mount."

Huw put down the bow and crouched low, allowing her to clasp him around the neck. Taking care, he stood up straight and with his hands gripped behind him to support her weight, he walked down into the stream. The water must have been as cold as ice, but all that he was aware of was the girl's firm body pressed against his.

"Do you often hunt wolves, Huw Gethin?" the girl asked in a teasing manner. "I could be riding again on the morrow and I would feel safer were you close at hand."

Scarcely believing what he was hearing, Huw waded carefully on until they reached the further bank.

"We don't see wolves every day, my lady, but when we do see them, I hunt them," he answered. "If you fear them and need protection, I could be found, tomorrow, upstream, near the path which leads to the high land. The best part of the day to hunt is in the afternoon, so

I've been told." Reluctantly he released his hold and she slipped lightly to the ground.

"Thank you, Huw," she said. "You deserve a reward, though all I can give is this."

Reaching up, she drew his head down to hers and kissed him on the cheek. "Now, help me get mounted."

Completely dumb-struck, he followed her over to her horse, which stood quite still at her approach. Cupping his hands beneath her foot, Huw helped her up into the saddle.

"Until the morrow, then," she said, looking down at him.

She tapped her heels into the horse's flanks then stopped as Huw caught hold of the bridle.

"I think you should know that I'm the Gethin who serves Glyndŵr," he told her. "You may not wish someone like me, whom they call a rebel, to protect you from wild animals."

"I had already guessed that it was you who served Glyndŵr," she said laughingly. "That fact will add to the thrill of the morrow's chase."

Reluctantly, Huw watched her ride away until she out of sight. That night, as he lay in bed, the winter wind howling round the old farmstead, Huw realised that he did not know the girl's name, and as he drifted into sleep, he remembered that his expensive yew bow still lay on the banks of the Hafren.

Chapter 12

"Then we are agreed, Edmund," Glyndŵr said, addressing Mortimer and relaxing in his chair. "All the lands south of your own and reaching to the Wash will belong to the Mortimers. North of this line, the lands shall be ruled by the Percy family. All lands west of the Severn and the Dee will belong to me and my heirs and will be recognised as an independent country in its own right. Should one of the three make a warlike move against another of us, the third must come to the injured party's aid. Finally, should any other persons seek to overthrow any one of our triple alliance, the remaining two will rally to his assistance."

Glyndŵr looked at those seated around the table; three were knights in the service of Harry Hotspur, representing the Percys, another was Edmund Mortimer, still technically a prisoner of Glyndŵr, and the fifth was Tudor, brother to Glyndŵr, the Prince of Wales. They had met to form an alliance. On his own, even with the following he had and the victories to his credit, Glyndŵr recognised the limitations of his campaigns. He needed the strength of the Percys and the Mortimers, if he was to continue to hold Wales against the English. The relief that he no longer stood alone against the English throne made him want to shout the news aloud for all to hear. With an effort, he contented himself for the present by ordering more wine to be served.

"You must make it clear to your master that we make our move together," he said, aiming his remark at Hotspur's knights who sat to his left. "Mortimer, my friend, has explained to us that he needs the summer months to organise his supporters, and I wish to secure Pembroke before next winter. A September campaign should suit everyone and I strongly urge that the Palatine of Cheshire be where our three armies join together. If we are to be successful, it is essential that we are all ready at the same time."

The three knights agreed that they would repeat Owain's exhortation word for word. None of the knights present wore any badge or coat of arms to show that they were Hotspur's men, for they were a long way from their northern stronghold. Hotspur's loyalty to King Henry had never been absolute and now that he was about to change his allegiance, it was vital to keep this fact secret for as long as possible. Owain had met Hotspur, the youngest of the Percy family, some years ago and had always admired his soldierly qualities. He was also aware that Hotspur could be impetuous as well as brave. He sat now, half listening to Tudor, Mortimer and the knights discussing the relative strengths of their armies. Owain was only too pleased to allow his brother, Tudor, to further this business, for he had other matters to attend to.

***

"I believe you have spoken to my daughter, Catrin, about your feelings for her," he said to Edmund, when they were again alone. Mortimer, during his captivity, had often spent time with those of Glyndŵr's family who had been able to travel with him. An affection had grown between Catrin and the young captive, feelings not discouraged by the Prince of Wales.

"Has my daughter accepted your proposal of marriage? I am displeased that you did not discuss your intentions with me first, but she has confessed her feelings for you, and I suppose she will not be gainsaid," Owain said with mock severity.

"Indeed she has," the young man beamed. "I told her that I had little to offer other than my love and she said that that was all she desired. I apologise if I have been guilty of a misdemeanour." He eyed Glyndŵr for a short while then took a deep breath. "You have not forced Catrin into agreeing to marry me, have you Owain?" he asked.

Glyndŵr's face lit up in a broad smile and he struggled to contain his mirth, for he had become fond of the young man. "Force Catrin," he chuckled. "You have much to learn in regard to my womenfolk, Edmund. They are very different from those grand ladies at the King's court, I can tell you. They all have a mind and a will of their own. I'd sooner wrestle with a dancing bear, than attempt to impose my will over theirs. Margaret will be pleased to hear this news, for she has grown fond of you over these past months. The future looks more assured now, than it did two years ago. I must tell you that today has been a great one for my cause. I have never believed that we could win on our own for we are too few to stand for long against the English throne. Now, I have two powerful allies; should things go as planned and with God's blessing, you could be the next King of England."

Later that day, Owain spoke with David at great length on various matters, two of which were close to his heart. He talked about founding a college in Wales, where students could study the old laws and be competent to put them into practice once again. He instructed his secretary to write to a number of learned men, asking that they meet with him to discuss his plan. He himself would be contacting the clergy, many of whom supported him and were anxious to create an independent Church of Wales, away from the imposed yoke of Canterbury.

"I shall join Rhys Gethin, my general, in the south, when early summer has arrived. It is in the Towy valley that I shall be proclaimed the Prince of Wales. Those who have given so much to our struggle wish to see me take the title, so I must comply with their demand."

The month of July, found Owain camped with his army close to the town of Laugharne. Rhys Gethin had led his men through the narrow valleys of Morgannwg, and received the acclaim of the people and the promise of more fighting men to join him. All Wales now stood firmly for Glyndŵr, though, as Rhys had learned to his cost at Brecon, a few castles still held out for the King. The risks and planning of the early days were now coming to fruition, and Owain felt a tremendous sense of exhilaration at each success. A further march through the troublesome land of Pembroke was his next move, after which he would go on to the English border, to aid Edmund Mortimer in his attempt to raise his own army. Finally, he would march north to Cheshire, where he would bring Mortimer and his men to the rendezvous with Hotspur.

Owain had retired to his pavilion and was making ready for bed, when the thud of galloping hooves and the cries of his sentries made him pause. Through the canvas, he heard David answer their challenge and he felt a stab of apprehension at the urgency in his secretary's voice.

Unmoving, he stood by the cot, holding his shirt, and saw the tent flap fly open. The look on David's face confirmed his feeling that something was amiss.

"My lord, it's news of Hotspur," his secretary panted out. "He has already made his move against the King."

Glyndŵr recoiled as though he had been struck a physical blow, then lunged forward and grabbed David's tunic. "In the name of God, what are you saying?" he choked out angrily.

"It's true enough. He is in Cheshire, recruiting bowmen, and there is nothing secretive about his actions for his knights are openly hiring men in the market places. They have not sent you one official word of this business," David said.

Suddenly becoming aware that his secretary was swaying with fatigue, Glyndŵr placed a supporting arm around him, led him to the cot and sat him down.

"I have ridden without rest from the Dee," David said. "I've changed horses wherever I could, even threatening some owners with your wrath before they would oblige me."

"You did right," Glyndŵr told him, then called for the sentries. "Summon my captains to attend me immediately," he commanded one. "Bring food and wine quickly," he told the other.

Within a short space of time, Rhys Gethin, John Leggatt and several other captains were crowded into the pavilion, where Glyndŵr broke the news to them.

"We have but a slender chance of reaching Hotspur before the King does," he said. "Yet it is a chance we must take. Have your men make ready to march at break of day. Leave behind anything that will hinder us; the wagons must follow as best they can. Now, go, there is not a moment to be lost."

When they had gone, he turned to the cot and saw that David was asleep, an empty flask still in one hand. Gently, he prised it free and spread his cloak over the sleeping secretary. All thoughts of resting himself were gone, so he sat listening to the noises outside.

At supper, all seemed to have been well; now his plans were in danger of collapsing around him. He held his head in both hands and stared unseeingly into the candle light, asking himself repeatedly why Hotspur had acted so impetuously, before all was ready.

***

"Wake up, Huw," John Leggatt ordered, nudging the sleeping bowman with his toe. "We are on the move shortly. There's hard marching ahead of us today, so be sure to put some food in your belly before we set off. Go and wake the others. I've much to attend to. I want the bowmen at the head of the army when we start the march. Rhys wishes us to set the pace. I shall join you when we move off."

They had cooked a sheep for their supper and Huw now cut himself a slice from one of its legs. Chewing on the mutton, he awoke the others, paying little heed to their curses and protestations.

"Go rot in hell," Idwal snarled. "It is not daybreak yet and I'm not moving until it is."

"That's your choice. You can argue it with John later," Huw retorted.

The covered figure remained motionless for a while, then, with another oath, Idwal scrambled to his feet.

"I don't know who is the cause of this disturbance of

my rest," he said loudly, "and should I meet up with him, I'll place an arrow in his arse. I've not had a moment of proper sleep all night."

With the memory of Idwal's snoring, long before he himself was asleep, Huw grinned into the darkness and returned to the embers of their cooking fire. Cutting another slice of meat, he handed it to Idwal, before making sure that his few possessions were safely in his satchel. With nothing more to do than wait, he sat down by the dying fire, his thoughts full of the girl he now knew as Elinor. They had met a number of times after the incident with the wolf, riding up to the high land or, when the weather dictated, sheltering in an abandoned holding. The more he saw of the girl, the more Huw wanted to be with her, and he had had a tremendous tussle with his loyalties when the day came for him to rejoin John Leggatt. He had not spoken of love and neither had Elinor, though she was in his thoughts every moment of the day.

Dawn came at last and the mercenaries made their way to the front of the forming column. John was already there and gave them a nod of greeting before placing himself at their head. At the start of the many marches that Huw had been on, there had always been a great deal of waiting, however, this one was different. The thudding of hooves heralded the arrival of Glyndŵr and his closest aides and, with no more ado, the Prince gave the signal to march. The pace, set by John, was the one now so familiar to Huw and his fellow bowmen, long, low strides that seemed to be almost a saunter, yet which covered the ground at a surprising speed.

Looking to the rear, Glyndŵr could see his army begin to string out. The bowmen in the van, pikemen, trailing their long spears, following. Behind the fighting men came a herd of horses and ponies, carrying provisions and bundles of arrows. He caught John's eyes upon him and smiled his satisfaction. They were on the move, they were making a good pace and there was nothing more that he or anyone could do now, so he settled himself into the saddle and tried to relax.

They marched all that day, pausing only to drink sparingly at streams that they crossed and eating while on the move. When darkness overtook them, they simply lay where they stopped. The following day was a repetition of the previous one, though now, the army was up on the high land, and had left the towns and villages behind. It was after the sun had peaked that men began to drop out of the march. Many of these were men no longer in their prime, others had some disability and could no longer keep up the telling pace. Glyndŵr now began to ride up and down the length of the column, encouraging his men and sparing a word for those who stood or lay aside. Halting by one grey-haired bowman, he gave a sympathetic smile.

"Have you food and drink?" he asked kindly.

"Aye my lord, enough of both," the other answered. "Though I'd gladly trade all for a new pair of legs right now. A little rest and I will catch up." He caught hold of Owain's sleeve as he urged his horse forward. "You were born too late for me," he said. "Whatever the outcome of this march, I beg you to fight on. There will be other battles to win. Never give in."

By the following day, it had become apparent that the army was in danger of becoming an exhausted rabble. Noon found the men strung out over a distance of several miles, with someone leaving the column every few paces.

Glyndŵr ordered a halt and held a hurried conference with his captains. The result of this, was that he would press on with the lightly armed bowmen and those pikemen who were still able to make good speed. He would also take some of the horses, which would be herded by young lads. Rhys Gethin would follow with the remainder when all had rested where they were now stopped.

On the move again, he sent mounted scouts on ahead with orders to seek out the Percy army. To two of these, who spoke some English, he gave further instructions. They were to find Hotspur himself and urge the noble to make for the safety of the Dee, where the Welsh would join him. The next day found his force on the hills above the Severn valley, where they followed an ancient road which ran towards England. It was night when his scouts returned, guided by their camp fires and bringing the news which Owain had feared. Hotspur was already in Shropshire, making for Shrewsbury, which was held by the King's fifteen-year-old son, Henry.

"There is only one course open to me, John," Owain told his captain. "I shall ride ahead and attempt to persuade Hotspur to march into Wales. His army can meet with ours along the Severn. Choose thirty of your bowmen to accompany me; we have horses to spare for that number. You will have to follow afterwards, as best you can. Make for the ford outside Welshpool and await my command."

He waited impatiently while the bowmen were getting themselves mounts, then the advance party moved off.

"Pray that I am not too late, John," he called back, as he urged his horse into a gallop.

He led his men down into the broad valley, where they

followed the Severn down stream. Skirting Welshpool, they parted company with the river and took the road which led to Shrewsbury. Other road users eyed the mounted bowmen nervously as they passed, though their fears were not warranted, for the Welsh gave them no more than a passing glance. Their road brought them to a wide, shallow ford and they splashed through before riding for a low ridge which lay in their path. Here, they saw that the river made a great oxbow to the north before reappearing directly to their front. Moving off the ridge at a steady canter, they rode for another mile, before Glyndŵr suddenly reined in his horse and pointed ahead to where a huge dust cloud was rising into the summer sky and slowly drifting towards the bowmen on a light, easterly breeze.

Huw had pulled up beside the Prince and dismounted at his command. Together, the two walked forward, away from the laboured breathing of their mounts. On the breeze, there came a distant sound which, over the past few years, had become familiar to both men, the sound made by the throats of thousands, the sound of battle.

Prince and bowman glanced at one another and sat wearily down in the lush grass. Behind them, the others dismounted and formed a semicircle around the pair. Not one man spoke a word, for all knew what the far off roar meant. Huw risked a glance at Glyndŵr and saw that the handsome face showed no emotion whatsoever, despite the turmoil that must be raging behind it. For what seemed an age, they sat listening to the far off noise, which rose and fell as waves on an unseen sea. Then, gradually, the sounds died away and the Welshmen got to their feet, as one of their number gave a cry and pointed across the river. Through the scattered trees, they caught their first glimpse of men running for their lives, making for the Severn. Without pausing, the fugitives plunged into the water, which reached up to their shoulders, and struggled across to the near bank.

Most of them ran on, swerving away from the group of bowmen, though a few dragged themselves out of the water and lay exhausted on the bank. It was to these that Glyndŵr gestured, commanding his men to bring them to him. When this had been done, he spoke to the dripping and terrified captives, who stood huddled and shivering before him.

"Whom do you serve and why do you flee the fight?" he asked, in the English tongue.

"We are men of Cheshire, my lord," the boldest answered. "We served Henry Percy as bowmen. We have lost the day and Hotspur is dead. I saw him fall myself. He fought like a lion, for it took a number of the King's men to kill him."

"The King is here?" Glyndŵr asked incredulously. "We were led to believe that he would be in distant parts this summer."

"I know nothing of that," the spokesman replied with a shrug, "yet his banner was clearly seen on the field. I beg you now to let us proceed. We need to distance ourselves from this place."

Glyndŵr told them to go, then mounted his horse.

"It seems that we must seek another ally," he said resignedly. Without looking again towards Shrewsbury, he rode for Wales, his heart full of bitterness that Hotspur's impetuousness had cost him a valuable ally and the life of a brave man. It had cost Owain one third of his hoped for strength.

Chapter 13

The months passed and winter brought campaigning to a close. After the disaster at Shrewsbury, Owain divided his rested men into three commands. The first returned south, the second marched west, while the third moved north under his personal command, to harry and attack the castles which still held out against him; however, he was thwarted by the King.

With the host that had defeated Hotspur, Henry IV left his base at Chester, marched into Wales and followed the coast as far as Caernarfon. From this stronghold, he made for Harlech, but dwindling provisions forced him to return to England. Glyndŵr refused to risk his much smaller force in battle, and King Henry avoided the mountain passes, for fear of ambush. Once more, Wales had cost the King a fortune and the loss of scores of men who had been picked off by unseen bowmen. On the last day in November, Glyndŵr dismissed his men with the order to muster at Corwen in the following Spring.

Begging leave from John Leggatt, Huw hurried home, where he received his usual warm welcome. When he asked the captain to join him at Argoed, John declined, saying that Glyndŵr may have need of him. Huw thought this a lame excuse but put it quickly from his mind, his head full of the prospect of seeing Elinor once more. On the first two mornings, he rode across the Hafren, openly walking his pony over Plas Hirnant land. Heading upstream, he followed the twisting waters until he came to the empty holding, where he waited for the girl to appear, but it was on the third morning when Elinor came to their meeting place, and he threw aside his natural restraint. After he had helped her to dismount, he held her in his arms and kissed her passionately.

"I've waited long enough for that," he told her. "Where have you been? One more day without seeing you and I would have been pounding at the gates of Plas Hirnant."

"I have had to be careful," Elinor answered. "The kitchen maids mentioned that you were home and I wanted to seek you out, there and then, which would have been unwise." She stood on tiptoe and kissed him fiercely on the mouth. "My brother is visiting our uncle," she said. "I dared not say that I was going riding, as he would probably insist on accompanying me. Should he even suspect that you and I were meeting like this, he would be wild with rage. He plans to marry me into some wealthy merchant family and, in his eyes, you are merely a peasant and a rebel."

"Where is this brother of yours today?" he asked softly.

"He and one of uncle's retainers have taken two cattle to the market in Llanidloes. I believe that Richard has money troubles and Griffith has given him the beasts." She released herself from his arms and looked around them. "Let's move further upstream," she said. "I feel that I want to ride for ever. I hate Richard visiting us; he does nothing but argue with uncle over some matter which they keep from me. He knows it upsets the old man and seems not to care."

Remounting, they rode up the Hafren until its banks narrowed, forcing them to dismount again. They tethered their mounts and began to scramble along the water's edge. Huw helped her over some of the larger rocks and, a short distance on, they came to a pool, created by the waters which tumbled some twelve feet in a sheer drop. Smooth gravel fringed the pool which, in turn, was surrounded by a wider strip of mosses and grass. Huw sat down, pulled Elinor down beside him and held her close.

"What of this rich merchant you are to marry?" he asked.

Silently, she looked up at the dark face so close to hers, threw her arms around his neck and kissed him. Now, there was a new meaning in her lips and he instinctively understood their message. In that secluded place, on the banks of the stream which divided their two families in hate and distrust, the two united in their love.

The following few days were an agony for Huw. At Elinor's insistence, he had agreed that, while her brother remained at Plas Hirnant, they would not meet. It had been hard for him to accept this and it was proving even harder to keep his word. From morning to night, he prowled around Argoed, frequently climbing up to the lookout post where he could see the Plas. His mood darkened as the days passed. When he was indoors, Morgan and Emma made small talk between themselves, casting puzzled glances at each other, while Hywel kept to himself. His brother's brooding silence reminded him of Emma, whenever she and Morgan had differed, and experience had taught the lad to keep out of harm's way.

Emma's intuition told her that a girl was at the root of her son's mood, but who she was remained a mystery. She was certainly not from Cwmdu, of that Emma was positive. No young man had ever kept his affairs secret from his neighbours in the cwm. Yet, if the girl was someone that Huw had met in his service with Glyndŵr, what was he doing here? One evening, unable to put up with his continuing silence, Emma asked him bluntly who was the cause of his unhappiness. Huw reacted by going outdoors without saying a word and he did not return until all were abed.

A week dragged by with no sign of Elinor and, unable to face another day mooning around Argoed, he saddled a pony and rode off. He had money in his purse and headed towards the Dovey valley, intending to visit the first inn that he came to. He had ridden some two miles when he heard the sounds of a horse galloping after him. Turning in the saddle, his heart leapt when he saw Elinor racing towards him. Reining in the pony, he leapt to the ground, his mood lifting the closer she came. Her manner of riding quickly replaced his exhilaration by a feeling of growing alarm. She was within a stone's throw of him, when Huw saw another rider heading for him at a furious pace.

The next few moments passed in a blur and a number of things happened very quickly. Elinor forced her mount to a skidding halt, flung herself from the saddle and stumbled into his arms.

"It is Richard," she cried out. "He has learned about our meeting. He has vowed to take me back to Shrewsbury."

Before she could say more, her pursuer was on them. Huw dived aside, taking the girl with him, as the horse thundered past. Such was its speed, that Richard was at least fifty paces away before he was able to bring the animal around and ride at them again. Pulling Elinor to her feet, Huw pushed her into the flank of her horse.

"Hold the reins," he shouted. "Use your horse as a shield."

He sprinted to his own pony, which was prancing wildly in fright, grabbed its mane and turned the animal, so that it was between him and Richard. The move had the effect that he had hoped for and he saw the charging horse swerve aside, forcing Richard to lean out of his saddle. He glimpsed a sword, swinging down at his head, and ducked low. The blade struck his pony's rump, which made it squeal in pain. It jerked free and bolted away. Before Richard could raise his sword again, Huw sprang upward and managed to lock an arm around his neck. The weight of the passing horse swept his feet from the ground and, gritting his teeth in desperation, he hung on. Frantically, Richard struggled in vain to stay in the saddle but he began to slide off his horse. The two men hit the ground with a bone-jarring thud which threw them apart. Both lay gasping for air for a few moments, then, scrambled to their feet. Richard's sword lay a short distance away and he made for it, with Huw lunging after him. Huw saw Richard's blonde head lower when he stooped to pick up the weapon and, still running, Huw lashed out and delivered a blow with his right foot that snapped Richard's head backward, so that for a moment he stood completely defenceless. Huw had learned a great deal about close fighting, while under John Leggatt's command. He quickly stepped nearer and kicked out once more, his foot aimed at Richard's groin.

With a cry of agony, Richard collapsed. Huw pinned him firmly to the ground, using his knees, and, with a free hand, drew his short sword. Richard face reflected sheer terror; when he looked into the emotionless face above him and saw the heavy blade raised, he knew that he was about to die. It was Elinor's scream that stopped Huw's hand.

"For the love of God, don't do it," she shouted. "Leave him be, I beg you."

The blade remained poised, and Richard knew that any move on his part would be his last.

"Please, my love, for my sake, let him live," Elinor pleaded.

Slowly the sword was lowered until its point came to rest on Richard's throat.

"Take his sword and throw it into the stream," Huw said, keeping his eyes fixed on Richard. He waited until she had moved away, then pressed fractionally on the blade. "Get yourself back to England while you are able," he hissed. "Elinor stays here with me."

Richard did not understand one word but nodded his head because it seemed the wisest thing to do. Huw stood back, keeping the blade pointed toward Richard while he struggled to stand upright. His horse stood a short distance away, unconcernedly cropping the grass, and when Elinor rejoined them, he limped toward it. Somehow, he managed to drag himself into the saddle, where he sat for a while, his body throbbing in pain from the kicks it had endured. Eventually, he tapped the horse with his heels and walked it closer to Elinor and Huw, who stood side by side, watching him.

"Get on your horse and come with me now," he told Elinor angrily. "Do as I say and we shall forget this foolishness."

"I am not going with you to Shrewsbury," she replied, shaking her head defiantly. "You can forget your scheme to enrich yourself with no thought to my happiness. I'm staying here, no matter what you wish."

Richard felt his rage overcome the pain and he longed to slap some sense into his sister. The tall figure standing beside her dispelled this urge, however, and, with a vicious tug on the reins, he turned his mount around.

"Then, stay with your rebel and rot," he yelled. "Don't even think of returning to Plas Hirnant. I shall see to it that Griffith will disown you. You can be sure of that."

Bracing himself against the motion of his horse he moved off, allowing it to set the pace.

Huw took his eyes from the horse and rider and turned to the girl. Elinor gripped his arms and pressed her body against his, her worry showing clearly on her face.

"He has banned me from the Plas, Huw," she said. "What am I to do? Where can I go? I was in despair, when I saw you on the meadow, and could only think of being with you. It seems that I've made my situation worse by doing so. Oh, my love, tell me what to do."

Elinor had to wait for the answers while Huw went to retrieve their mounts.

"There is only one place we can go, and that is Argoed," he said. "I've had enough of hiding my feelings for you. Should we not be welcomed there, we shall go north to Corwen. A few of the other bowmen have their women with them and they would accept us, of that I'm sure."

Elinor made no reply and he saw that she had a strange look on her face.

"What is wrong?" he asked.

"You have not spoken of marriage," she answered. "I want to be with you and will gladly follow you anywhere but it must be as your wife."

Huw swung up onto the pony's back and coaxed the animal alongside hers.

"You are forcing my hand," he said, his smile widening. Leaning toward her, he kissed her lightly on the cheek, and added seriously, "I want you for my wife more than anything in this world. We shall marry, I promise you. For the present, though, we had best see what awaits us at Argoed."

They rode slowly for Cwmdu, Elinor asking questions, Huw grunting an occasional answer. He had no idea how his family were going to react and he became increasingly uncommunicative, the closer they came to Argoed. He felt that he could rely on his father's loyalty, to a certain extent, though Emma's reception was an unknown quantity. Inwardly, he steeled himself against whatever would happen. He was leading Elinor towards the doorway, when a shutter opened and his mother leaned out.

"Oh it's, you," she called. "We were not expecting to see you until nightfall. What made you change your plans? You seemed determined to ....." Her voice trailed off when she saw who stood behind her son. Emma had heard talk of the light-haired girl who lived across the Hafren but had never actually seen her. She stared at Elinor for a few moments, lost for words, then glanced at Huw, who was watching her intently.

"This is Elinor Lloyd of Plas Hirnant," he said bluntly. "We love one another and are going to be married."

Emma felt her head begin to spin and grabbed hold of the sill for support. She now knew the reason for Huw's dark mood. Her first feeling was a mixture of shocked disbelief and anger, the latter directed at her son. Huw had suddenly revived the threat from Griffith Lloyd, after three years of peace from that quarter. She looked again at the girl, studying her more closely. Elinor held Huw's arm tightly and she looked very scared and lost. Emma's anger evaporated, when the blue eyes met hers, to be replaced by compassion.

"You had best come in to me," she said to the girl. "Go and tell your father, Huw. You will find him at Iolo's."

When he returned to the house with Morgan, Huw found the two women seated by the hearth. Elinor seemed more at ease now, and Huw was glad to see her smile at his father, when the two men seated themselves at the table. For a while, the women chattered together and ignored the men, until Morgan gave an impatient cough and Emma look in their direction.

"Well now, my husband, what do you make of this matter?" she asked. "I take it that Huw has told you of their predicament?"

Huw had indeed done just that and had been both worried and relieved, when Morgan had simply said that they should get home as quickly as possible. His father stood up and crossed over to the hearth, from where he looked appraisingly at Elinor. It was no wonder that his son had fallen in love with the girl, he thought; she could captivate any young man's heart. She looked up at him and gave a tentative smile. That was all that it took to place the big man under her spell.

"You are welcome here," he told her kindly. "You may be from Plas Hirnant, girl, but you cannot be blamed for your uncle's greed."

He was pleasantly surprised at his wife's apparent friendship for the girl.

"What are your feelings on this, Emma?" he asked, needing to be certain.

"They are of an age to marry if they so wish," she answered. "Who am I to say no. I pray only that this will not provoke Griffith Lloyd into some rash action."

"Have no fears on that account," Huw assured her. "Remember that you have Glyndŵr's protection. Griffith would be signing his own death warrant, should he act foolishly."

"Have you given thought to where you will live when you are married?" Emma asked. "Argoed is not built to shelter two families."

"'I shall look for a holding somewhere along the Hafren," Huw answered. "At the moment, I have only a little money and have decided to serve Glyndŵr for a further year or two. It would enable me to save enough for us to start on our own."

His parents glanced quickly at one another, aware of the risks of his occupation, aware, too, that he had very little choice. In comparison with most holdings, Argoed was successful but, as Emma had said, it could not support two families.

"Until the day comes when you can marry, Elinor must live with your Uncle Iolo and Aunt Morwen, Huw," Emma said. "They have room to spare and would welcome her presence in their home. It would not be seemly for her to live under the same roof as you."

"You had best pay Iolo a visit," Morgan told Huw. "Your mother is right in what she says, though it would be wise to ask for his help, rather than assume it will be forthcoming. While you are making your way there, tell Hywel to bring the flock home. You will find him at the top pasture."

Before Huw had gone far, a whistle sounded from the look-out, on the ridge above. The man waved his arms and gestured towards Plas Hirnant, which sent Huw running back to the house, where Morgan came out to meet him. Huw dashed inside, pulled down his bow from the rafters, grabbed a fistful of arrows and joined his father. He detached the short sword from his belt and held it out to Morgan, then quickly strung the bow and notched an arrow. Watched by the women, who had come out of doors, the two men hurried to the track leading down to the meadow, but halted when Griffith Lloyd appeared, riding up the track towards them.

He reined in beside the two Gethins but made no move to dismount. "I come alone and unarmed, as you can see," Griffith said. " I am not breaking my pledge to Glyndŵr. I wish to speak with Elinor in private. Your son is here, so she must be close by." The old man's voice was feeble and he seemed to have grown sicker then ever.

"She is here, right enough," Morgan told him. "Though, whether she wishes to hear you out, or not, is up to her. Go and tell her of our visitor, Huw."

While they waited, Morgan studied his neighbour and was shocked at the physical change in the man, who had put on a lot of weight and whose complexion was marred by ugly, red veins, which contrasted with his sickly pallor. Elinor and Huw approached, and the girl ran to her uncle, her face filled with concern.

"What are you doing, Uncle?" she remonstrated. "You know full well that riding causes your chest to pain."

Griffith turned his horse and beckoned her to follow him down the track. "I need to speak with you alone," he said. "Tell that young man he has no need of his bow. I intend you no harm, I can scarcely sit on this animal, as it is."

Elinor motioned to Huw to put down his bow, then followed her uncle part way down the track.

"What is it?" she asked, when they were out of earshot

of the others.

"I am here to find out if what Richard has told me is the truth," he said, when they came to a halt. "He is drinking himself into a stupor and seems to be talking nonsense. He claims that you left us because you want to live with that rebel back there. Tell me that he speaks this way merely to make mischief."

"He is telling you the truth," Elinor replied. "Huw and I are to be married as soon as possible." She saw Griffith stiffen in the saddle and his face tighten with rage.

"Think of what you are about, girl," he spluttered. "It is being arranged for you to marry into a wealthy family. You will have fine clothes to wear and servants to attend your every whim. What can this bowman offer you, Elinor? Tell me, I pray."

"Love and happiness," Elinor answered simply.

"You will soon find that you cannot live on that alone," Griffith snorted derisively. "Listen to me. I have plans for all our futures. This upstart called Glyndŵr cannot defy the King much longer and, then, when he has been hanged, I shall be free to carry out these plans of mine. You will find that you have made a terrible mistake, should you stay here with these people. Do so, and I will not be held responsible for your well-being. Come home with me, now, I beseech you."

"I am staying, Uncle." Elinor replied firmly. "I have made my decision and nothing you say will change my mind. My life would be without meaning were I to leave Huw."

Griffith looked down at her and bowed his head. He was genuinely fond of his niece and felt pain at losing her. Then his anger seethed once more to the surface and he looked back up the track, to the cause of his hurt.

"May you rot in the bowels of Hell, with the rest of your rebel friends," he shouted at Huw. "Listen to me and listen well. Take the girl from this place and never return."

Realising that he might easily say too much in his rage, Griffith's jaw snapped shut and he began to ride down to the meadow. Elinor had made her choice and would have to live with the consequences. There was nothing more that he could do.

After his departure, the Gethins and Elinor walked up the cwm, to call on Iolo. They were nearing his holding when they met Hywel driving the flock down to Argoed. The lad was struck dumb for some moments when he saw Elinor, and stared at her open mouthed. Then came a flood of questions.

"Later, lad," Morgan told him, "you will learn all there is to know. For now, take the sheep down to their pen."

Arriving at Iolo's, they were greeted warmly, as was usual, The two kind people listened to Morgan's request for them to take the girl into their home and, as Emma had predicted, they agreed to do this without any hesitation. In Morwen's case, Elinor's arrival brought out the maternal instinct, which only showed briefly whenever her two nephews paid her a visit. Her face beaming with pleasure, she fussed over the girl, telling Huw that he could call to pay court in the manner of any sweetheart. The memory of their love-making sprang into Huw's mind and he quickly averted his eyes, grunting his thanks.

That night, Huw offered up a silent prayer of gratitude for the way his family had taken Elinor to their hearts. He wondered about her feelings this night, living in a new home and lying in a strange bed, and he longed to be with her. As an afterthought, he prayed that Glyndŵr's cause would continue to succeed, so that the Gethins would always enjoy his protection.

Chapter 14

They came from nowhere, the English, in a sudden thundering of countless hooves which shook the earth. John Leggatt's bowmen cursed and leapt to their feet, scattering the supper bowls as they began to string bows, which they had little or no chance to use before the enemy knights and men-at-arms were in the midst of the scattered groups of men. Huw saw one mercenary reel away from a flashing sword, clutching a gash in his neck from which blood sprayed up in a fountain. Another went down beneath the cruel hooves of the attackers, his scream cut short as he disappeared before Huw's horrified gaze. He saw Idwal swing wildly with a bow staff at a mailed horseman, who fell sideways out of the saddle. As if he were a spectator, Huw stood rooted to the spot and saw Idwal's weapon splinter into pieces, while the Englishman's body flopped like a rag doll and was trampled by a following rider. A rough hand pushed Huw aside and the flank of a charging horse brushed past him, sending his bow flying.

Before one Welsh arrow was loosed, the horsemen had passed and ridden on through the Welsh encampment, which lay along the floor of the narrow valley. Huw retrieved his bow, looked wildly around and felt his heart stop beating for a moment for, a few paces away, John Leggatt lay face down and motionless in the trampled grass. Huw knelt down at his side and cried aloud with relief when he saw that the captain was breathing. Blood was already seeping through his leather jerkin and he was calling Idwal's name. Huw gently opened the garment and noted that the shirt beneath it was badly torn; there was an ugly wound, which ran across John's ribs and ended under his armpit.

"Is he still alive?" Idwal panted, appearing at Huw's side. "Then we must move him into cover now. The English will be back at any moment. You can be sure of it."

Tearing a strip from Leggatt's bloodied shirt, the two bowmen quickly rolled it into a wad which they placed over the wound. Between them, they heaved the semiconscious captain to his feet and fastened his jerkin as tightly as they could, to hold the makeshift dressing in place. Haste was essential, for voices began to call out a warning, and Huw saw that, at the far end of the encampment, the English had wheeled their horses and were preparing to charge again. Men started to run for the shelter of the thickly wooded slopes that lined the valley, in the hope of escape. Some fifty paces from the mercenaries, a body of pikemen formed themselves into a tight circle and, carrying their long spears pointed upwards, began to climb. Supporting John between them, the two bowmen made for this temporary haven. The pikemen opened their ranks without dissent, allowing them to pass inside and, scarcely were they inside this temporary haven, than the first horseman came up to the spears. To have ridden head on to them would have been suicidal; the knight swerved aside and waited for support. When the enemy numbers grew to a score and more, they drove their horses onto the spears, attempting to break the circle, but only one of them succeeded. He was quickly pounced upon and, with a flashing of steel, soon dispatched.

Slowly, the circle of men moved into the scrub oaks, where they halted. Huw and Idwal set the captain down gently and pushed through the pikemen, notching an arrow in readiness. At the bottom of the slope, the main body of mounted men were making ready for yet another charge along the valley floor. The two bowmen drew back their bow strings and loosed at this perfect target. Their arrows sped true and they had the satisfaction of seeing two horses rear up and fall, trapping the riders. The nearest Englishmen looked up at the bowmen and some began to ride up the slope, only stopping when a clear voice called out a command. The voice called another order, at which the horsemen charged over the body-strewn ground, their lances and swords at the ready. It was only after they had passed from view that Huw could see the extent of their terrible work. Not one foot soldier remained on his feet in the wake of this third charge. A few riderless horses wandered aimlessly through the carnage and Idwal made to move down the slope.

"Stay with John," he called back. "I'm going to get us a mount. We can't carry him far and I am not leaving him here."

Huw watched Idwal run down the slope and make for the nearest horse. The animal reared its head, drew back, then shot forward with a terrifying snapping of teeth, and narrowly missed Idwal's out-stretched hand. Next, with incredible speed for its size, the charger whirled round and lashed out viciously with its hind legs. The bowman was equally fast and dodged aside as the hooves sliced the air above him. Wisely he backed away, recognising that the beast was in shock. He walked slowly up to another charger, which was calmly cropping the grass. The big horse raised its head at his approach, allowed Idwal to take its reins and lead it towards the pikemen.

The English had made no move to intervene, but seemed to be fully occupied in searching amongst the dead at the far end of the encampment. Huw remembered that it was in that area where Tudor had set up his small pavilion, and he prayed that Glyndŵr's brother had got clear. He felt a hand on his shoulder and turned to see one of the pikemen standing beside him.

"Your friend has recovered his wits," the man said. "You had best attend to him, for we are moving off before the English come at us again."

Huw waited until Idwal rejoined him and, together, they returned to the captain, who now sat with his back against a tree. The glazed look had gone from his eyes and he gave them a wan smile.

"Praise be, you are unhurt, lad," he croaked at Huw. "I thought that you had been flattened in that first moment."

"So, it was your hand that pushed me aside," Huw said, kneeling down.

"Aye, though don't count on me repeating the act," John replied, wincing with pain. "That English lance almost skewered me."

The pikemen were already starting to make their way through the trees, so, between them, Huw and Idwal lifted Leggatt onto the horse's back. Then, one on either side of the charger, they began to follow the other troops. Until now, it had seemed as though they and the pikemen were all that remained of the Welsh force but, as they progressed, more men joined them, in twos and threes.

Huw was relieved to find that a number of these were his fellow mercenaries, but some familiar faces were missing. There had been no discussion about where they were heading; the pikemen were from the distant mountains of Gwynedd and it was to these that their faces were now turned.

Back in the valley, the heir to the throne of England approached one of the groups of men-at-arms searching amongst the dead, whose exultant cries had caught his attention. He saw one of the men raise a battle-axe and bring it sweeping down. The next moment, the man was hurrying toward him, triumphantly holding high a gory head.

"It is Glyndŵr, sire," he called out, beaming broadly. "I served with him as a squire under King Richard. I'd know him anywhere. Your troubles are over in this Godforsaken country."

Young Prince Henry averted his gaze from the bloodied prize and smiled with satisfaction. He had caught the Welsh napping at Grosmont, three days ago, driving them back into the hills, then, with a small force of some five hundred mounted men, he had repeated his success in this wooded glen near Usk. His own losses numbered no more than one hundred, a trifle to pay for ending this costly sore in the King's side. Steeling himself, he looked once more at the head of the man the Welsh had called their Prince. From this day, they would have to recognise the true holder of that title, himself.

"Take the head to Hereford," he commanded. "Show it in the market place, for all to see. Let it remain there for seven days, then move on to Shrewsbury and do the same. In that way, the people of the Marches will know that the war is over."

***

Huw and his comrades spent a miserable night, huddled together, afraid to risk a fire. There had been no sign of pursuit, yet no man amongst them complained. The second surprise attack had unsettled the boldest amongst them.

"I'd wager that those men were led by the King's son," a pike-man said, as they talked over the day. "I am sure that some of the men-at-arms wore the Bolingbroke crest."

"What of Tudor?" another asked. "It will be a bitter blow to Glyndŵr should he have been taken."

None had any news of Owain's brother, Tudor, and Huw remembered the group of Englishmen searching amongst the dead but kept the memory to himself. There was no point in idle speculation; the men's spirits were low enough as it was. He spent the night lying by John's side, with Idwal on the other. They had bathed the captain's wound and bound his ribs with fresh linen but had been unable to stop the bleeding completely. They were all aware that the wound was in need of proper care but that would have to wait. The following day, they continued northwards. John's condition worsened during the night and he could only remain in the saddle by being supported every moment. The motion of the horse, gentle as it was, caused his wound to open and the bleeding to increase but he refused to call a halt. They were still too close to the Usk for that. It was well past noon when they reached the high lands of Epynt and, at the first isolated holding, they decided to halt. Although the men had eaten little that day, they refused their host's offer of food. A man had only to take one look about him, to see that the smallholders could barely support themselves.

The woman of the house tenderly removed the blood soaked material from John's wound, and after she had bathed and cleaned it, she disappeared into an out-building. When she returned, she was carrying cobwebs in both hands; these she firmly pressed into the deepest part of the wound. Within moments, the bleeding had stopped and, when she had rebound his ribs to her satisfaction, she motioned Huw to one side. "Your friend reeds rest and food," she told him. "I shall make some broth, which he can have in the morning. Have you a safe place near by to which you can take him?"

In Huw's mind there was only one such place, and that was Argoed. His only concern was whether John could survive the journey, for it would take the best part of two days to reach Cwmdu. He voiced his feelings to the woman and asked what she thought of John's chances, were he to be moved.

"That would be in the hands of God," she answered. "He seems to be a fit man, apart from his wound, and the further north you can travel, the safer he will be."

Later on, he spoke to John about making for Argoed and asked whether he could survive the journey.

"Keep me on that horse and I will," the captain answered.

It was the evening of the second day when they came to the falls of Cwmdu, John's wound had begun to bleed again and his face was deathly pale. The party halted at the head of the narrow path; the pikemen, born amongst the peaks of Snowdonia, had no fear of the sheer drop down to the valley, but it was obvious that John would have to be carried, and a make-shift stretcher was prepared from the spears, which they had carried for so many miles, threaded through the sleeves of some bowmen's leather jerkins. Four bearers lifted Leggatt clear of the ground and set off down the track, followed by the others. Hugging the cliff side, Huw kept his eyes firmly fixed on the back of the man in front of him. From behind, he heard the clatter of hooves, as Idwal brought up the rear, leading the horse down, its eyes covered by his tunic, to stop it shying away from the precipitous pathway. The animal was worth money, and was part of Idwal's spoils of war.

The party reached the bottom safely and John was again lifted onto the charger's back. He was semiconscious and would have fallen from the saddle, had several pairs of hands not held him. Huw felt a tremendous feeling of relief sweep through him as he took the lead and started off down the cwm. The captain was in a very poor state, yet still alive, with the prospect of care only a short distance away.

At Argoed, they carried John into Hywel's room and placed him on the spare bed. Emma immediately took charge, ordered Idwal to heat lots of water and told Huw to fetch Morwen to help. A number of people were gathered outside the house, questioning the other members of the party, and his heart leapt when he saw Elinor approach. Conscious of the curious stares, they embraced briefly before he led her indoors. Once inside, however, the two clung fiercely to each other, each welcoming the touch of the other's body. It was Idwal's polite cough which finally caused them to break apart. He had heard Huw casually mention a girl's name, once in a while, and he now gazed admiringly at her.

"So, this is the lady you have spoken of, Longshanks," he said. "I admire your choice. Count yourself lucky that you found her before I did." His face twisted into its awful grin. He poured hot water into a bowl and moved towards the bedroom. "I will leave you to it, for now," he said, giving Huw a wink. "Maybe you will introduce me later."

No sooner had Idwal left the room, than Morgan and Hywel hurried in, followed by Morwen.

"I can see that you are not hurt, lad," the big man said. "Thanks be for that. You had best stay here, Hywel, for the present. Let the women do their work in peace. Morgan joined his wife and left the younger son outside. He spent a long while in the bedroom, before returning with Idwal.

"That man must be made of oak," he commented. "It is a wonder that he survived the journey here from the south. I'm sure that, now he has a place to rest, he will live to fight another day. Tell me what happened to you. Two defeats in such a disastrous manner are hard to accept."

Huw told him of the new tactics that the English had used on both occasions, how they had been caught by surprise and the bowmen, having no opportunity to form a line, had been scattered like chaff in a high wind, and that Glyndŵr had lost hundreds of his best men, while the King was easily able to replace any loss of his men-at-arms. He kept his suspicion of Tudor's death to himself. If his fears were well-founded, he did not want to be the one who broke the news to Owain.

With the coming of darkness and the stock and Pero safely secured for the night, the Gethins and their guests, which included Iolo, sat down to a late supper. Iolo reported that some of Leggatt's men were resting at his holding and the others had been taken in by the people of Cwmdu. After the meal, they talked late into the night, Emma or Morwen occasionally looking in at their sleeping patient.

"I have some news which should cheer you and your comrades, Huw," Morgan said. "We hear that Harlech has fallen to Glyndŵr at long last. Iolo Goch himself gave the news to the townsfolk of Machynlleth. The Prince will use the castle as his new home. You should tell the men to make their way there in the morning."

Huw gave up any hope of being alone with Elinor that night and contented himself by holding her hand in his; he was, therefore, delighted when she managed to whisper that she would be going riding on the morrow.

The following morning, Idwal and the others set off for Harlech.

"You can keep my horse for John to ride," he told Huw. "His need for the animal is greater than mine, for the moment. Take good care of both of them, Longshanks." They saw Elinor riding past. "And, take care of yourself," he added, with a wicked chuckle.

Huw waited until the last of the pikemen had disappeared down the track, then hurriedly saddled one of the ponies and rode down to the meadow. He found Elinor waiting for him at the empty holding and they rode towards the secluded pool. Here, on the mossy bank, they made love with an urgency that left them breathless. It was well past noon when they rode slowly back to Cwmdu and parted reluctantly.

They enjoyed four more such days before John Leggatt announced that he was ready to travel on to Harlech. His stay at Argoed, although short, had done wonders, his strength had returned almost completely and, unaided, he was able to walk for a short distance. Thanks to the care given by Emma and Morwen, the wound had closed cleanly, showing no sign of infection. On the morning of their departure, he refused all offers of assistance and climbed stiffly onto the charger's broad back. From here, he smiled and thanked his hosts for their hospitality and care.

"I owe you a great deal," he said. "It is something that I shall not forget, and I shall count you all amongst my truest of friends."

Standing slightly apart from the others, Huw held Elinor close to him.

"Take care, my love, and return safely," Elinor said softly. "You will be in my thoughts day and night."

Before taking his leave, Huw drew some coins from his pouch and pressed them into her hand. "Keep these somewhere safe," he told her. "They are for our home. It is precious little, I know, but it is a beginning."

Over the past months, he had been paid three pennies a day and, by taking care, he had retained almost half of the total sum. Kissing her lips, he turned away and took his place beside the great charger, then, captain and bowman set off down the track.

Chapter 15

Owain Glyndŵr slumped against the tower battlement and stared unseeingly out to sea. Far below him, a fine stretch of sand ran northward, only to turn west to follow the Lleyn peninsula, which jutted out toward Ireland. He wondered briefly what his position would have been had Wales been an island, and decided that, probably, things would not have been much different. The ambitions of the Kings of England were not thwarted by a stretch of water, no matter how wide; they were as much a curse on the Irish as they were to his own countrymen.

His men had done well this past year, and they had now taken this great stronghold of Harlech castle and the castle at Aberystwyth, both of which had long been a thorn in his side. He chose to make Harlech his home and base, for the mountains of Snowdon lay an easy march away. The Dragon standard floated proudly over the length and breadth of the land and, to bring credibility to his title Prince of Wales, he had held a Parliament in Machynlleth. In the spring, the war-weary people of Shropshire had sued for peace, to which he had readily agreed. In his search for a new ally, he had sent envoys, led by the bishop of Saint Asaph, to France and, to his delight, he had received a letter of support from the French. They were already finalising plans to dispatch an army to aid the Welsh in their war against their mutual enemy, the English.

Yet, whenever his cause came close to succeeding, fate stepped in and dealt him a cruel blow. As at Shrewsbury, he had now suffered another setback, this time it was truly heartbreaking, for his brother, Tudor, had fallen in the fight near Usk, and his head had been paraded through the Marches. The English were jubilant, for they believed that the head of Tudor was his own, and that the war was as good as over. The Prince had not flinched when the news was brought to him but it was as if a dagger had been thrust into his heart, which was why he stood, brooding sadly and alone, at the highest point in the castle.

Unobserved, he allowed his grief to take over, his shoulders rising and falling with the force of his sobs. God only knew how much he would miss his brother. From childhood they had always been close, sharing their thoughts and dreams, while they grew into young men under the roof of Sycharth. For a long while he remained there, before he was able to control the anguish in his mind. He turned away, dried his tears and began slowly to descend the steep steps, which spiralled around the tower walls. The lower he went, the faster his feet moved, and when he came to his bed chamber, his servants brought Margaret to him. She held him tightly, silently; kissed his face and shared his grief.

Huw awoke late and found himself in an unfamiliar chamber, from somewhere within came the sound of gentle snoring, emanating from two still figures, cocooned in cloaks. With an effort, he raised himself upright, his head throbbed and felt as if it were about to explode. He sat on the edge of the bed, praying for the pain to subside, afraid to stand, until the chill air drove him to get dressed. He looked down and smiled at the cherubic set of David's face, smooth and boyish in repose. The remembrance of the previous night brought a grin to Huw's face. He had only been in Harlech one day when David Mostyn arrived from France. The secretary spoke in private with Glyndŵr for most of that day, and, with his business completed, he sought Huw out. He had a hundred questions to ask and as many items of news to impart, but one pressing need was paramount.

"Let's find a tavern," he said. "I've had my fill of the wines of France and crave for a tankard of good ale. So much travelling and talking makes a man thirsty."

Huw drank sparingly at first, while he gave his companion news of events in the field, news of his family, and then, he made the mistake of mentioning Elinor. David had consumed several mugs of ale at this stage and his eyes twinkled mischievously when he heard her name.

"Your romance must have shattered the peace in Cwmdu," he chuckled. "I pray you, tell me all."

He listened attentively while Huw told him of the fight with Richard, her estrangement from her own people, and of how his family had warmed to the girl and given her shelter.

"I smell a marriage in this business," David remarked, when Huw had finished his tale. "A solemn matter, indeed; it calls for serious celebration. You have spoken more tonight than ever before and your throat must be as parched as my own."

He was ordering more ale when the tavern door swung open and Idwal entered. The mercenary's face lit up at the sight of the two young men and, not waiting for an invitation, he joined them. The three drank steadily, late into the night, David regaling his friends with tales of the riches of the French court.

"The King has agreed to send an army to help Owain," he told them. "He promises a force of some ten thousand men. We are arranging for them to land at Milford and, with that number beside us, we can match the English in the field."

The two bowmen reminisced over past battles, confusing the fights as the ale took hold.

"I am fortunate to be here, David," Huw said, slurring his words. "I've had Idwal to thank for my life since Hyddgen, and now I owe it also to John Leggatt. I can only wonder why he risked being skewered on a lance to save me. What friends I have."

"The captain thinks much of you, my friend," David replied loudly. "Is that not so, Idwal?"

"Indeed he does," the mercenary answered, getting to his feet. "I'm for my bed now, lads, if I can find it. The castle is like a rabbit warren and a man can get lost even when he's sober."

"You must be my guests tonight," David said.

Huw thought briefly about the strange look Idwal had given him, when he had answered David's question. He was too drunk to bother with it for more than a moment, and it was quickly forgotten. He followed the others out into the darkness.

In the centre of the inner ward, with the walls of Harlech castle towering above them, David decided to compose a verse. The moon hung large, a sprinkling of stars sparkled in the night sky. Inspired by their beauty, he began to declaim his ode, his voice echoing from wall to wall, until, from every quarter, came cries of protest.

Undeterred, the secretary continued his drunken poetry. The appearance of a familiar and imposing figure, in the doorway leading into the great hall, finally quietened the aspiring bard. Hands on hips, his head thrust belligerently forward, Glyndŵr called for silence. Huw heard David draw breath, as though to reply, and clamped a hand over the open mouth, lifted him clear of the ground and staggered into the tower doorway leading to David's quarters.

He smiled ruefully now at the recollection He made his way down the steps to the inner ward and crossed the yard, the smell of baking drawing him irresistibly to the kitchens. The bakers and cooks were too busy to pay heed to his entry. A tray of freshly baked oatmeal cakes lay on a table and swiftly Huw grabbed a handful, his eyes already searching for something to drink. In one corner stood a large earthenware urn full of milk. He took up a wooden ladle, lowered it into the creamy whiteness and brought it full to his lips. He felt the coolness as the milk slipped down his parched throat. Aware that people were watching him now, he put down the ladle and casually sauntered outside. He sat on a bench, rested his back against the stone wall and began to eat. The pain in his head eased a little.

He watched the bustle of activity going on around him; two of his fellow mercenaries passed him and one asked if he had heard the news just arrived from England. Huw said he had not. The man perched beside Huw on the stone bench and, lowering his voice, told him that Glyndŵr had learned of the death of his brother. Huw's stomach tightened into a knot and he put a half-eaten cake on the bench beside him. Ever since the fight at Usk, he had hoped that his suspicion of Tudor's fate would prove to be false; he felt as though he had just been struck a physical blow.

Through one of the narrow slits in the wall of his chamber, Glyndŵr looked down at the seated bowman. He recognised the young man from Cwmdu and was reminded of when he and his men had rested there on the march to Hyddgen. So much had happened since then, so many emotions experienced. The elation of a victory, the dejection of defeat and, today, the agony of a personal loss, his dear brother, the loyal Tudor, butchered and humiliated. With a twinge of envy, he watched the bowman get to his feet and walk out of sight. Not for him the problems that a Prince had to face, every day of the year. At that precise moment, Glyndŵr would have given much to change his lot for that of Huw Gethin's.

Collecting his bow from the room that he shared with Idwal and two others, Huw made his way down to the sands. He thought about waking his scar-faced friend but he knew that Idwal was never at his best in the mornings and, after the revelry of the previous night, he would probably wake like a bear with a sore head. Once on the beach, Huw joined some of the other bowmen, who were practising their archery. As John was not yet fully fit, no-one was in charge and Huw leaned contentedly on his bow staff, daydreamed about sharing a holding with Elinor, and of owning a fine herd of beef cattle. He appreciated that he would never be wealthy, but when things improved, he would be able to buy her fine things for their home. He was lost in his imaginary world, and when one of his companions nudged his arm, he realised that the others were making their way up to the castle. The sea air and his lazy morning had helped to clear his head and he already felt fitter and more than a little hungry.

Huw was walking toward the eating hall when a commotion broke out from the direction of the main gateway. He looked in that direction. Under the great archway, a handful of men were kneeling around someone who had apparently collapsed and, as he drew closer, Huw saw two of them pick up the limp figure. They did so with ease and, as they passed him, he saw that they were carrying a lad of some fifteen years of age. The lad's head rolled to one side and Huw gave a surprised gasp when he recognised the face of Wynn, a friend of Hywel.

Huw followed the bearers to a wooden bench, where they laid their burden gently down. "Get him some water," he said, kneeling down. "He seems to have fainted."

While one of the men ran to the well, he took a closer look at the lad. There was no sign of injury but his breathing was fast and shallow. He called the lad's name and saw the eyelids flutter in answer. The man returned, carrying a pail and, while Huw raised Wynn's head, he began to flick water over the pale skin. His actions soon brought a response, the lad opened his eyes and looked fearfully about him.

"Easy now, Wynn," Huw said soothingly. "You are safe and in good hands."

The lad's eyes stared up at him for a few moments then filled with recognition. A croaking sound came from his throat and the man with the pail held a cupped hand to his lips.

"You are Huw Gethin," Wynn said weakly. "It's you I have come to see. My pony collapsed when we reached the sea and I have run the last miles. I thought that I should never reach you."

With Huw's help, he sat upright and drank some water

from the pail.

"I bring bad news," he said. "Cwmdu was attacked last night. There was no warning and we had to flee for our lives. Some of the people are hiding above the falls, your mother and the lady Elinor amongst them. It was they who sent me with a plea for help."

"What of my father and Hywel?" Huw asked, with growing alarm.

"I know nothing of them," the lad answered. "It could be that they are with some of the other men. There were several that did not get as far as the falls. They may well be in hiding somewhere down in the cwm."

"Do you know who attacked you?" the man with the pail asked.

"I saw no-one," Wynn answered. "I fled with my family when we heard the raiders approach. Those who did see them, swear that they were English soldiers."

The idea of an English force in the very heart of Wales seemed quite ludicrous to Huw, and even if the story were true, why would English soldiers attack harmless smallholders, who would be no threat to them?

"I doubt that these men are soldiers," a familiar voice growled, his thoughts obviously on a parallel track to Huw's. "We would have known of their presence long ago."

"I agree with you on that, Idwal. Take the lad to Glyndŵr, let him tell his story and see that he is cared for. Make sure that you tell the Prince that the people of Cwmdu are in need of him." He went to pass Idwal who threw out a restraining hand.

"Where do you think you are going?" the mercenary asked.

"To Cwmdu. Where else?" Huw answered, brushing his hand aside. "I'm taking a mount from the stables."

Idwal watched him walk away and, with a despairing sigh, followed. "You can do no good on your own. Wait here until we have raised a force to accompany you."

"No, Idwal. I made a vow to my mother when I left Cwmdu and I am going to keep it. I pray that I shall not be too late." Huw called back, striding on purposely.

Idwal broke into a run until he drew level and clutched Huw's sleeve.

"Then you had best take my horse. He could do with a run," he said. "Besides which, the beast has emptied my purse, buying him oats."

Between them they quickly saddled the horse and, apprehensively, Huw swung up onto its back. He had not ridden a mount as large as this one before, and felt encouraged when the big head turned slowly to look at him. Idwal handed him his bow and led the horse across the yard to the main gate.

"Go with care, Huw," he said. "We shall follow as soon as possible."

Standing aside, he slapped the horse's rump with an open hand and the animal started off, clattering over the bridge. Once clear of the huddle of cottages at the foot of the castle walls, Huw tapped his heels into the charger's flanks and the horse found a steady stride. The motion was easy to cope with and Huw gave the animal its head. After they had travelled about four miles, he dismounted and led the horse at a walk for another mile, to ease its breathing. Remounting, he followed the coast line, the miles slipping by. Riding a few miles and walking one, Huw came to the Mawddach and turned inland, following the estuary until they reached a tiny hamlet, which stood close to where the river split into two. Crossing both streams, Huw rode into Dolgellau, where he allowed his mount time to drink from a water trough in the main street.

Outside the town, they began to ascend a winding track which skirted Cader Idris, and came, eventually, to an inn that stood at a fork in the road. Turning to the left, Huw rode slowly now, as the road climbed uphill towards a narrow gap in the montains. Here he dismounted and began to lead the charger carefully down a steep, stony track, man and beast slithering and sliding on the loose surface. Although the day was cool, Huw was sweating profusely when they reached the bottom of the pass. He stripped off his leather jerkin and shirt and splashed his body with cold water from a stream. The floor of the valley was almost level, with a gentle slope in his favour. Huw remounted and urged the horse into a run, which soon saw him on the banks of the Dovey. He slowed the horse to a walk and followed the river downstream.

He was headed for Machynlleth, some fifteen miles distant, and had covered two of these miles when he reined in. He would not reach Cwmdu that day, were he to continue on this road. During one of their marches in the previous year, a local man had shown Glyndŵr's men a little used path which led to the Hafren, and Huw turned toward it, forded the river, rode up to a scattering of cottages and stopped at the first one. A woman and two lads came to the door in answer to his call and promised to watch for Idwal and the others.

"Tell them I have taken the shorter way," Huw told them. "Say also that I urge them to do the same."

"You may rely on us," the woman said. "My man has served Glyndŵr's cause from the beginning."

His way ran through a thickly wooded valley and his

eyes watched for gnarled roots, which broke the uneven surface. The big horse was tiring and Huw allowed it to walk at its own pace, until they came to an earthen mound in the centre of what had once been a clearing. It was here that Glyndŵr's men had rested on their march. Huw dismounted and led his mount toward a dense thicket of hazel which grew around the perimeter of the clearing. It took him a while to find the path he wanted. It led steeply downwards to a stream. Across the water, the narrow path twisted and turned beneath over-hanging branches, hanging so low that Huw gave up any idea of remounting. The branches brushed against the horse's head and he became fretful. For some three miles, Huw cajoled the fractious horse along the path. Then, as his strained nerves were about to snap, they broke clear of the trees and before them lay a wide, shallow valley, stretching into the distance, the smooth pasture of long, wild grass broken only by an occasional blackthorn tree.

Wincing at the growing soreness between inner thighs, Huw swung himself up into the saddle once more and set the horse into a steady run. Daylight was already fading and it was with a growing anxiety that he urged the tired charger on. He rode for more than two miles before the horse came to a stop, its great head bowed low, while it sucked in air. Huw slid down and loosened its girth, then sat himself down in the grass. He felt as if he were aching in every muscle of his body, there was a nagging pain behind his eyes, the hangover from his late night drinking bout. For a long while he sat motionless, his head resting on his drawn up knees, until the horse's breathing began to ease. Getting stiffly to his feet, Huw stroked the animal's silky neck for a few moments, feeling its sweat stick to his hand, then picked up the reins and began to walk the horse on along the valley.

It seemed an age before he saw a line of trees ahead of him and knew that they were nearing the Hafren. His tiredness vanished and, lengthening his stride, he soon found himself standing on the river bank. He slid into the water, followed by the horse. On the far bank, he turned upstream and walked quickly through the gathering gloom. He guessed that Cwmdu lay six miles away and that the route he had taken, although a difficult one, had shortened his journey by at least fifteen. He was forced to slow his pace after nightfall and was cheered when they reached the place where Elinor had encountered the wolf. After two more miles, Huw stepped out of the trees and onto the familiar meadow, where he stopped, in order to prepare himself for whatever lay ahead.

Stringing his bow by touch, he slipped its string over his shoulder and checked that the arrows were still secure in his belt. Satisfied, he patted the short sword in its scabbard. The night sky was dappled by broken cloud and the moon not yet risen but Huw was on familiar ground; he mounted the charger and rode slowly into the open, guiding the horse toward Argoed. The only sound was the soft swishing of the horse's hooves in the lush grass, otherwise, silence pervaded the darkness. Then, to his right Huw saw Plas Hirnant, every window ablaze with light. Coming to the track, he slid to the ground and pondered what to do. His aim was to find Morgan and help him to drive off the unknown assailants. He had no idea where his father might be, and it seemed sensible to start his search at Argoed. Leading the horse by its reins, he began to climb the track.

There was more skylight as he neared the top, where he stopped again and was able to make out the shape of

Argoed, standing dark and strangely forlorn. Huw felt the tension mounting within him as he dropped the reins and moved silently forward. Reaching the cattle byre, he drew his sword and pressed himself close to the wall. Slowly, he edged himself to the doorway and whistled softly. No answering sound came from within, and he knew that Pero was not in his usual place. A sound, however, came to him from another quarter and he turned quickly, to see the outline of a man carrying a short pike appear around the corner. Huw sensed, rather than saw, that the pike was being thrust toward him. He struck out blindly with his left arm, felt it strike the wooden pike-shaft and heard the man give a cry of alarm. His shout was in English and, in an instant, Huw stepped forward and drove his sword blade upward, feeling it bite deep into the man's chest. The man grunted and sagged against him, before collapsing to the ground.

At the other end of the house a door crashed open and voices broke the silence. Risking a glance around the corner, he saw a number of men, some carrying freshly lit torches, run out into the yard. He did not wait to count heads but ducked back out of sight and, as he did so, there came the twang of a crossbow, and a bolt struck the stone wall, sending up a shower of sparks. He heard the sound of running feet coming towards the corner and, bending low, he ran for the horse and flung himself up onto its back. Another bolt whined past as he kicked the horse's flanks savagely, and the animal leaped forward. Huw had a brief glimpse of upturned faces as he whirled the horse around; then, he was galloping crazily down the track. They had almost reached the bottom when the big horse lost its footing and began to slide forward, its front legs splaying wide. Huw was scarcely able to free his feet from the stirrups before he was pitched over its head.

He hit the loosely packed earth with a bone-jarring thud, and heard the bow staff snap beneath him. A moment later, he heard the horse fall with a resounding crash. From the top of the track, torch lights began to move down towards him, and flinging his useless bow aside, he scrambled to his feet. A few paces away, he saw the horse rise up and he staggered toward it. The charger had had enough of war, however, and it trotted down onto the meadow and out of Huw's sight. Reaching the bottom of the track, he came to the pasture land that flanked the Hafren. Behind him, the torches began to spread out, as his pursuers formed themselves into a line.

He knew that if he were caught in the open, he would have no chance against so many and, throwing caution aside, he ran for the dimly seen line of trees. Once in their shelter, he slowed to a walk and moved upstream. With Argoed in the hands of these unknown assailants and the entry into Cwmdu barred to him, Huw decided to make for the sheep track, which led to the higher ground. If he could reach this safely, he would wait until daybreak, then seek out Elinor and his mother. The torches were now some way off, so he risked a brief halt, to take stock of his condition. His left shoulder had taken the brunt of his fall and he was aware of a burning sensation down his arm. Both his hands had the sticky wetness of blood on them, whether his or the pike-man's he could not tell. Otherwise, he seemed to be unharmed. To his surprise, he found that he still held the short sword in his right hand.

He saw that the torches were heading towards the river, drawing closer to him, so, forcing himself to keep to a walking pace, he set off once more upstream. He had barely covered twenty paces when he came to stop and sank to the ground. From ahead of him, a voice cursed loudly in English, and there came the sound of laughter. Huw saw three men outlined against the night sky, and he held his breath until they had passed by, only ten yards from where he lay. When the sound of their passing had faded away, he moved on.

From behind a huge cloud, the moon emerged again; taking advantage of its light, Huw lengthened his stride and soon came to the start of the sheep track. He had climbed half-way up when another cloud obscured the moon. He paused to see how far the torch-bearers had come. Their lights were almost directly below where he stood, stretching in an uneven line from the hillside to the Hafren. The torches gave enough light for Huw to see the men who carried them and, as his eyes followed the line, his blood suddenly ran cold. The man walking in the centre had momentarily moved slightly ahead of the others, and Huw clearly saw the ash blonde hair. How long he stood there watching Richard Lloyd he did not know, but his astonishment was replaced by a sense of fear for the safety of Elinor and his family and he resumed his climb. The question of who had attacked Cwmdu was now answered, but he found it hard to accept the idea that the Lloyds had dared to defy the might of Owain Glyndŵr. At the top of the path, he passed the rock ledge where he had often sat, and walked on until he came to a gap in the waist-high fern. The path was worn smooth by the passing of countless sheep and Huw broke into a trot, his aching muscles protesting at every step, his mind in turmoil, anxious about Elinor and his family, and a feeling of foreboding took hold of him, strong enough to make him scream in terror when a huge, dark figure suddenly rose from the fern and seized his sword arm in a grip of iron; a hand was clamped over his mouth, silencing his scream.

"Quiet, Huw. In God's name, be silent," a familiar voice hissed in his ear. "It's Iolo. We heard the shouting and saw the lights below. I guessed you would be coming here and was about to send help. Follow me now, we must not tarry here."

Iolo led off along the path, giving Huw no chance to speak but, cursing under his breath, Huw followed, and was aware of other men, breaking cover behind him. His uncle set a fast pace, and Huw was hard pressed to keep up. When he tried to ask for information about his father, Morgan, his uncle ignored him.

Eventually, the sounds of the waterfalls reached his ears, promising an end to his fears. They passed the place where the waters tumbled over the precipice and turned right, to a place where the land formed a natural bowl. A rough shelter stood in its centre, a small fire lighting the scene, which did nothing to dispel Huw's fears, for the people of Cwmdu were seated around the fire, their faces full of despair. Huw searched frantically amongst them, and his heart leapt when he saw Elinor's head of blonde hair. He made his way to her, called her name and saw her turn to him. She sprang to her feet and looked up at him for some moments, then buried her face into his chest and began to cry silently, her body wracked by sobs. Huw asked her why she wept so bitterly and, when she gave no answer, he looked at Emma and Morwen, who had been watching him. Seeing his glance, they moved close and he extended his arms to clasp all three to him.

"What has happened, mother?" he asked in a strained voice. "I beg you to tell me all."

"Your father is dead, my son. Hywel also. Slain by a gang of cut-throats."

Emma's answer came so quickly that Huw scarcely grasped her meaning.

"It's true," Morwen confirmed, seeing the blank look on his face. "They came the night before this. There were a score of them, at least. Morgan had no chance to hold them off."

Huw was utterly stunned, now that he understood what they were saying.

"They were led by Richard," Elinor said. "Oh, Huw, can you ever forgive me? That it should be my brother who brought such sorrow to you, who have all been so kind to me; I deserve to die."

"You must not blame yourself, girl," Morwen snapped. "When we heard the clamour, Huw, Elinor ran down to Argoed, before we could stop her. Some of the murderers had forced your mother into the bedchamber and this brave girl made her brother set your mother free. Who knows what might have happened, otherwise."

Huw looked at his mother and she lowered her head, but not before he saw her pain and anguish.

He gave a howl of fury, released the women and made as if to move back to the path. For the second time that night, he felt the strength of his uncle. Iolo had stood back, unable to tell Huw the tragic news himself, and now he held the young man in his powerful arms.

"Control your anger, lad," he gasped as Huw struggled to free himself. "You can do nothing for the moment. Go down there alone and you will be killed for certain. Think on it. It's just what Richard Lloyd wants you to do."

Gradually, Iolo prevailed and Huw stopped his futile struggle

"It was Wynn's message that brought you here?" Iolo asked. "It was a lot to ask of someone so young but I could not spare another man. We tried to fight them off, Huw, and lost two of our own in the attempt. There are other families here, too, who have much to mourn." He released his hold on Huw, placed a comforting arm around his shoulders, and asked, "Will your comrades in Harlech come to our aid? Glyndŵr did give us his word that they would."

"They will come, you may count on it," Huw answered, in a grim voice, "though they will not reach Cwmdu until late tomorrow."

"Then, until they do, we shall remain here," Iolo said. "Had you not received my message, I was intent on taking the women to Machynlleth tomorrow. There, they would have been safe from those fiends down below." He tightened his arm affectionately around Huw's shoulders and added, "So, now we wait, lad. You can have your revenge, when your friends arrive. Go to your women, now. They are in need of you."

Exhausted though he was, the night seemed endless, for he could not rest, but sat between his mother and Elinor, sharing their common grief. He could not quite believe that he would never see his father and brother again. His father had always seemed to be indestructible, and Hywel so full of life and joy. He wished that he could cry, to relieve his pain, but no tears came. With the passing of the night, he formed a resolve, which grew stronger as the new day dawned. Whatever happened in the future, he would somehow exact his revenge on Richard.

Chapter 16

Richard Lloyd was sitting on a bench beneath a narrow, semi-opaque window, drinking wine. He moved his position a little, until he had a narrow view of the yard and stockade outside. The sound of voices raised in argument reached him and a look of contempt swept over his features. All that day, the dregs of the border country, whom he had hired, looted the holdings along Cwmdu; now, they were squabbling over their share of the loot. Tomorrow, he would pay them off and they would be away down the Hafren, and although it would leave him almost penniless; it was, he decided, money well spent. The lush pastures on both sides of the stream were now his, or would be soon, and, by theft, he had more than doubled the size of his uncle's herd, all in one nights work.

He shuddered at the memory of the attack on Argoed. Morgan Gethin had fought like an enraged bull, killed two men with an axe before he went down under a welter of swords and daggers. His son, Hywel, had stuck a knife into the belly of the man who was about to slit his throat; the fellow had died in agony a short while ago. The mental image of the Gethin woman, clawing like a wild cat, her bodice torn to the waist, returned to his mind. He had appealed to Walter Harding, the leader of these scum, to intervene, but the ex-mercenary had merely shrugged and the woman had been flung onto a bed. It was not until

Elinor burst into the room that Richard had acted, laying about him with his sword and yelling that he would not pay them a penny. They had reluctantly released the woman, but the look which Elinor had given him, as she led the woman out of the holding, would stay with him for the rest of his days.

Richard was evil, but he had been fond of his sister, and now his cheeks burned with shame when he reflected that it was she who had discovered what he was allowing to happen. He banished the thought and returned, in his mind, to the rest of the attack on the homes in the valley. There had been another brief fight, in the darkness, with the men of Cwmdu, and two more of Walter's men had died. With one exception, Richard considered that his plan had worked well: he had hoped to find Huw Gethin at Argoed. Richard knew that someone had killed one of the guards at the holding, and he was sure it had been Huw Gethin but what could this rebel do now? With Glyndŵr's head on a scaffold in Shrewsbury, Huw Gethin must surely be busy saving his own skin. His reverie was broken by voices, and when he went downstairs, he saw a priest talking to one of his uncle's retainers.

"You have need of my services, I hear," the brown-robed man of God said, at Richard's approach. "It is fortunate that I am visiting the Church of Our Lady to celebrate a Mass, and also fortunate that I have some knowledge of your language. What do you require of me, my son?"

"It's my uncle, Griffith Lloyd," Richard answered. "I fear that he is nearing his end. He has been of poor health and, this morning, he was found senseless in his bed."

To say that the old man had collapsed during the night in which Richard had arrived with Walter Harding, the leader of the rabble band, would only lead to more questions, so Richard told the lie without hesitation. He led the priest upstairs and ushered him into Griffith's room. His uncle seemed to be unconscious but his eyes flickered open when the priest placed a hand on his forehead. For a few moments, Griffith stared up at the priest, then saw Richard; his eyes glittered with unspoken accusation and he gave a dry croaking sound, when Richard quickly moved back to stand directly behind the priest. From the yard came the sound of another argument between some of Walter Harding's men.

"Your servants seem to be an unruly lot," the priest commented. "May I ask why you employ so many?"

"They are here to protect my uncle's property," Richard answered glibly. "When we received news of the death of Glyndŵr, we feared that some of those who served him would come this way in search of plunder."

The priest was about to kneel beside Griffith but, instead, turned to look at Richard with astonishment.

"You are mistaken, my son," he said. "The Prince is alive and well. He mourns the loss of his younger brother. I saw Glyndŵr myself, four days ago. Your fears are groundless."

Richard felt giddy when he heard this, and he grabbed the priest's arm for support. "Do you say that it was his brother's head that I saw in Shrewsbury?" he asked.

"Sadly, that is, or was, all that remains of Tudor," the priest answered. "The lord Owain was devoted to him. When I saw him, he was in a vengeful mood; I would not wish to face his wrath."

Richard felt his fear churn his bowels, and released the priest arm. "You must excuse me for the moment, Father," he said, trying to hide the panic in his voice.

"There is a matter that I have to attend to. I will return shortly."

Closing the door behind him, he leaned heavily against it. The priest's news that Glyndŵr still lived had turned his world upside down. All his scheming had come to nought, for to stay here at Plas Hirnant would be to sign his own death warrant. It crossed his mind to run for safety, but he immediately discarded the idea. He had not yet paid Walter Harding, and his men watched every move that Richard made outside the house. He had arrived here in the dead of night and, like it or not, it would be night when he departed. In the darkness, he would retrieve his uncle's money from the garden where he had hidden it, then slip away and leave these cut-throats to their fate. He had lost Plas Hirnant for the present, and the consolation was that the money he had taken from his dying uncle would keep him in comfort for a long while. Another idea suddenly came to him, an idea so outrageous that at first he rejected it, then, on further reflection, he found himself warming to the thought. It would be a desperate act indeed, yet, the position that he was now in called for desperate measures. With a flicker of hope in his breast, Richard went downstairs and out into the yard, where Walter's men, who had quit their quarrelling by now, stood or sat in small groups, most of them drinking ale which they had looted from the houses in Cwmdu. The moment that he stepped from the doorway, he became aware of them watching him and he forced himself to walk slowly toward the gates. A group of three men sat with their backs against the timber palisade and, as he drew near, he recognised one of them.

"How are your wounds?" he asked, feigning concern.

The man looked up sullenly and then spat in the dust. "Sore. Sore as boils on your backside," he answered. "You should have warned us about that hound. If it were not for Thomas here, that crazy animal would have ripped my throat out. Pity you did not have the chance to kill it, Thomas."

Thomas licked his lips and set his tankard down. Richard nodded at the pair of them and moved on casually. The first fellow to whom he spoke had been one of those ordered to take the cattle from the byre at Argoed. It had been his misfortune to be the one who opened the door and met the full fury of a maddened Pero.

At the gates of Hirnant, Richard paused for a few moments and gazed out over the meadow. Somewhere, up on the opposite hills, the surviving men from Cwmdu would be watching the Plas, but everything looked quiet. The gates were heavy and demanded all his strength to swing them shut. They came together and the young man dropped the bar into place.

"I want you to stand guard tonight," he called to three of Harding's men, who stared at him in astonishment. "Let no man in. The priest may wish to leave, and you may open the gates for him alone."

One of the three murmured inaudibly to his companions, who burst into laughter. Richard knew that their mockery was directed at him but he chose to ignore it and began to walk back to the house. As he crossed the yard, he felt the first chill of evening touch his cheek. The priest's wiry pony stood close to the stable wall, its reins looped through an iron ring, which is what he had hoped to establish. Before long, he would be far away from this death trap, the pony bearing him on its back.

He returned to the house and entered the kitchen,

where he prepared a plate of food, which he took to his uncle's room. The priest accepted the food gratefully and watched in silence as Richard knelt beside the bed. Such apparent devotion from nephew to uncle was reassuring to the priest. Richard was, indeed, praying that Griffith would live a while longer, although it was for purely selfish reasons. The room was darkening when he got to his feet, and he lit two candles, which he placed one on each side of the bed.

"You will stay with him, Father?" he asked. "I shall rejoin you later."

"Rest assured, my son," the priest told him. "I will be here to bring comfort when the end comes."

Richard went back downstairs and into the kitchen, from where another door opened out onto the garden plot at the rear of the house. He let himself out and stood still for a while, until his eyes grew accustomed to the darkness. The chill air was more noticeable now and, from the other side of the house, he could hear the crackle of firewood, as someone lit a fire. With a deliberate step, he walked ten paces along a path, turned to his right, measured another five paces and then sank to his knees. The soft earth gave easily under his searching fingers and, within a few moments, he stood up, a small metal box in his hands. He looked around, satisfied himself that no-one had seen him, and he returned to the kitchen.

Once inside, he locked the door and was about to cross the room, when he realised that Walter Harding sat at the kitchen table, testing the edge of a knife with his thumb. The old soldier's eyes bored into Richard's and his mouth widened in a mirthless smile.

"You've been digging for your dinner, master?" he asked mockingly.

Richard looked at Walter's knife, while trying to act calmly. He carried nothing but a small dagger in his own belt, but he doubted that, even if he had a sword, he could get the better of this man who barred his way.

"This is better than turnips, Walter," he said, with a forced laugh. "The box holds what I owe you, and a little more. I was about to seek you out so that we could settle our agreement." He walked over to the table and put the box close to Walter. "Count what is yours, my friend," he added. "I will go and find some wine, for we must celebrate."

Walter took hold of the box, shook it so that its contents rattled, then visibly relaxed. "That's a fine idea," he said, burying the point of his knife into the table with a thump. "I think we have earned that much. I have made a tidy profit, for I've six less of the scum out there to be paid than when we started."

Richard left him emptying the box and went down to the main door; he peered out and observed that Walter's men were seated around a fire, which burned merrily in the centre of the yard. To his joy, he also saw white wisps of mist rising from the earth. Soon, the meadow would be wearing its shroud of white, which was to his advantage. He then went into the room in which they used to eat their meals and poured two goblets of wine. He drank the contents of one goblet, feeling the warmth spread through his belly, then refilled it and carried both of them to the kitchen, where he put them down on the table.

Walter was busily counting the coins, which he was arranging into small piles, and absently drank some of the wine. "I've been thinking, master," he said. "There is nothing to stop me taking the lot, is there?" He smiled at his sword and ran a hand gently over the piles of coins.

His words gave Richard the spur to action that he badly needed; he drew his dagger and thrust its point, with all his strength, into the man's back and into his heart. Walter Harding died instantly, his body falling forward onto the table. Thick, dark blood seeped from his open mouth and mingled with the red wine spilled from his overturned goblet. The liquid ran amongst the coins. With a curse, Richard brushed them clear and felt the stickiness of blood and wine on his skin. For a few moments, he stared unbelievingly at the body, then went over to the door leading to the garden. He unlocked it, rushed back to the table and took a firm grip on the body, which he dragged out into the garden, where he let it fall. The body slumped to the ground, invisible in the darkness, and Richard stepped clear, convinced that only a deliberate search would discover it.

He hastened back into the kitchen, turned the door-key in its lock, removed it and hid it behind a stack of basins on a shelf. A pail of water stood ready for use on the narrow table used for bread-making. Scooping up the coins, he hurriedly rinsed the blood and wine from them and put them back in their box. His own goblet still stood, full to the brim, on the table and he drank its contents down, his hands shaking. For a long while, he stood by the table, and when the trembling ceased, he took a deep breath, left the kitchen and started to climb the stairs. So intent was he on his own deeds and plans, that he failed to notice the main door standing open and, beyond it, the night sky glowing red.

Chapter 17

From above the falls, the people of Cwmdu had watched in dismay as their homes were systematically looted. There were only six men of fighting age amongst them, far too few to tackle the invaders, and they could do no more than crouch in the ferns, their anger mounting at their helplessness. Huw, who was almost demented by grief and frustration, rallied the men and led them some miles due east, through the long grass and heather, and down the steep, wooded slope to the Hafren. He searched the path here for signs of anyone passing recently, but he saw only his own footprints and the charger's hoof prints, which indicated that Idwal had not yet reached this place. He ordered the men to rest and sat himself down, his back against a tree trunk, clearly in no mood for conversation, so Iolo and the others left him alone and conversed quietly amongst themselves. Huw recalled that this was where Pero had found the wolf, reminded of that incident by the amazing and unexpected appearance of the hound, earlier that day. Pero had trotted out of the ferns, gone to the shelter where Emma rested, nuzzled up to her, and spread his length at her feet. He had refused food, and any attempt to coax him away from his mistress was ignored. When Emma left the shelter to bid Huw and the other men farewell and good fortune, Pero remained at her side.

His reverie was disturbed by the men moving. They were staring downstream, their weapons held ready. At a short distance, two men stood. Despite the poor light, Huw recognised one of them as Idwal. His relief and joy on seeing the mercenary was almost overwhelming. He leaped up and hurried towards him.

"It's all right, Idwal," he called softly. "You are amongst friends. These men are from Cwmdu. Thank God you got my message."

Idwal sent his companion hurrying back down the path, then approached Huw. "I got your message, when we came to the cottages near the Dyfi," he said. "The two lads who delivered it almost dragged me across the stream to their home, where their mother told me of your passing by. Now, what news of your father?"

Huw quickly told him of the deaths of his father and brother and of the looting of Cwmdu by Richard Lloyd's hirelings.

"They must think themselves safe behind the stockade, Idwal. We saw the gates being closed and no guards were posted out on the meadow. How many men are with you?"

"Thirty all told, and your friend the secretary amongst them. I told him that he would be a hindrance and he flew into a rage. John Leggatt advised me to bring him along, to give those we left behind in Harlech some peace from his eternal questions. So far, he has done all that I've asked of him. Let's hope that he continues to do so." He looked earnestly at Huw then added, "I'm sorry for your loss, lad. I truly am."

A line of Idwal's men filed up the path towards them and Huw told the Cwmdu men to head off for the meadows.

"We must surround Plas Hirnant as soon as possible,

Idwal. Should those inside receive any warning of our presence, they could try to escape. A favour, too, my old comrade-in-arms, I would beg of you. When the fighting begins, leave Richard Lloyd to me. Tell your men that he has a very fair head of hair. There will be no mistaking him. He and I have scores to settle." Huw and Idwal clasped hands and the older man, his scarred face grim, moved back to his men.

David came to Huw's side and listened in stunned silence as his friend told him what had taken place in Cwmdu, David wanted to hug his friend, to comfort him and dispel the demons that were tearing at his heart, but such things are not done by warriors in the field. Instead, he put an arm around Huw's shoulder, for a fleeting moment only.

The meadow was buried in a deep covering of mist, and here they came to a halt. From the direction of Cwmdu, a deep red glow lit the entrance to the valley; with a sickening feeling, Huw guessed that Argoed was burning. Tearing his gaze away, he walked ahead of the others, to what remained of the sycamore. As he had done with his brother, in the happier days of his youth, he slid into the cold water but this was not the time for play, and Huw waded across to the far bank. When everyone stood on Plas Hirnant land, he and Idwal split the men into pairs and told them that they would make the attack on the stockade at daybreak. With David at his side, Huw took a position some two hundred yards from the Plas, then began to wait.

The mist thickened during the night, gently soaking everything and everyone and making the waiting band invisible. From time to time, a man rose up, to check that his bowstring was still snug and dry around his belly.

Occasionally, distant voices came from Plas Hirnant and flames from a rekindled fire would silhouette the stockade. Otherwise, there was the sound of the Plas gates creaking open and falling closed again, at some time late in the night. Huw and David heard the sound, but could only speculate about why they had opened. It was Idwal who said that the men on night watch had reported to him that they saw a priest ride out from the Plas. He gave them a blessing in Latin, the men reported, when they challenged him. Huw remembered being told that a priest had been seen riding into Plas Hirnant and, apart from wondering if Griffith Lloyd had died, he thought no more of the matter.

When daylight touched the meadow and the cold mist thinned, men stirred themselves, stretching stiffened limbs. Bows were strung, weapons checked, and the battle line was formed. At Idwal's command, four men hurried to the stream, where they felled a sturdy, young tree, which they fashioned into a battering ram. The ring of their axes sounded through the mist and reached the ears of those inside the stockade. The bowmen heard the first cries of alarm from within. When the four returned and had taken their place in the centre of the column, the line began to move towards Plas Hirnant, using the mist as cover. It allowed them to approach to within thirty paces of the stockade, where the men stopped, to draw back on their bow strings. Huw found himself opposite the gates. He ducked when a crossbow twanged. Several heads appeared over the stockade and, not waiting for an order, the men nearest to him loosed their arrows. The heads disappeared behind the timbers and, seizing their opportunity, the men carrying the makeshift ram sprinted toward the gates.

They had not quite reached their objective, however, when the gates were flung open with a loud crash and several men ran out from the yard, jumped into the ditch, huddled together, raised their arms in surrender, and called, in Welsh, for mercy. Scarcely giving them a glance, Huw dashed into the yard, leaping over three inert figures. Complete panic had seized the remaining men inside the stockade. While he surveyed the scene, he was conscious that David was once more at his side. From all around the stockade, men were jumping to the ground and running for the main door, their faces contorted with fear. One of them showed some spirit, for, as he ran past, he threw a double headed axe at the two Welshmen. His aim was off the mark, and the weapon buried itself into the timber of the stockade.

Not one of the terrified defenders remotely resembled Richard; Huw searched around the yard in vain. The bowmen were pouring through the gates, shooting at their foes, who were fleeing towards the house; the doorway became jammed with pushing, fighting men, who formed a target that no archer could possibly miss, and their shouted curses turned to screams as arrow heads bit deep into flesh. A few, realising the futility of attempting to enter the house, scattered and made for the stables, two of their number leaping into the air as they were struck by the deadly shafts. Followed by David and a few of the bowmen, Huw began to run for the doorway of the mansion, his short sword at the ready. Without pausing, he trampled over the bodies heaped around the door, then, bending low, charged into the hall, unopposed, and stood aside to allow the others to rush past him.

To his left was a closed door, which he was curious to see beyond. As he neared it, he heard a warning cry and somebody pushed him roughly aside. The twanging of a crossbow and a bowstring came simultaneously and, regaining his balance, Huw saw David beside him, staring up the stairs, where they saw a man sway drunkenly to and fro and then pitch head first into the hall. He saw Idwal notch another arrow, grin at him, then motion him towards the door, but the room behind it was empty. David, meanwhile, had checked the opposite room and shouted that he had found three men cowering inside. These offered no resistance, and Idwal and the other bowmen quickly trussed them up. A search of the kitchen also proved fruitless; if Richard was still in Plas Hirnant, he had to be upstairs.

Taking the stairs three at a bound, Huw opened the first door and burst into a bed chamber. He stopped immediately at the sight before him; illuminated by two guttering candles, Griffith Lloyd lay peacefully on his death bed, a rosary wound around his folded hands. Behind him, Huw heard Idwal enter the room and curse.

"That's your old neighbour, is it not?" the mercenary asked.

Huw nodded, looked around the room and left again, pushing past David, who stood in the doorway. Idwal and David listened as Huw flung open one door after another, searching frantically for Richard.

"Open a window, David." Idwal said, keeping one eye on the door. "The stink from these candles is turning my stomach."

The secretary crossed the room and swung the window frame open. Idwal was snuffing out the smoking candles, when a noise caused both men to freeze and look at each other. Holding a warning finger to his lips, Idwal tiptoed over to a corner of the room, where a large wooden chest stood in the shadows. Signalling David to be ready, Idwal lifted the lid, to reveal the bed chamber's second surprise of the day. Bound and gagged and wearing only a rough shirt, a shaven-headed man stared up at them appealingly.

"God's blood, it's a priest," David cried out. "Hold still, Father, and I'll set you free." He carefully cut through the ropes, removed the gag and helped the priest to his feet. "In the name of God, Father, how did you end up in there?" he asked.

Behind the chest, David could see a number of items of clothing, which had obviously been tossed there in a hurry, and a long robe, which he handed to the priest.

"What happened here, and how did you hurt your head?" David asked, helping the shivering priest to dress himself.

The priest slipped the robe over his shoulders, then tenderly touched an ugly bruise on the back of his head. "I was sent for to come and give comfort to Griffith Lloyd, who was nearing his end," he croaked, closing the lid of the trunk and sitting down on it. "He was still alive when his nephew joined me at the old man's bedside. I asked him to join me in a prayer, instead of which, he struck me senseless with some object."

His eyes roved around the room, as though seeking something. "I cannot see the wafer and wine, my holy water, the chalice, the things I use for the Sacrament," he said, agitatedly. "The scoundrel has taken the holy objects along with my robe. He will be cursed to roast in Hell for his deeds."

"A lot of people have already said that of him, Father," Idwal told him. "Take care of the priest for now, David. I must go and see to those outside."

Idwal went downstairs, calling Huw's name; an

answering shout came from the yard and the two bowmen met in the doorway.

"He's not here," Huw cried out savagely. "I've searched everywhere, but can find no trace of him." He began to look amongst the bodies lying in the doorway, but stopped when Idwal told him of finding the priest.

"Richard Lloyd has foxed us, Huw," he said. "It was he, dressed in the priest's clothing, who passed through our men in the night."

Huw closed his eyes for a few moments, taking stock of this development, then, without a word, he ran for the stables. Idwal stayed where he was, having guessed Huw's intention and knowing that he could not be dissuaded from carrying it through. Huw reappeared, leading a horse, which one of the mercenaries saddled for him. He sprang onto its back and galloped out onto the meadow.

Idwal shrugged his shoulders, picked his way through the bodies and went into the yard. The men who had opened the gates and then taken refuge in the ditch, were now standing together, and he walked over to them.

"We are Griffith Lloyd's men," one of them cried out. "Not one of us took any part in the attack on Cwmdu. He could not stop those Englishmen, they were too many for us to do that. It was his nephew, Richard, who brought them here."

Idwal eyed the speaker up and down then looked coldly at his companions. His orders were to kill every man involved in the attack, and the lives of these frightened retainers meant nothing to him. Yet, he believed that the man was saying only the truth.

"Then, leave here now and never return," he told the spokesman. Their faces lighting up with relief, the men exclaimed their gratitude and scuttled out of the yard.

"You are getting soft, Idwal," one of the bowmen growled. He gestured to five men, who were slumped on the hard packed earth, watching and waiting to learn their fate "What of these? They are from over the border and there's no doubting they had a hand in the killings."

"Then, there should be no doubting as to what must be done, my friend," Idwal replied. "Hang them."

His face void of expression, he watched as the prisoners were dragged to their feet and their hands bound behind them. Struggling and pleading, they were hustled through the gates and forced towards the nearest tree. Ropes were brought from the stables and, within a short space of time, the five were kicking in mid-air. David and the priest joined him in the yard, the latter, though pale, seemed none the worse for his ordeal. Crossing over to the stables, Idwal chose a horse, saddled it, then led it back to the pair.

"This is for you, Father," he said, handing over the reins. "It's the best of the bunch. I reckon you deserve this much."

The priest thanked him and with David's help climbed into the saddle. "I feel that they should have a Christian burial, my son," he said nodding towards the dead lying in the doorway.

"They shall have just that, Father," Idwal replied quickly. "It will take some while to dig their graves and you had best get home and rest yourself."

The priest thanked him again for the horse and then rode out slowly onto the meadow.

By now, the men of Cwmdu had gathered all the stolen cattle together and, beckoning to David to follow him, Idwal walked over to them.

"Tell your people to take what is rightly theirs, Iolo,"

he told the big man. "You will have to take care of your brother's beasts for the present. I suppose that they now belong to Longshanks."

"I will do that gladly," Iolo replied. "I shall tend them as though they were my own." Fondly stroking the ears of one of the big white cattle, he stared eastward, his brow creasing in a worried frown. "I pray the lad is safe," he said. "He is so intent on revenge, that I fear he will take any risk, even hazard his own life. Do you think he is safe?"

"I'm trying hard not to think about him," Idwal answered. "Should anything happen to Huw Gethin, I shall have to answer for it." He saw Iolo's expression change to one of puzzlement and added quickly. "That is for me to worry about. You have much to attend to now, my friend. Take your cattle and your families, and return to Cwmdu, for you have the women and children to care for."

He waited until Iolo and the others were nearing the Hafren before he turned back to the Plas. Griffith Lloyd's herd was now unattended, so he told two of the bowmen to care for them.

"They are now Glyndŵr's," he said. "No doubt they will end up in your bellies someday."

"What of the dead?" one of the men asked. "'We cannot leave them to rot in the open.

"Dig a grave large enough for one," Idwal answered. "Put the old man from the bedchamber in it. After that, my lads, take what's valuable from the house. Anything that we can carry must go to Harlech with us. The remaining dead we shall put in the hall. I think it's a waste, but Glyndŵr commanded that this place be put to the torch. The stockade must come down also, those posts are well seasoned and will add to the fire. That will also take care of our dead friends, who shall have a funeral pyre.

It was long past noon when the various tasks were completed. Griffith Lloyd had been laid to rest in the garden, where the two bowmen discovered Walter Harding's body. How he came to be there was a mystery, for there had been no fighting at the rear of the house; however, his body now lay piled with his men, in the hall of the mansion. The timbers from the stockade had been stacked around them, or flung randomly through opened windows. Straw from the stables was heaped into every available space, and the bowmen were now fashioning torches in readiness for the final destruction.

Idwal was about to raise a spark from his tinder box, when David shouted at him to stop. The secretary was pointing across the meadow, to a distant figure leading two horses.

"It's Huw, I'll wager," David called out. "It seems that he caught up with Richard Lloyd."

This, however, proved not to be the case for, as Huw drew nearer, Idwal recognised one of the horses.

"He's found my charger," Idwal announced, grinning cheerfully. "To tell the truth, I'd forgotten about the animal."

"I did not meet up with Richard Lloyd," Huw explained, sinking wearily onto one of the bloodstained steps. "I rode to Llanidloes and they told me that no rider had passed through the town. Richard must have turned off the road somewhere." He eyed the torch in Idwal's hand and then looked into the hall. "You and the others have been busy," he remarked. "Did Glyndŵr command you to do this?"

Idwal nodded and struck the flint, sending a spark onto the torch. "I fancy you should be the one to do this," he said, blowing gently on the tiny flame.

Huw got to his feet, took the brand from him and climbed the few steps up to the doorway. "Bring me more fire, Idwal," he said, tossing the burning torch into the hall. "Give me the lot. This house has been a curse on my family for long enough."

He was still standing exultantly in the doorway, when the hall and stairway were well alight, and it took all of Idwal's strength to pull him away from the increasing heat.

Chapter 18

Jean de Rieux took a mouthful of wine, showed his displeasure with a grimace, and emptied his goblet onto the grass. During his service as Marshal of France, he had frequently done without many of the finer things in life, but having to drink this wine, he thought, had to be his worst experience.

"Pray inform your Prince that I shall attend him as he requests," he told David Mostyn, who stood before him. "I trust that you will be at the meeting, to translate for us?"

"That I will, my lord," David Mostyn assured him. "The Prince speaks some French, as you know, though his knowledge is limited."

The Marshal waited until David had departed, then instructed a servant to summon the more senior of his knights. The day was sultry, with a hint of thunder in the air, and he loosened his fine linen shirt in an attempt to cool himself. A group of Welshmen passed his pavilion, their brown homespun opened to the waist, and he snorted with disgust.

"Peasants," he growled, as the first of his captains joined him. "I tell you, Jean, I am not happy at having such men for allies. They do not even look like soldiers, and God alone knows whether they can fight, should it come to it."

"Their Prince has defied the King of England for five years with men such as these, my lord," his companion replied firmly. "You must remember that they are free men and would not be here, were they not willing to fight. You are well versed in the history of war, Marshal, and know that it was men such as these who fought against us at Crécy. It would be wrong to underestimate their skills on the field of battle."

The Marshal bit his tongue at the mild reproach, and thought it wise to make no further comment. Jean de Hengest was not a man to be treated lightly. Master of the King's crossbow-men, experienced in war and held in high esteem by the court, the Gascon was a man of few words, and was usually proved right when he did speak on a matter.

"The Prince requests that we meet with him. It would seem that he is as anxious as we are to come to some decision as to our next move. I, for one, would be glad to leave the situation in which we presently find ourselves."

When the other knights were assembled, the Marshal of France led them through the encampment and up a gentle slope to where Glyndŵr awaited them. He knew every man in his following, and it saddened him that not all of them were here to fight for his beloved France. The majority were in this adventure for personal gain, hoping to get rich on ransom payment. He joined the Prince of Wales, who stood beneath his Dragon standard, which flapped idly in the slight breeze.

"A good day to you, Marshal," Glyndŵr said, looking to David to translate. "The arena is empty, I see. Has not one of your knights received a challenge this morning?"

"It would appear not, my lord," the Frenchman answered. "Maybe the English are as tired of this charade as we are."

Glyndŵr shrugged his shoulders and motioned the

Marshal nearer. "We must decide what is to be done," he said. "The English grow stronger with each passing day. It would be folly to wait any longer. We must either attack today, or return to Wales. I have settled my mind as to what is wisest, though I wish to hear your views."

Jean de Rieux looked at the now familiar scene facing the allied armies. To his front, the ground dipped into a large bowl before rising to a ridge similar to the one on which he was standing. There, the English army sat at their ease, as they had sat for the past seven days, waiting for the allies to attack them. Behind them lay the town of Worcester, ready for looting of its riches. Yet, the place might have been on the moon, for all its proximity. Woodbury Hill was the cause of the stalemate between the opposing armies; to advance down into the bowl and then up the opposite slope would expose the attackers to their foe's bowmen. Indeed, the only fighting in this area had been individual combat between French and English knights.

The Marshal took one more searching look along their foes' battle lines, then sighed deeply. "I feel sure that to advance would be to sign our own death warrants," he said finally. "Our supplies are already dangerously low, while, as you say, the enemy grows stronger by the day. There is no choice." He looked earnestly at Glyndŵr and laid a hand on his shoulder. "We shall have to return to your country, my lord. Though, were you to order an attack, I and my men would obey."

The Prince gave a sad smile, while his eyes showed his appreciation of this noble offer.

"My thanks for that, Marshal, " he said. "Your words serve to confirm what I know must be done. Tonight, we shall build our fires high, then, we shall start back for

Wales. We must wait for another day to defeat Henry Bolingbroke."

Now would have been the moment to criticise his allies for their lack of support, for they numbered but three thousand men, one third the army promised by the French King. Glyndŵr, however, said nothing about this disappointment. There seemed to be no point in chastising the nobleman. When the day drew to a close, the allies slipped quietly away. The move was greeted with relief by most of the Welshmen, for they felt themselves exposed, being so far from their mountains. Huw shared this feeling, as the men marched west along a well used road, each step taking him closer to Elinor and Emma, who were now at Harlech, and he was impatient to be with them. Fixing his eyes on the back of the man in front of him, he thought over the happenings of the past weeks. Morgan and Hywel now lay in the churchyard on the road to Machynlleth. The day of their burial had been the worst day of his life, leaving him emotionally drained. Iolo and the other men had not allowed Emma or him to see the bodies, for they had been charred in the flames, when Argoed was set on fire. How the fire had started was a mystery, most people thought it was accidental. Whatever the cause, only the stone walls of Argoed now remained.

Glyndŵr had commanded that Emma and Elinor be brought to Harlech, where they would be under his protection, and both women had gladly obeyed. The prospect of staying in Cwmdu was more than Emma could face, while, for Elinor, it meant that she would be close to Huw.

They had been in the castle for only one day, when Margaret Hanmer summoned them to her chamber. Glyndŵr had stopped at his sentry post afterwards, and asked Huw bluntly if he was in love with Elinor. Huw confessed his love for the young woman, and, thus, it was arranged that the two young people were to be married, after a suitable period of mourning. Huw thought to rebuild Argoed, but had dismissed the idea, eventually. Once back in Cwmdu, he could easily find himself trapped in the routine of farming, and his chances of meeting up with Richard Lloyd would be nil. Besides which, John Leggatt acted as though Huw would never wish to leave his fellow bowmen, and Huw doubted if he had the courage to tell the captain otherwise.

The allies marched until noon, when the order was given to halt and, gratefully, the army settled down to rest, the French immediately building cooking fires. The only sign of the English troops were small groups of horsemen, who kept their distance, apparently content to keep watch on the direction of march. Huw was pondering on how these Frenchmen could eat so much at mid-day, when he was joined by David.

"I feel the need of better company," the secretary said. "Glyndŵr has scarcely spoken since we began our march home, and his mood is darkening with every step. I have never seen him so despondent. He has just told us that he is returning to Harlech with a small escort of mounted men. He is placing Rhys Gethin in command and we are to march through southern Wales. He is concerned that our people may believe that we have been defeated, and he wishes to make a show of strength in those parts."

He grinned suddenly and waved an arm at the other mercenaries. "I have to stay with you, to act as interpreter, so you will have the pleasure of my company. I feel sure that your captain will be delighted. Apart from which, someone has to look after the prospective bridegroom and bring him home unscathed."

The allies continued their march, passing close to the town of Leominster. Not one man in the army thought of searching the place for easy pickings, for the people of Herefordshire were, in the main, sympathetic to the Welsh cause. Also, the county was still influenced by Edmund Mortimer, and Glyndŵr would have had the head of anyone foolish enough to upset their unsigned truce. By the following evening, they were camped by the Monnow. Rhys Gethin had learned the lessons of Grosmont and Usk well, for he sent out small parties of mounted men, to circle the camp at a distance of several miles. It was one of these scouting bands that brought news which stirred the resting men. The King had taken up the pursuit, his army strengthened by levies from Gloucester and Wiltshire.

When Jean de Rieux heard of this, he hurriedly sought out the Welsh commander. "What now?" he asked anxiously. "We are greatly outnumbered, should this news be true."

"It's true enough, Marshal," Rhys answered cheerily, after David had translated. "It seems that Henry Bolingbroke has learned nought about waging war against us. He simply relies on large numbers of men, which only causes him problems in our mountains. Were the English commanded by his son, then I would be concerned." He poured some wine into a goblet and handed it to the Marshal, who sipped it apprehensively.

"We shall fight them on our terms," Rhys explained. "Inform your knights that they shall have the combat that they crave for, although they must be patient. We will choose the right place and set the trap." He smiled at the dismay on the Frenchman's face. "This is how we make war," he explained. "We are usually outnumbered, so we use the land to our advantage. You must understand that the king can field five men for one of ours. Do not worry yourself, Marshal. Your men will have the honours they desire. I shall see to it."

Jean de Rieux took a mouthful of wine and looked into his goblet. Unlike his favourite, full-bodied, red wines of France, this was white, yet very pleasant on his tongue. His appreciation showed clearly, and Rhys offered to deliver more to his pavilion.

"It comes from a grape grown on slopes overlooking the Irish Sea," he said. "I think it compares with any grown in Europe."

The Marshal thanked him for the offer, then took his leave. Watching him walk away with the other noblemen, Rhys little realised that he had now made a friend of his ally.

Anxious to reach the safety of the mountains, Rhys increased their speed of march and soon the allied army was winding its way through the narrow valleys of southern Wales. They had come to a particularly deep valley when it began to rain. Low clouds hugged the mountain tops, emptying their contents into the dozens of tiny streams which fed the rivers. These, in turn, filled rapidly and, as the rains continued, became raging torrents. The Welsh commander ordered his army to take to the high ground and seek shelter on the thickly wooded slopes. The rain was a misery for the Welshmen, though, for the French it quickly became a living nightmare. Whenever a flat piece of ground was discovered, they often came to blows, arguing over who should erect his pavilion on the site. Most however, copied their allies and lopped limbs from trees to build shelters, using bundles of fern as thatching. Though these crude huts leaked in a score of places, they did keep off the worst of the downpour.

Henry Bolingbroke was in an even sorrier state. His way forward and back barred by floods, he was forced to sit the weather out, while his army devoured its supplies. To search the countryside for food was a waste of effort, as he had already found to his cost. Warned of his approach, the local people had driven their farm animals up into the hills, far beyond his reach. The soldiers sent out in pursuit had been picked off, one by one, by unseen bowmen, and the remainder returned empty-handed, after losing more than a score of their number.

The rain continued for seven days and nights, swamping the English encampment and when it finally ceased, Bolingbroke had had enough. He waited two more days for the waters to subside, then gave the order to retire back into England. He did make some use of his presence in these sodden valleys, however. Not far distant stood Coity castle, which still held out against Glyndŵr, and he determined to relieve its garrison, which was under seige. Four carts were filled with provisions, arrows and bolts, material for clothing, tools for building repair and whatever food could be spared. Then, hidden beneath the contents of one of the wagons, Henry included a richly woven doublet with rubies sewn into the collar, a reward for his loyal captain. This valuable garment was wrapped around a heavy wallet, which held the long overdue pay for the soldiers of the garrison. To ensure safe delivery of this costly wagon train, Bolingbroke detached a force of more than three thousand men to escort it.

In the hills, Rhys Gethin sent a large number of his remaining men to harry the English army, now wending their way to the border. "You must not confront the enemy," he ordered. "Split into small groups and attack their foraging parties. When night falls, shoot your arrows into their camp, so that they have no rest."

Many of his men had already returned to their homes, as he had expected and, in his heart, he could not blame them. Wet, cold and hungry, the temptation to be seated in comfort by a blazing fire and with a roof overhead that did not leak had proved too strong. Accompanied by David, Rhys Gethin climbed an adjoining hill, on which the Marshal had set up his pavilion, and spoke with him.

"I will wager my life that the English wagons are making for Coity, to lift the seige." he said. "Your knights can have their moment of glory at last. There is only one road suitable for them to take and some of my men will show you where I suggest that you bar their way. When the English show themselves, charge their front. My men will rush their flanks and rear, when they least expect it."

Their pace set by the slow-moving oxen drawing the carts, the relieving force moved down the valley. The further south they advanced, the wider the level ground became, showing promise of open country ahead. It was here that they found the French drawn up in splendid array, their battle lines drawn across the width of the valley. The English captains were not given the opportunity to assess the situation, for the French knights immediately urged their horses forward and charged headlong at the now stationary column. The King's men were desperately forming themselves into line when the charge struck home, smashing great gaps into their ranks. Further down the column, more Englishmen rushed forward to support their comrades, leaving a widening gap between themselves and the wagons.

At the rear, the wagons' guards watched anxiously as the gap widened further and, within moments, they found themselves isolated from the main body. Casting searching looks at the wooded slopes, they urged the oxen forward, to shorten the distance, but no amount of shouting and whip-cracking would make the big beasts move any faster. They had scarcely covered fifty yards when the woods became alive with brown-clad figures. A volley of arrows fell on the wagon guards, who instinctively ducked low to protect themselves and, when they looked up, it was to find hundreds of pikemen rushing towards them. Despite losing some of their number to a following volley, the English men-at-arms managed to form a body before the pikemen reached them. They were heavily outnumbered, however, and the scene soon became one of scattered groups of men, thrusting at each other with lances, or hacking with swords.

Standing at the edge of the trees, Huw and the other mercenaries searched for targets before loosing their arrows. Here and there, men were struck and fell into the churned-up earth, others tripped over their bodies. To and fro the fighting swayed, until a gap appeared in the press and gave John Leggatt the opportunity to lead his bowmen, in a wild slithering rush, inside the defending circle. Keeping close to the captain, Huw found himself alongside one of the wagons. He hauled himself over its side. The driver took one look at the dark figure towering above him, gave a yelp of fear and leapt blindly into the bunch of struggling men on the ground. Much of the wagon's load consisted of sacks of grain and, balancing himself on these, Huw began to rain blows with his bow staff on the helmeted heads within reach. He was soon joined by Idwal, who also began to lay about him, a smile of sheer enjoyment twisting his ravaged face.

The men-at-arms were heavily outnumbered by now and, reluctantly abandoning the wagons, they began to fight their way back up the valley. The attention of many of the Welshmen was fixed firmly on the captured wagons, for the supplies they contained. This kept them occupied and, within moments, the King's men were able to continue their withdrawal in an orderly manner. Giving up any hope of forming a pursuit, John clambered up beside Huw and Idwal, who were now searching amongst the sacks. It was when he joined them that Idwal gave a low cry of astonishment.

"By all that's holy," he gasped. "Would you look at this?" Standing erect, he held a green doublet at arm's length, the better to admire it, but it was not the exquisite cloth which held the three men's eyes, it was the deep red rubies, which glowed brilliantly in the collar.

"Shares for all, friends," a voice growled menacingly behind them.

Spinning around, the three bowmen saw that the wagon had now filled with men, who stared greedily at the doublet.

"I reckon we have earned some reward for the misery of these past few days. What say you, lads?" the speaker called out, glancing quickly over his shoulder.

There was a general cry of agreement, at which the man stepped toward Idwal.

"Stay where you are," Huw said softly.

The man was no coward but, despite himself, he came to an immediate stop. There was something about this tall bowman that called for caution and he forced a smile to his lips.

"We can split those gems between us," he said. "One each would buy us all the comfort we need for a year or more."

"They belong to Glyndŵr," Huw replied flatly. "He has fed you these past months and you owe that to him."

At the rear of the wagon, the others began to push forward and Huw drew his short sword, pointing the heavy blade at the spokesman's belly. The man frantically attempted to hold them back, but to no avail, and Huw braced himself to strike.

"Take it and be damned to you," Idwal shouted from behind him.

Before Huw could protest, the doublet was tossed over the side of the wagon and, in the blink of an eye, the three bowmen stood alone.

"Don't argue," Idwal snarled, as Huw turned angrily toward him. "Give me a hand with this sack."

Taking hold of one end, Huw helped his friend to move the heavy bag, until Idwal gave a grunt of satisfaction. The mercenary then sat down on it and gestured to the others to do likewise.

"Let them squabble over those pretty stones," he chuckled. "We will sit here until they have finished their business."

"What game are you playing, Idwal?" John asked harshly.

"No game, I assure you," the mercenary answered. "Be patient and you will see that I acted wisely. It would have been a cruel twist of fate if any of us had been killed by one of our own."

After a while, the men around the wagon moved off, still arguing amongst themselves. Idwal waited until they were some distance away, then, with Huw's help, he stood the sack on its end, revealing the wallet which had been hidden underneath the other things.

"I think you should take care of this," he said, picking

it up and handing it to John. "My nose tells me that there is a small fortune there, and I doubt if I can trust myself with it."

John untied the bindings of the wallet, knelt down and carefully tipped some of its contents onto the wagon's floor. The coins that tumbled out caused him to catch his breath, for amongst the silver there came the gleam of gold. "A fortune fit for a Prince," he said quietly, after a stunned silence. "No wonder the English fought so stubbornly around these carts." He picked up a handful of coins and let them trickle through his fingers. "What now?" he asked, looking directly at each man in turn. "You could live a life of ease for the rest of your days with this in your purse."

There was a long silence while his two comrades thought about what he had said, and it was Huw who spoke first. "It's a temptation I admit, but I say it goes to the man who pays me. To cheat him of it would only bring bad luck to me and mine, of that I'm sure."

Idwal stared at him for a few moments then sighed and gave a twisted grin. "You are probably right, Longshanks," he said. "The odds are, that I'd drink myself to an early grave. So, put the coins away, John, and don't mention them to me again, ever."

Leggatt felt his muscles relax and he scooped the coins back into the wallet. What he would have done if the other two had wanted to keep a third share each he did not know, and he thanked God that he did not have to find out.

"They should bring much cheer to Glyndŵr, my lads," he said. "Now, let's be away from here and get this wallet to a safer place."

The sounds of battle drew nearer as they jumped down from the wagon, and instinctively they sought cover on the wooded slope. Here, in the shelter of the trees, they waited, and as the din grew louder, they could distinguish individual voices, shouting in fear or anger. Then, the first of the English soldiers passed by, shuffling backwards, shoulder to shoulder, their spears levelled. These were followed by men-at-arms and bowmen, who sometimes paused, to shoot down the valley. Then came the French, who charged, rallied, charged again, while their crossbow-men let fly their bolts from close range. The three watched with professional interest as the battle lines passed their hiding place and began to move slowly out of sight and earshot. Then, John led them out of the woods, to go in search of Rhys Gethin.

He found the fiery commander in the company of Jean de Rieux, who was in a buoyant mood, and it was with some difficulty that Leggatt eventually managed to speak privately with Rhys about the wallet of coins. The commander agreed that the money should be taken to Glyndŵr at once.

"It saddened me to see our Prince in such low spirits, when he took his leave," Rhys said. "Be sure to tell him that the French fought well and proved their worth. The news may ease his disappointment at their lack of numbers. I shall continue the march, when we are rested, and move on to Carmarthen. With good fortune we shall meet again at Harlech in the late autumn." He put out a restraining hand as John made to leave and shook his head sorrowfully. "I feel that we have missed a great opportunity," he said. "Had the King of France dispatched ten thousand men, as promised, we would have changed the course of history, when we were at Worcester."

Chapter 19

Huw steadied the pony while Elinor mounted. No matter how often he saw her, the sight of the girl filled him with pride in the knowledge that he was the envy of many men, and wonder that someone so wonderful could love him so passionately. He watched as she swung herself gracefully up onto the side-saddle, turned his own pony's head and led the way out of the castle.

Away from the towering walls, they rode side by side, allowing their mounts to walk at their own pace. There was no need for haste, the whole day was theirs to do with as they wished. Tomorrow, things would be very different, for they were to be married in the castle chapel. Emma and the other women were excited at the coming event, and it was to escape their attentions that Elinor had suggested this ride. Always eager to be alone with her, Huw had agreed with alacrity, having first sought John Leggatt's permission to leave the castle.

They followed a track that led down to a fine stretch of sands and, as was their custom, they followed the beach northward. Elinor was unusually quiet, lost in her own thoughts. No doubt, her head was full of the morrow, Huw concluded. Hoping to cheer her, he urged his pony into a run and called out for her to follow. He had galloped some hundred yards when he discovered that she was not riding after him. Reining in, he turned; Elinor was still following at a sedate walk. Somewhat concerned, Huw turned his pony and raced back to her side.

"What's wrong?" he asked. "Are you feeling unwell, or worried about the morrow?"

Elinor shook her head, smiled at him and brought her pony to a halt. "I have never felt better, my love," she answered. "Would you help me down please."

Huw took her weight as she dismounted, a feeling of alarm sweeping over him. "Something is wrong," he said forcefully. "I've never had to help you before. You are usually out of the saddle before me."

Elinor broke free from his arms and walked over to a small sand dune, motioning for him to join her. " Sit yourself down, Huw," she said, giving him a strange smile. "There is something that you should know."

His alarm increasing by the moment, Huw seated himself and looked anxiously into her eyes.

"I am with child," she said.

The words came so quickly that they did not fully strike home, and Huw continued to look at her without speaking.

"Did you hear what I said?" Elinor asked, after a few moments. "We are going to have a child. A boy. I'm sure of it. You are not angry, are you?" she asked, with apprehension at his continued silence. "You knew that there was always a chance of it happening."

The dark face in front of her suddenly lit up with a smile of sheer joy and she was almost crushed as Huw held her close to him. "Angry, sweetheart," he exclaimed, and he burst into laughter. "How could I be angry? You have made me the happiest of men. It is the most wonderful news that I have ever heard."

He fell silent for a while, then held her at arm's length while he composed himself. "Think on it, Elinor, I'm going to be a father. I can scarce believe it. Do you know when?"

"Mid summer," Elinor answered. "We shall have been married but seven months, by my reckoning."

"One month longer than my parents, when mother gave birth to me," Huw replied, with another laugh.

They sat for a long while, talking and planning, both aware that their future lay in the hands of others.

"I shall give up soldiering," Huw said at one stage. "You will need me close to you from now on."

"We must wait and see about that, my love," Elinor replied. "The only home we have is here, in Harlech castle, and this war cannot go on for ever. Besides which, if I know John Leggatt, he will be the last man to send you into danger when he learns that I am with child."

Later, as they made their way back to the castle, Huw had to agree with what she had said. Elinor, like his mother, was very practical in her ways, and he thought that their best course was to do as she had suggested. Only one thing annoyed him, that he could not yet tell anyone that he was going to be a father.

"Exaudi Nos, Domine Sancte," the priest's voice filled the small chapel and reached out to those who stood in the ward. Inside, Owain Glyndŵr glanced at some of the faces fixed on the young couple who knelt before the altar. He noticed that the mercenary captain, John Leggatt, stood beside Emma Gethin, and it occurred to him that he had seen them together quite often of late. His secretary, David Mostyn, was in a rarely seen serious mood and Owain stifled a smile, wondering how long this would last. He had grown used to David's presence, and the young man

had become sleek and plump in his service, sharing the prince's table and avoiding most of the rougher side of military life. Several of the groom's comrades were present, looking somewhat out of place amongst the wedding finery, and Glyndŵr thought regretfully of their dwindling numbers. Of the men who had first joined him with John, only half now remained in his service. Those who were missing this day, lay buried in shallow graves across the length and breadth of Wales. His attention switched back to the priest, who concluded the service by announcing that Huw and his bride were now one, having been joined together on the twenty-fourth day of January, in the year of Our Lord, fourteen hundred and six.

Later that day, the people were invited to join in a feast, and Glyndŵr, appointing himself as patron to the newly wedded couple, saw to it that no-one was wanting. Musicians played, jugglers amused the crowd with their manipulations, strong men wrestled one another to the floor. Men drank and ate their fill, then drank again. As the celebrations went on, the music became wilder and people began to dance, wheeling happily around the great hall. More at ease in these surroundings, the mercenaries grew more boisterous as the feasting went on and, more than once, Huw squirmed in his chair at some ribald remark aimed at him. Anxiously, he looked at his bride, but Elinor appeared to have heard nothing untoward and sat by his side, smiling serenely at those around her. Relaxing, with his family around him, Glyndŵr enjoyed every moment. Many of those present had been with him from the beginning, and he was using the feast to show his gratitude.

The revelry was at its height when Huw saw David

look toward him, then give a slight nod of his head. Taking Elinor's hand they joined the dancers, making their way across the floor, towards the doorway, where they broke out of the ring. David was waiting outside, holding the reins of two ponies, and while he steadied them, Huw heaved Elinor up into the saddle of one. They were cantering out of the ward, when Idwal appeared in the doorway, leading his companions in mock chase. Their shouts and whoops of glee followed the riders as they clattered between the two massive towers of the gate-house, finally fading away when they were clear of the castle walls.

A friend of David's father, who made his living from the sea, had offered them his tiny cottage, while he went to stay with the Mostyns, and this was their home for a week. No-one-came near, and though the castle could be seen standing on its great rock, it could well have been a thousand miles away. Only the tragic events at Cwmdu marred Huw's happiness, but he never mentioned them. The seven days passed delightfully, and it was with a wrench that the two young people made their departure.

In the castle, a room had been allocated to them, adjoining Emma's, and the two women began immediately to transform the bare walls into a home, while Huw resumed his light and frequently boring duties as a member of the garrison. His dislike of being confined within the thick, stone walls was a feeling that he shared with most of the men, but it was compensated for by Elinor's welcome at the end of his day's duty. This was a period of peace and contentment for both of them. Elinor had arrived at Harlech with only the clothes that she had on her back and, under Emma's tuition, she learned the crafts of weaving and sewing. Neither came easily to her, yet she persisted until, eventually, her efforts began to win praise from the other women. Huw occasionally marched through the countryside, escorting Glyndŵr on some business or other and, though these escapes were of short duration, he was able to enjoy the open spaces.

He went once to Aberystwyth castle, travelling by sea, which was a novel experience for him. The Irish sea had been relatively calm, though the swell of the water came broadside on, causing the ship to roll. Although he was not taken ill, as some of his companions were, Huw did not enjoy the trip and was glad to return to Harlech.

On the fourth day of July, Elinor gave birth to a son, as she had predicted. To Emma's delight, they named the baby Morgan, after his grandfather. Peering down at his fair-headed son, as he lay in his cradle, Huw smiled into the blue eyes, which stared solemnly back at him, and marvelled at it all. At first, he was nervous when holding the infant but, as the months passed, Morgan became as familiar in his hands as a longbow.

Winter came and went, with no change in their pleasant routine. The baby grew sturdily and soon became the favourite of those who garrisoned the castle. John Leggatt and David Mostyn doted on him, vying for his affection, although, strangely, it was Idwal who caught his attention most. The young Morgan seemed fascinated by the mercenary's scar, and would pluck at the ugly groove with plump fingers, screaming with delight when Idwal made a face at him.

It was early June when their routine was disrupted by a party of horsemen who thundered into the castle, flung themselves to the ground, hurried into the great hall and demanded an audience with the prince.

"Something is amiss," John said to the Gethins, who

sat in the sunshine. "I'd best attend Glyndŵr."

Lifting Morgan from his knee and handing the baby to Elinor, he crossed the ward and arrived at the hall with Glyndŵr. He took his place by the Prince's side.

"The English are at Aberystwyth, my lord," one of the new arrivals said. "They have laid siege to the castle and are building machines to break down the walls."

Prince and captain stared in astonishment at the man for a few moments.

"The English are there?" Glyndŵr finally cried out. "In the name of God, how did they get to Aberystwyth without being seen by our men? Who commands them? Come, speak up, man."

The spokesman took a pace backward as the Prince moved toward him, his anger mounting.

"We believe that they came through the hills of Radnor," he answered. "They had no wagons with them and carried little. They number some five hundred, all knights and mounted men-at-arms. The people of Llanbadarn told us that they rode fast, ignoring everything around them."

"You say that they have siege engines with them," John said. "How can that be? You said they had no wagons."

"They were brought by sea," the spokesman answered. "When the English reached the castle, they lit a signal fire on top of Pendinas, and a number of ships came close to the shore in response."

""Who commands this valiant five hundred?" Glyndŵr asked.

The man shuffled his feet and flung an appealing look at his companions before answering. "We spoke to some of the town's people who had fled, and they are sure that the English are led by the King's son."

"He who calls himself Prince of Wales," Glyndŵr growled. "It would seem that the young Bolingbroke can catch us napping whenever he has the mind."

He began to pace the width of the hall, his brow creased in thought. The landing by sea was something that he should have foreseen. Jean de Rieux, yielding to the demands of his knights, had returned with them to France. With their departure, the sea now lay empty of a fleet capable of opposing any English intrusion into Cardigan Bay. Despite himself, Owain had to admire the younger Henry for seizing the opportunity so quickly. He ceased his pacing and laid a hand on John's arm.

"In truth, the young man has moved with great speed, and we must do likewise, old friend. With good fortune, we will catch him at Aberystwyth. Send out my summons to arms and tell the men to gather at Dolgellau. We shall make the young Henry pay dearly for his audacity. Edmund will take command of the castle garrison while we are away. Now, get your bowmen ready; we shall march this very day."

The castle ward was soon ringing with noise, as voices called out commands and men bustled around in haste. Food and weapons were issued to each man, bundles of arrows were tied to the backs of sturdy ponies, weapons checked and re-checked. Wearing part-armour, Glyndŵr joined the men and rode out onto the road which led south. Huw had time for the briefest of farewells with Elinor and his mother, before he hurried over the bridge, to find the Dragon standard already moving down the road.

They waited for one day in Dolgellau, as men arrived in answer to the call, then, impatient to be under way, Glyndŵr marched for Machynlleth. Here, the men of

Powys were gathering, and with his force now numbering some fifteen hundred, he led them down the Dyfi valley. By noon of the following day, the Welsh stood on the banks of the Rheidol, where mounted scouts were sent forward. While they waited for their return, a local man ran up with the news that the English were already gone. Suspecting trickery, Glyndŵr told John to hurry forward with a body of bowmen.

"Beware of a trap," he said. "Should you see as much as a single Englishman, rejoin me straight away."

Close by the church of Llanbadarn, the bowmen met one of their scouts, who confirmed that the enemy had indeed fled. "They left in haste, as you will see," he said. "They destroyed their siege engines and, what is more, they have abandoned some of those new weapons, things which shoot stones out of a metal barrel. I've never seen the like of them before."

Telling the man to ride at speed back to the waiting army, John led his bowmen towards the castle.

"What are these engines?" Huw asked, as they strode along. "Have you seen them during your service in foreign lands?"

"I've only heard talk of some new and terrible weapon which can make a hole in the thickest of walls," the captain answered. "I was told that they were equally dangerous to those who use them. They use a powder, I heard, which has to be used with the greatest of care."

When they stood before the castle, they saw, gathered around the burst remains of two of these new weapons, some of the garrison, who excitedly told the bowmen what had taken place.

"The English fired several rounded stones at yonder tower," one said, pointing over his shoulder. "It was as though they had harnessed both thunder and lightening. I must confess that the noise frightened me out of my wits. They were firing one of these, when it burst into pieces, and those who were standing near were blown into the air like chaff. The other engine also burst, shortly afterwards, killing more men."

John looked around the now empty bay, then stared down at the abandoned siege equipment which lay scattered around. "When did the English leave?" he asked.

"They were here when darkness fell," another answered. "There was a lot of movement in their lines during the night, and at dawn, they rode off in a body along the Ystwyth. The tide was running high by then, and their ships cleared the beach and took sail. You will have little chance of catching; up with those who went inland, for they only took some spare mounts with them."

While they waited for Glyndŵr to arrive, the bowmen examined the destroyed siege engines. It was obvious that their foes had left in haste, for they found abandoned weapons everywhere, and even discovered a cache of food.

"There is little doubt that they left as speedily as they arrived," John commented. He took another look at the deserted siege lines, his brow creasing in a frown. "I fear this young Bolingbroke will cause us much mischief in the years to come, lads. He is proving to be a bold commander and a lucky one. He has certainly had good fortune in this venture, even though he failed to take the castle. Had he stayed here until noon, we would have caught him."

The Prince echoed his captain's words when finally he arrived with his force at the castle. "He is either a fool or a man who is prepared to take risk, should the reward be great enough," he said. "I do not believe that he is a fool. Had he succeeded in taking the castle, he could have turned it into a thorn in our side." He struck his fist into an open palm, giving vent to his frustration. "Hell's fire. Can you imagine our position had we taken him captive? Not even the King of England would have been able to ignore his plight. We could have bargained for our independence in return for the release of his son. I would no longer have to ask any man to shed his blood for our cause."

He stared out to sea for a while, alone with his thoughts, then gave a wry smile. "His capture would have more than made up for the disappointments I have experienced over these past few years. However, it was not to be. I will call on my garrison commander now, but must return to Harlech as soon as possible. I have a meeting with the Bishop of Saint Asaph to attend. Stay here with the bowmen for two days, then follow me home. I will dispatch a force into Radnor, to discourage young Bolingbroke."

On the second day of their stay in Aberystwyth, Huw asked John for leave to visit the town's market. He had a little money in his purse and wanted to buy some coloured ribbons for Elinor.

"No reason why you should not go," John answered, and as Huw turned to leave, added. "I've a mind to come with you, if you do not mind my company."

Together, they walked the short distance into the town and found its narrow streets thronged with people. Many were here to see the aftermath of the brief siege, others had come to sell or buy a variety of wares. On occasions, Huw tried to strike up a conversation with his friend but, after several unsuccessful attempts, he gave up. The captain seemed to have something on his mind and would merely grunt a brief reply, before relapsing once more into silence. He was probably brooding over the missed opportunity to join battle with the King's son, Huw concluded.

He found and bought a bunch of ribbons and suggested that they might as well return to the castle. John nodded in agreement, then looked about him at the crush of people.

"Let's walk along the shore," he said. "I need to talk with you and I cannot do so with this mob around us."

Without waiting to see if Huw was agreeable, he began to push his way along the street, lengthening his stride as he drew clear of the crowd. Reaching the shoreline, he changed direction and made for the castle, his pace quickening. Not once did he look to see if the tall bowman was still with him, and only when Huw grabbed his arm, did he come to a sudden halt.

"I thought that you wanted to speak with me," Huw said, his voice tight with annoyance.

The captain turned toward him and Huw saw that his normally tanned face was now pale. He gulped nervously then with an effort said, "I want to marry Emma. I've asked her for her hand and she has consented. She is concerned about your feelings on this matter, though. I'm telling you now, I am going to marry her, despite any objections from you or anyone else."

Speechless, Huw stood rooted to the ground. He and John had been as close as two friends could be, and while living in the confines of Harlech castle, they had been thrown together more than ever. Yet, he had no idea of the strength of John's feelings for his mother.

"Well, say something, lad," John demanded. "This is ridiculous, you know, I've never felt so nervous in my whole life."

"I do not know what to say," Huw stammered. "You certainly succeeded in keeping this to yourselves. Mother did not even hint that you and she cared for each other."

"That was her wish," John said. "She wanted her mourning to run its proper course. We both pray that you are agreeable, although, as I've said, I am determined to make Emma my wife."

Huw saw the concern in the captain's eyes and felt his affection for the man sweep everything else aside. "Then I would not dare to stand in your way, John Leggatt," he replied with a grin.

The two continued to stare at one another for a few moments, then both suddenly laughed, John with relief, Huw from sheer happiness.

"I don't know about you, but I badly need a drink," John gasped, when their laughter subsided. "My throat is as dry as sand. Come on, let us find a tavern."

The one drink led to another and it was late in the day when they returned to their temporary camp close by the castle walls.

The following morning, John led his bowmen back to Harlech. They were just clear of Llanbadarn when he called Huw and Idwal to his side.

"I'm taking one of the horses and going on ahead," he told them. "I must tell your mother my news, Huw. You will take command. You know what to do as well as any man here and you, Idwal, will take good care of him, as always."

"What did he mean by that remark?" Huw asked, as the captain rode off.

"Simply what he said," Idwal answered. "Surely you must have noticed that either he or I have always been close whenever there was any danger threatening you. He worried over your safety as though you were his own son."

Huw was thinking about this when Idwal tried to explain how it was.

"It might be that I should not say this, but John has loved your mother for years. He never spoke of it, but when you know someone as well as I know him, you can tell the signs. I'm glad that you feel as you do about their love and welcome their marriage. He is a good man, although you don't need me to tell you that." He looked over his shoulder at the waiting bowmen and smiled. "Well now, my captain, your men await your command. I suggest that we get them moving."

Huw waved the men forward. He was pleased that his mother now had someone to share her life with. Her loneliness had been a secret source of sorrow to him, a feeling made stronger by his joy at having Elinor. His mind turned to his father, and the familiar, cold anger took hold. No matter how often good fortune came the Gethin family's way, as it had now, he would never know real peace of mind until Richard Lloyd had paid for his crimes.

Chapter 20

Hundreds of miles to the north of the British Isles, massive snow-laden clouds drew together, then, nudged by a northerly wind, began to move south, over the cold sea. On the mountains of western Scotland the leading clouds began to shed their heavy load, covering the rocks and heather in a thickening whiteness. The increasing strength of the wind moved the banks of cloud on, blotting out the landscape in their passing. The further south they moved, the fiercer the wind became, until, when it came to the Irish sea, the storm had the proportions of a blizzard.

It struck the northern coast of Wales, raged through the mountain passes, building up huge drifts, which covered many of the holdings in its path. The blizzard swept over the Rhinogs and much of the Berwyns, howled across the open spaces of the Cambrians, blasted over the Black Mountains and into the deep valleys of the south. Somewhere between Wales and Cornwall, the blizzard lost its momentum, eased into separated snowfalls, before finally exhausting itself. In its wake, most of Wales lay covered to the depth of a man's hips, and, where the snow had drifted, it stood ten to twelve feet high. As the winds dropped, a hush came over the land and the temperature plummeted. That winter of 1408 was one of the worst to hit Britain in decades.

Huw braced himself, before throwing back the covers and swinging his feet to the floor, leaving his wife asleep. The cold struck immediately and he shivered as he hurriedly dressed, his breath forming clouds of moisture. He drew back the covering from one of the narrow window slits in the wall and peered out. The ward lay under a thick fall of snow. He watched a hunched figure struggle through it toward the kitchens, another flurry of snowflakes whirled through the air. The fire in their room had long burned itself out and he knelt before the hearth, to light it once more. He placed some dry kindling in the centre of the ashes and began to strike sparks from his tinder box. His efforts were soon rewarded and he quickly had a cheerful, crackling glow, which he banked with some peat. Satisfied with his handiwork, he let himself out of the room, smiling to himself as a wailing call came from Morgan's cradle.

Carefully, he descended the spiralling steps and came out into the ward, flinching at the bitterly cold wind, which cut through his clothing as he crunched over the snow. He followed a trail of footprints to the kitchen and had his breakfast of oatcakes and milk, welcoming the heat given off by the ovens, then, reluctantly took his leave. The night guard waited in the gate-room, huddled around a glowing brazier; although his companion for the day's duties had not yet arrived, Huw told the others to go. Tired from their vigil and with thoughts of a warm bed in their minds, the men did not linger. Within moments of their leaving, the door crashed open, to admit his fellow guard and a blast of cold air. Huw grinned a welcome.

The grizzled old mercenary snorted a reply and,

brushing snow from his grey beard, walked stiff-legged over to the brazier.

"Aches and pains are all that's left to me, lad," he groaned. "This cursed weather only adds to my discomfort." He sat on a stool, groaning at the twinges from his complaining muscles, and began to massage the back of his neck. "What, in God's name, am I doing here?" he asked. "I should be back on the southern shores of France, where the air is as soft as a woman's touch."

William was the oldest of the surviving men who had travelled back to Wales with John Leggatt, and he was held in high regard. His age was more than fifty years, and he had spent many of these drifting around Europe, fighting in one war or another. He had led a hard life and bore the scars to prove it, but his knack of survival was such that, despite his constant grumbling, everyone respected him. Drawing his stool closer to the heat, he gave Huw a crafty, sideways look.

"One of us had better try to clear the snow," he said dolefully, and shifted his gaze to the brazier. He made no attempt to move and, with a chuckle, Huw patted him on the shoulder.

"You tend to the fire, William," he said. "It's by far the most important task on a day such as this."

The snow was falling even more heavily when Huw went outside, and he had to fight his way through the clinging whiteness to reach one of the store rooms. Even with the body heat caused by his exertions, the cold already pinched at his nose and fingers. Never in his life had he felt a coldness such as this. Selecting a spade with a long handle, he went back outside and began to try and clear the area around the gates. He stuck to his task until his arms and shoulders were aching in protest, then he abandoned the work, for no sooner had he cleared one patch, than a gust of freezing wind covered it with snow again. Leaning the spade against a wall, he re-entered the gate-room; William had not moved from brazier.

"What do you make of this storm, William?" he asked. "I cannot recall weather such as this."

The old mercenary got stiffly to his feet, walked over to the door, opened it part way, and peered up at the leaden sky. When a blast of cold air rushed into the room, he hurriedly slammed the door shut and resumed his seat.

"It makes me think of a land far to the East," he said. "They call the people who live there the Hungry Ones. Our employer was campaigning against them, when winter caught us. That wind outside is like the one we had there, and you had better pray that it soon stops. We had to retreat because of the cold, and a number of our comrades were frozen to death. It was a nightmare of a march, lad, I can tell you. I was lucky to be alive at the end of it."

Not until much later in the day, with the help of dozen or so of the garrison, did they finally manage to get the great gates open. During the morning of the following day, the snow clouds cleared Harlech, leaving a dull, blue sky behind them. The wind, however, came back and blew for another two days, probing every nook and cranny in the castle, making life a misery for those within its walls. Wherever a man lay or sat huddled by a fireside, there was no escaping from the freezing draughts, and the men of the garrison looked like dancing bears, as they added more and more layers of clothing. The wind piled the fallen snow into great drifts, which, unless cleared quickly, became as solid as the castle's stone walls, and the men were hard put to keep the approaches to the gates passable. When eventually the wind dropped, the garrison was presented with an incredible sight. Here and there, large areas of the frozen ground lay bare of snow; in places which had been sheltered from the wind, it had drifted to a height of twelve to fifteen feet. Any cottages in the vicinity of the castle were almost totally buried, and, under the command of Edmund Mortimer, all available men were sent to free those occupants who were trapped.

The terrible cold continued for days, and appeals for aid reached the castle from many places. In response, many of the garrison were sent out into the hills, to do what they could for the suffering populace. The plight of the smallholders was pitiful to see, and although the men did what they could to help themselves, the seriousness of their situation began to dawn on everyone. Much of the winter feed on which the animals depended lay buried beneath a thick sheet of frozen snow and it took days of back-breaking labour to dig down to it. Every smallholder told of losing some stock. Others expressed their fears for neighbours who had disappeared during the blizzard. Wrapped in his warmest cloak, Owain Glyndŵr presided over a meeting of captains and notables.

"We have been advised that much of Wales is in the same plight as we in Harlech are," he said. "Messengers have risked their lives to get here and all say that conditions for travelling are fraught with danger. As there is nothing that we can do for those who live any great distance away, we must concentrate our efforts in helping the people of the locality. The castle gates will remain open as from today and nobody who seeks shelter will be turned away."

"A word of caution, my lord," Edmund Mortimer said quickly, when the Prince paused. "Though we are provisioned in case of a siege, I doubt that we can feed any number of mouths for long. It is only January and there is no telling how long this cold will last. We should not risk using all our stores too soon."

The meeting discussed his advice and finally agreed to a suggestion made by Iolo Goch, that those who sought shelter within the castle should hand over what food they had.

"I place you in charge of this matter, Edmund," Glyndŵr said. "Think how to best control our supplies and implement it straight away. John, you have the task of informing our people of our decision. Give them all the help you can."

Huw, Idwal and their fellow mercenaries, with one exception, were chosen to accompany the captain on the first of these missions. Standing in the ward while they made ready to leave, poor, old William was a picture of dejection. John guessed the man's feelings and ordered him to stay with the gate guard. Marching out of the castle shortly afterwards, one of the men remarked that he had not seen William move so fast for many a year.

Their march soon degenerated into a line of slipping, cursing men, struggling over the frozen snow, as they took the path to the holdings along the Dwyryd. By noon that day, the bowmen had covered some ten miles and John wisely decided to turn about. Most of the people they called on decided to accept the offer of refuge in the castle, and Huw and the other men now helped to drive the surviving stock to Harlech, their progress painfully slow because the animals' hooves could get very little purchase on the ice, and the men spent time helping one beast after another back onto its feet. They were still a mile from the castle when darkness fell. Guided by torch light, they passed through the gates at last, every man in a state of exhaustion.

Throughout the months of February and March the killing, relentless cold persisted. Tales of sorcery began to spread amongst the four hundred or so people who had sought refuge in and around the castle, the King was spoken of as the likely source of this evil. Although the garrison made light of these rustic fancies, the tale persisted. Glyndŵr, to scotch the rumours, called for a day of prayer. His chaplain prayed to the Almighty and asked Him to hasten the coming of spring. By now, the countryside had been emptied of game, either through poaching or because the fauna had starved and perished in the cold. It had become necessary to begin slaughtering the livestock. Glyndŵr only consented to this last resort when he learned that a hunting party had been greatly troubled by wolves.

"Those farmers will hold me responsible for their loss," Glyndŵr told Edmund Mortimer, as they watched two smallholders protest angrily as their animals were butchered. "How can I ask them to take up arms on my behalf again?"

Edmund Mortimer made no reply, for he knew that Owain's words would prove to be true. Men usually found someone to blame when misfortune struck.

***

His feet and legs bound in thick layers of sack-cloth, Huw made his way cautiously over the jagged blocks of ice thrown up by the frozen sea and fetched in by the incoming tide. The huge blocks stretched from the base of the castle rock, for a distance of roughly thirty yards, until they reached the open water. For a man to get this far, he risked being badly gashed by a fall, or sustaining a broken limb. Ahead of him, two figures sat huddled together on a slab of ice, close to the water, and as he drew near, one of them swung a long pole into the air and examined the length of twine attached to one end.

"The fish are too cold to take a bite of my bait," he heard Idwal call out. "I swear that I heard their teeth chattering a few moments ago."

Huw heard Idwal's companion snort in derision as the two turned to see who was approaching.

"You would be better employed gathering fuel for your fire," the second fisherman said, as Huw joined them.

Dressed similarly to Idwal, it was the voice that identified the speaker as William. The old mercenary was literally swathed in reams of homespun which covered all but his eyes.

"It is mutton again tonight, for a certainty," he moaned. "Should I live through this frozen hell, which I doubt, my lips will never taste that greasy excuse for meat ever again." Taking his line from the water, he flung his pole aside and sat staring glumly out over the sea. Idwal gave Huw a wink and motioned him to sit beside him.

"I hear that you found another who had died, when you were out searching yesterday," Huw said to him.

"Aye, more's the pity," Idwal replied. "It was the strangest thing I've ever come across. We had to dig our way into the holding and there was this old woman, sitting in a chair, frozen solid. A man, who must have been her husband, was lying dead in bed. It sent a shudder down my back bone, I can tell you."

He was about to say more but remained silent, his head cocked to one side as he listened to something.

"Tide's beginning to come in, I think. Listen carefully and you can hear the ice creak."

Huw heard a faint grinding sound and when he got to his feet, he felt the ice move slightly beneath him. "The fish may come in with the tide," he said hopefully.

Unwinding his line, he laid it on the ice behind him, baited the hook, and was about to swing his pole over the water when something touched his cheek. Puzzled, he looked at the others, who were preparing to cast their lines, obviously unaware of anything unusual. With a shrug, he forgot about it and swung his pole. The gust of warm air caught him full in the face and, with a cry of disbelief, Huw stared out to sea. The surface of the water which had lain like a sheet of dulled metal for months, was coming alive with tiny ripples of white foam.

Aware that the other two were staring at him as though he had gone mad, Huw pulled back his hood and began to laugh almost hysterically. "The wind," he shouted out. "Feel the wind, William."

It was Idwal, though, who first removed the homespun from his face and tentatively sniffed the air. Huw caught a flash of white teeth, framed in a black, stubble-covered face, before Idwal let out a whoop of joy and swung old William off his feet. Not knowing whether to continue laughing, or burst into tears, Huw joined the two in a wild, crazy jig, completely ignoring the slippery surface. Arm in arm they whirled, William's pleas to spare his aches and pains only served to spur on their antics. Their foolery ended in a predictable manner: one of them lost his footing and brought the other two down in a tangle of arms and legs. Their joy was in no way lessened by the fall and, giggling to themselves, they made their way slowly back to the castle rock.

The castle itself might well have been mistaken for one which had successfully withstood a siege, such were the scenes of relief which greeted the three on their arrival. Eager to share the moment with Elinor, Huw rushed ahead, to find her waiting for him, carrying their son in her arms. During the hardships of the past months, Elinor had maintained a cheerful spirit but now she wept openly. For a while, they clung to each other, then, at her suggestion, they made their way to the nearby church and gave thanks for their deliverance.

The weather became milder with each passing day and though the temperature dropped at night, there was a continual slow thaw. A south-westerly wind began to blow, increasing in strength and bringing the first rains of spring with it. The warm rain washed the land and, reluctantly at first, the frozen snow released its grip. As though anxious to speed its departure, nature summoned up a week of heavy rain, which added to the melting snow until the rivers and streams were unable to take the combined volume of water. Now, on top of all else, the smallholders were faced with the hazards of flooding, their misery made worse by the sight of their dead sheep and cattle, which had lain buried since the first fall of snow.

Once more the garrison was called upon to help, and again they struggled from one holding to another, driving the few remaining stock up to higher ground, for if famine was to be avoided, these precious animals had to be saved from the flood waters. Turned loose to forage amongst the dead grass, they had to be guarded day and night against attack by wolves. Elinor saw little of her husband, and his brief time in the castle he spent eating whatever hot food she could provide, or collapsing into the luxury of a dry bed, with her at his side.

It was the middle of May before the waters receded sufficiently to allow safe movement in the low lying areas. During one particularly sunny day, John and Huw received a visit from Glyndŵr, who, in company with several of his closest friends, was making a tour of inspection. When he rode up to where the two men guarded a straggle of thin sheep, his face showed concern. He shook his head in dismay at what he saw in the valley below, for the rich, productive bottom land had been turned into a quagmire.

"We have suffered a disastrous setback, John," he said in a tired voice. "The men will be hard put to provide for their families, this year and next. I fear that we cannot count on their support as we have in the past. Even the urgings of Iolo Goch will have little effect; we must pray that the King will not move against us now."

"'He will have troubles enough of his own, my lord," John replied. "Our men who are keeping watch on the border report that the Marcher lands escaped the worst of the snows, but floods have created havoc along the Severn."

The Prince gave a troubled sigh and John could see from his face the strain he was under. "It is not the border lands that concern me," Glyndŵr said. "It is the sea that could be our danger. Young Bolingbroke knows full well that, since the French ships set sail, he can come and go as he pleases in our waters. All that we can do is wait and pray."

He remounted his horse and looked once more at the devastation below. By this cruel twist of fortune, the weather, which had often been his ally in the past, had succeeded in doing the King's work. For, despite this welcome sunshine, Wales lay broken. Raising a hand in salute, he began to ride slowly down into the valley.

Towards the end of June, Emma announced that she wished to visit Cwmdu. Despite the numerous travellers calling at the castle, no-one had heard how the people there had fared during the winter, and she was determined to find out. Glyndŵr was as busy as ever and it was through David that the Gethins received the Prince's permission to make the journey.

"He hopes that you will find everyone safe and in good health," David told John. "However, he urges that you and Huw will not remain long in Cwmdu. He feels that he may soon have need of every man that he can get. I wish that I could accompany you, but there is so much to attend to here, that this is not possible."

With the two women seated in a borrowed cart, drawn by a sturdy pony, they set off soon after daybreak on the following morning. Huw had nailed Morgan's cradle to the floor of the cart and the infant lay cosily wrapped, occasionally cooing with delight as something caught his eye. They followed the coastal road and accepted the greater distance, rather than use the mountain passes. After Dolgellau, they followed the Mawddach down to the sea and continued south until they came to the Dyfi estuary and Machynlleth, where they gathered their first news of Cwmdu, which had been completely isolated during the winter. Facing due north, the cwm had caught the full force of the blizzard, the snow had drifted high at the entrance, where the burned-out shell of Argoed stood. Fearing the worst, they travelled on, reaching Cwmdu late on the fourth day of their journey.

Their concern was justified, when they finally brought the cart to a stop outside Iolo's holding. Alerted by the sound of the cart's wheels, he appeared in the doorway, and they were shocked by the change in the big man. His shoulders were bowed, as though under a great weight, his face, once glowing with health, was now gaunt with weariness. For a few moments, he stared in disbelief at his visitors, then came to Huw and embraced him.

"I cannot believe my eyes," he said. "I have prayed for help and God has sent you in answer. Come inside, the sight of you will be a tonic to Morwen. She is tired beyond belief and is resting."

Morwen's condition was worse than her husband's. The once bustling woman, who had been so full of life, was now a pale shadow of herself. Her first reaction when they entered the kitchen was to rise and give a welcoming smile; after a moment, she slumped back in her chair and began to weep.

While Emma comforted her, Elinor cooked a frugal supper of broth, using the last of the provisions they had brought in the cart. After they had eaten, Iolo told them of their ordeal during the snows.

"It took us the whole day to dig ourselves out of here," he said. "Then another day to free the animals from the byre. They were weak from thirst and I failed to get them down to the stream that day. Morwen melted snow over a fire and that saved them. It took all the men in Cwmdu to make a path and break the ice on the stream, before we had enough to drink."

He unashamedly wiped tears from his eyes, swallowed his grief and continued his story. "I have lost most of my stock, Huw," he said. "Those that survived the cold have died of starvation. When the rain came, what hay I had left went mouldy and they could not eat it. Your father's whites died a month back."

That night, Emma and John Leggatt discussed the plight of their hosts and agreed that Emma would not return to Harlech, for it was obvious that Morwen had reached the limit of her endurance and needed help in her tasks.

"I did not dream that we would be parted so soon, my husband," Emma remarked. "Yet, with summer soon upon us, you will be off soldiering. I shall be of more use here than sewing or weaving, alone at Harlech."

When they told the others of their decision, Elinor declared that she, too, was willing to stay. "I can work and ride as well as any man," she said. "In truth, I would welcome the freedom from the castle walls. Do not deny me, Huw, I beg you. Emma and Morwen can mind little Morgan while I am working on the land."

Huw saw the flicker of hope in his uncle's eyes and, shrugging off his dislike of being parted from Elinor, gave his agreement.

He and John stayed for two days, working around the holding. They gave what money they had to Iolo, who, with Elinor, journeyed over the hills to Llanidloes in the cart. They returned with a few provisions, a cockerel and eight hens.

"Your wife could prove to be our salvation," Iolo announced. "The traders are charging what they like for their goods, yet she was more than a match for them. Indeed, the man who sold us these birds was thankful to see the back of us."

When the two bowmen were about to take their leave, he spoke again with Huw. "I cannot thank you enough, lad," he said warmly. "Elinor's presence has given me new hope. I know now that we shall survive and see better days."

He gripped Huw's forearm in farewell and looked affectionately into the dark eyes. "Take good care of yourself and come back soon."

John urged the pony into a walk and headed up the rise. At Huw's request, they stopped at the little church, so that he could visit the graves of his father and brother. John had stayed in the cart, allowing Huw to have privacy. A grave which held loved ones was a place where people wished to be alone, John thought. Huw was not long at the graveside, and on his return to the cart, his face showed determination.

"Well lad, it is back to fending for ourselves for a while," John said, attempting to lighten the other's mood. "Think on it, we can retire to our beds whenever we wish and have nobody to answer to." He saw Huw glance quickly at him and he grinned in amusement. "I reckon many a married man would envy you and me, yet I'd wager that neither of us is a happy man."

"Do you think that we shall see more fighting this year?" Huw asked, obviously not wanting to make small talk.

"I hope and pray that we do not," John answered, in a serious voice. "You saw how weary the people of Cwmdu were, and there must be thousands like them in Wales at this moment. Should the English come, we will be unable to oppose them."

On their return to Harlech, they spent much of the next few weeks helping the local smallholders in their struggle to raise crops. That summer, the earth yielded little in return for their efforts, everywhere, the people's chief concern was how to find food for themselves and food for what little livestock remained. Returning to the castle late one evening, the bowmen heard the news which they had dreaded. Gathering a fleet at Bristol, the younger Henry had sailed unopposed up the Irish Sea and laid siege to Aberystwyth. Knowing that his summons to arms was little more than a gesture, Glyndŵr called on the men from the north to rally at Dolgellau. Their numbers were what he had expected, for scarcely six hundred gathered around the Dragon standard. At their head, he led them south towards the beleaguered castle, where all that they could do was watch the besieging army from afar. Sick with frustration, he managed to get word to the garrison that he was unable to help them, then, unwilling to wait for the end, he marched back to Harlech.

Chapter 21

The rain dripped steadily from the great oak, pattering softly onto the damp earth, and, seeking what little shelter the leafy branches offered, Thomas Matthews cursed the ill luck which had brought him into these godforsaken mountains. He had done no more than to show his face in the castle ward, yet it had been long enough for him to be ordered to join the escort for a supply train; not a task that he relished in the finest of weather; supply wagons were a prime target for those Welsh who still fought for Glyndŵr. Certainly, their numbers grew smaller with every passing month, but the remainder fought on with a ferocity that brought fear to the bravest of the King's men. At this moment, Thomas would have been happy to allow these remaining rebels to keep their sodden country. He would greatly prefer to sit in a tavern in Chester, with a girl on his knee and a fire to warm him. Wiping the drops of moisture from his brow, he glanced enviously in the direction of the parked wagons where his companions were preparing for sleep. A movement nearby caught his attention.

The cowled figure, which had appeared from nowhere, was twenty paces away; it caused him to start with fright and he felt the fine hair on his neck rise as the spectre moved toward him.

"Hell's fire! Who are you?" he challenged, his voice

pitched higher than was usual. "Stop, or I will skewer you."

The figure stopped moving, and Thomas took a step forward, leaving the protection of the massive tree trunk, his pike held level. That movement was the last he ever made, for a hand clamped firmly over his mouth, forcing his head back, and a razor-sharp blade flash across his throat and bit deep into the flesh. Huw Gethin held the dying man firmly for a few moments then slowly lowered the body to the ground and wiped his blade on the wet grass. Turning his face to the sky, he stood unprotected, welcoming the rain's cold freshness on his skin. He held the pose for a while, as though trying to cleanse every part of his being, then beckoned the cowled figure, who had not moved. The man glided nearer, throwing back the cowl, to reveal David's bearded features. The two friends listened for any cry of alarm to come from the wagons and, when none came, Huw cupped both hands to his mouth.

The screech of a hunting owl split the silence, echoing through the trees, and at its sound, men began to move, wraith-like, towards the wagons. The killing began before the owl-call finally faded into the damp night air. Such was the swiftness of their rush, that the Welshmen caught the soldiers and wagon-drivers completely off guard. Most died where they lay under the big carts, those who managed to flee, ran headlong into a line of hill-men waiting in the trees. Mercifully, it was over quickly and the victors were soon busily examining their booty: grain for flour, cheeses, salted meat and a small amount of money.

"A good night's work, lads," David called out. "There's food enough here to last us a month."

The men ignored his words and, instead, busied themselves with the task of dragging the dead clear of the wagons. Spluttering fires were coaxed back into life and the soaked men gathered around these in a vain attempt to dry their clothing. David gave up after a while and wearily crawled under one of the carts, where he was joined by Idwal.

"They are losing heart," David said in a low voice. "I wish that I could see them regain their old enthusiasm."

"Who can blame them?" Idwal asked. "I'm surprised that there are still men who are willing to fight for Glyndŵr's cause. You know full well, secretary, that that terrible winter we had four years ago weakened the people's will, and young Bolingbroke is making the most of the opportunity to finish us. No matter how often we chase him out of Wales, he comes back for more and, as you also know, he is beginning to keep what he gains."

David grunted in agreement and tried to make himself comfortable. The old mercenary, who seemed to be only interested in where his next meal and pot of ale would come from, was, in truth, a very perceptive person and David Mostyn thought about some of the things they had discussed together. Things had, indeed, gone from bad to worse after that terrible winter, and even now, the memories of that gripping cold made him shiver. First, they had lost Aberystwyth and its castle and then, in the following year, they had been struck a blow from which Glyndŵr had never really recovered. While leading his small army against the English in Morgannwg, an enemy force made a furious assault on Harlech. Edmund Mortimer died in the fighting and, when the castle fell, Margaret Hanmer and three of her daughters were made captive.

For days after learning the news Glyndŵr had kept to himself, refusing to see anyone, and his closest friends began to fear that he would lose that spirit which had sustained him for so long, against considerable odds. When, finally, he rejoined them, however, they found him filled with a quiet determination to continue with his campaign to make Wales independent of English rule. His personal losses in this war were painful to bear, he told them, yet there was much more than his family at stake and the struggle would continue. He was still the people's idol and wherever his Dragon standard was raised men answered the call, though no longer in their thousands.

David forced his thoughts back to the present. Several of the men were now resting under the cart, huddling close together to keep warm. He saw Idwal point toward the nearest fire and he could make out the tall shape of Huw framed against the flames.

"The years have certainly changed that one," the mercenary said. "He has changed inside as well as in appearance. He's not a man I should welcome as an enemy. Mind you, a dozen years in a trade such as ours hardens any man, if he lives that long. You know, when we came back to Wales, all those years back, there were about twenty of us. Now there's only him, me and old William left, not counting John Leggatt, that is. Makes you think, doesn't it?"

David agreed with Idwal. He had watched Huw kill the sentry with less emotion than David would have shown wringing a chicken's neck.

Huw turned away from the fire and walked over to the wagon where David and Idwal were; he crawled underneath and leant his back against one of the wheels.

The three made no attempt to converse, they sat in silence, waiting for sleep to overtake them. Huw closed his eyes and thought of Elinor. Once the castle at Aberystwyth fell to the English, he had decided that Harlech was no place for her and urged her to remain at Cwmdu. He had discussed it with John Leggatt, who had been less willing, at first, to leave his own wife there but had finally conceded that Emma was as safe there as anywhere. Both men frequently thanked God that they had made this decision, for either, or both, could have become widowers when Harlech was taken.

The women had stayed with Iolo until the past winter, when Elinor had insisted on joining Huw in the hills of northern Powys. When she presented him with another son, they named him after David, much to the secretary's delight. Gradually the tensions of the day eased away; Huw lay down, pulled the hood of his homespun jerkin over his head and, within moments, he fell into a deep sleep.

He awoke to a different world, finding bright rays of sunshine lancing through the trees, and immediately he was up and about, anxious to leave the ambush site. Urging the men to eat quickly, he began to cover the dead under mounds of wet leaves, doing the same with the camp fire ashes. His sense of urgency was relayed to the others and, before long, the plodding oxen were drawing the big carts steadily up the valley. Six miles on, they arrived at the prearranged meeting place, where John Leggatt waited with more men and a string of pack horses. Working together, they transferred the captured provisions onto the horses' backs, turned the oxen loose and systematically smashed every solid cartwheel. Once satisfied that not one cart would move again, the

Welshmen led the horses into the tangle of hills.

The day was fine, warm for October, and Huw took off his worn leather jerkin and hung it over a horse's back.

"It went well, from all accounts," John said, as they strolled along.

"Well enough," Huw replied abruptly.

The captain gave him a sideways glance and slowed his pace until David caught up with him.

"The lad's in a strange mood today," he remarked. "Do you know of any reason?"

"I do not," David answered.

"Not one of us has had a friendly word from him all morning. It's been do this, do that and be quick about it, since daybreak. He was quieter than usual after the attack last night. Maybe, he is beginning to feel like many of the men, weary of the war. Do you think that we shall lose many more of our number this winter?"

"The Lord forbid," John answered. "With so many taking the pardon that the King is now offering, there will be no need for him to take the field against us. He will be able to forget about Wales and Glyndŵr and concentrate on his other enemies. I cannot believe that Huw would take the King's pardon. He is simply tired. We have had a hard campaign this summer and it does take its toll on everyone."

Up ahead, Huw was thinking much the same thing. He did feel tired, not so much in the physical sense, but of the seemingly endless campaigning and killing. No matter how many skirmishes or ambushes he and the others took part in, the English always came back, led on many occasions by the King's son. Throughout these small but bitter actions, the Welsh had grudgingly come to respect the younger Henry's skills in the field of war. He had learned the futility of marching cumbersome armies through the mountains and from the day that his father had placed him in total command of the Marches, he had struck again and again with small mobile forces. It had been on his insistence, that the King had finally agreed to offer a pardon to the men who fought for Glyndŵr.

For Huw the turning point in the war had been the expression on a particular face, seen during what was now termed the Great Raid, two years after that terrible winter, when Glyndŵr had led every available man into Shropshire, with the aim of re-stocking the depleted cattle herds in Wales. Having faced the prospect of starvation, the Welshmen acted ruthlessly, taking more than cattle and killing anyone who attempted to deny them. On the second day of the raid, Huw rode past a farm which had been pillaged and saw a small group of people kneeling beside the dead body of a man. A lad of some fifteen years had raised a tearful face and turned on Huw a look of such hatred, that he had turned his head away in shame. This was the face, seen as clearly now, as he saw it then.

Huw led the way westward, to begin the climb towards the bulk of Aran Fawddwy, swinging south before they reached the mountain itself. The route followed a narrow ridge and when he came to the furthest end, he waited for the pack train to catch up with him before he set off down a steep path which brought him to a narrow valley far below. He was overcome by vertigo and could not wait to see if the men and horses were following but when he reached the bottom, he glanced briefly upward. He traversed the valley floor, which presently veered to his left, and soon came to a wide, pleasant meadow, partly tilled, at the edge of which stood a number of cottages.

Huw gave a shout of greeting to the cottagers.

A number of people emerged at his call, amongst whom he caught sight of Elinor's blonde hair. She began to run toward him, followed by a small child, whose short legs pumped furiously in an attempt to overtake her. Elinor reached him first and Huw held her close in a fierce embrace.

"Gently my love, you are hurting me," Elinor gasped.

Huw released his grip and kissed her tenderly on the mouth. "I'm sorry," he said. "I did not intend to hurt you. I have been aching all day long to hold you."

Before he could say more, he felt a tug on his sleeve and saw Morgan smiling up at him. Handing his bow to Elinor, he swung the boy high, holding him at arm's length for a moment before placing him on his shoulder. Together, they walked over to the watching women. Emma was holding his other son.

"John is well, mother," he said, answering her unspoken question. "All the men are safe. Hardly a scratch amongst them."

Emma smiled down at the baby. Huw set Morgan on the ground, held out his arms for the infant and began to study him closely. Little David really was a mixture of Elinor and himself, he thought, with his mother's fairness in looks and a temperament much like Huw's. Kissing his son on the forehead, he handed him back to Emma and walked towards the cluster of dwellings.

"Come Elinor, I must bathe myself," he said. "I need to wash away the stench of blood."

Scrubbed clean and dressed in fresh clothing, he rested on the bed while Elinor heated a bowl of broth. Watching her move around the sparsely furnished room, he marvelled at the way in which she accepted this new life.

Long gone were the days when she had sat at a fine table and enjoyed the good things that money bought, yet she had uttered no word of complaint at her changed circumstances. The only complaint came when he was about to leave her and the children and take part in yet another ambush.

He reviewed this latest attack. Everything had gone smoothly enough, the men acted without any need of commands; after so many years of carrying out similar actions, this was not surprising, but the last ambush had left him in the darkest of moods. Normally, he would have been elated at striking the enemy another blow, but last night had left him wondering when, if ever, the war would end, and when it ended, would it have achieved its objectives. He found it impossible to give an honest appraisal, and the consequent doubts that he had would not bear closer scrutiny.

A few days later, the Gethin's were seated outdoors, enjoying the late evening air. David was already asleep, Morgan, seated on his father's knee, was being taught simple arithmetic. The scene was one of tranquillity and provided a rare pleasure for the family, each member of which was enjoying every moment. Their peace was disturbed by the sound of a horse being ridden at a gallop, making for their dwellings.

"Someone brings important news," John said, getting to his feet and watching the approaching rider. "Unless my eyes deceive me, the messenger is Secretary David Mostyn. Nobody in the whole of Wales rides a horse quite like he does."

When his horse crossed a stretch of broken ground, David bounced in the saddle and both feet came out of the stirrups. When he breathlessly brought his mount to

237

a stop, he was almost pitched to the ground. For a few moments he remained mounted, regaining his breath, his chubby face showing his excitement.

"The King is dead," he exclaimed, slipping to the ground. "His son has succeeded him to the throne of England. Glyndŵr does not know what bearing this will have on the future of his campaign, and wishes to meet with his captains. He has sent messengers to all those who still serve his cause."

After David had eaten supper, the three men talked late into the night, pondering over the possibility of a peace being negotiated.

"Owain's quarrel was with Grey and the late King," John declared. "I feel that he would be wise to seek terms with the new one."

At John's insistence, Huw accompanied him to the meeting with Glyndŵr, which was held in a large house near Dolgellau.

"You have fought for him more or less from the beginning," the captain said. "It is only right that you should be present."

When they were all gathered, some expected to find the Prince exultant at Bolingbroke's death; instead, they found him in sombre mood.

"We have had a letter, dispatched from Shrewsbury two days ago," he told them. "It informs us that the new King has confirmed that the pardon is open to all of you. It also says that he prays that you will accept and return to his arms as loyal subjects."

The men sat quietly for a while, each lost in his own thoughts, and it was Glyndŵr who broke the silence.

"The pardon is not extended to me. I must tell you that, and I would not accept it, had it been offered.

However, any man here who wishes to take it may do so, with my blessing. You have all served my cause well and for longer than I ever expected. I shall always look on you as my friends, no matter what you now decide." Glyndŵr looked at the floor, unwilling to meet their eyes and put pressure on them to make a decision they might regret.

No-one present made his decision immediately and, when they had taken their leave, John took Huw and returned to the Prince.

"It saddens me that you are not included in the King's pardon, my lord," he said, "but it makes my choice easy to make. I have always been your man and will remain so while you have need of me."

"I thank you for that, John," Glyndŵr replied. "The struggle has become more of a private matter between Henry and myself. I feel that he respects me, even as he calls me a rebel; this respect would be lost were I to give up. What of you, Huw Gethin? Will you carry on the fight?" Glyndŵr asked, turning to Huw.

Startled by the sudden questions, Huw glanced frantically at John for guidance but found none in his friend's face. "I've not thought the matter through," he stammered. "I admit that I sometimes feel tired of this endless war, but while John serves you, so shall I, my lord."

The Prince smiled warmly and placed a hand on Huw's shoulder. "Then, we shall never be defeated," he said cheerfully. "I am truly grateful, for you have lost as much as I and I shall not forget your decision."

Chapter 22

No peace was announced at any time in the next two years, no truce was signed, no call came to muster under the Dragon standard. It was an uneasy interlude after so much fighting. News came occasionally of a skirmish further north, but for all it affected the lives of the men and women living beside the meadow, these could have taken place a thousand miles away. No longer did they set ambushes for English provision trains, and it seemed as if Glyndŵr was content to allow the King to maintain in peace his castles in Wales. Neither did King Henry attempt to seek out his adversary and bring him to battle, for he, too, seemed ready to accept a stalemate, although he still pursued his policy of granting pardons to those who wished to surrender.

The unreality of this new phase in the war was summed up when, one day, John Leggatt and twenty bowmen were returning from a scouting mission along the Hafren and crossing an expanse of heather-clad hill top, when a mounted patrol of English men-at-arms appeared over the crest and made straight for them. In a moment, the bowmen formed a line and were notching their arrows, when the horsemen veered to one side, rode out of range and reined the mounts to a standstill. For a long while the two groups watched each other, not a man making a move, until John growled out a command to march on.

Before they dropped over the rise, not one of the Welshmen, Huw included, had been able to resist the urge to look back over his shoulder. The English, however, sat motionless astride their horses until the last bowman had passed from sight.

The Gethins made the most of these days together, visiting Cwmdu on several occasions, where they found that all was well with their relatives, Morwen had fully recovered and was once more her usual cheerful, bustling self. Huw enjoyed these days in Cwmdu more than he would admit, although painful memories returned during every visit, and he thought of his father and brother, both lying in the cold soil. Whenever they passed the overgrown ruins of Argoed, Elinor noticed the muscles in his face tighten into hard lines. He never mentioned her brother, Richard, but she knew that it was the memory of his terrible deed that distressed Huw. The others spoke a great deal about returning to the holding for good, and he found the idea attractive, the only obstacles being John's promise to stay with Glyndŵr and the lack of money.

They returned from one such visit and found David waiting for them. When he saw his friend's serious expression, Huw guessed that something unpleasant had happened during their absence.

"It is Glyndŵr," David announced. "He has been taken ill. He was dictating a letter to me when he had some kind of seizure. He cannot move his left arm and could not speak for two days; it is still very difficult to understand what he says. He desires that you both attend on him as soon as possible; there are matters to be discussed."

The two bowmen and David Mostyn immediately rode to the Prince's quarters, where they found Glyndŵr seated in a high-backed chair, a housemaid feeding him broth and, at his signal, they waited until he had finished eating. When the maid departed, he motioned them closer to him and began to speak, with great difficulty. At first, Huw was so shocked at the change in Glyndŵr, that he failed to hear what the Prince was struggling to say. The once handsome face now hung slackly, while the eyes held an empty look.

"I want you to escort me to my daughter, who lives in the County of Hereford," Huw finally heard him say. "Alice is married to one of the Scudamores, a respected family. No-one will suspect that they are sheltering me. They intend to use their influence to obtain Margaret's release. I feel sure that the King will be sympathetic, when he realises that the fighting is over. I must ask you to tell no-one of my whereabouts, not even your wives. The more people that know my plan, the more chance there is that the wrong ones will learn of it."

He fell silent for a while, obviously exhausted by the effort to speak, then, forcing himself upright in the chair, he pointed toward an oak chest which stood near the hearth. "You will find two pouches in that chest, John," he said. "Bring them to me if you will."

Leggatt did as Glyndŵr asked, and placed the pouches on the Prince's lap.

"These pouches are lighter now than on the day I received them," Glyndŵr told them. "Do you remember the occasion?"

"Can these be the ones we found in the King's wagon, so long ago?" John asked in surprise.

"They are indeed," came the answer. "They are somewhat lighter now but there is still a considerable sum left. One is for you, John, the other for you, Huw

Gethin. Do with the money as you wish. I would suggest that you use it to build a new life for yourselves and your women folk."

The two bowmen began to protest at his generous gifts, but he waved them aside and began to talk of the past. Despite his difficulty in pronouncing some words, he seemed to relax as he spoke and, in a short while, the three men were conversing, not as a Prince, a captain and a humble bowman, but as friends. They talked of Hyddgen and Bryn Glas and other battles; of Hotspur and the French, the taking and losing of castles, the cruel winter of 1408, and the great raid into Shropshire. They spoke of men who now lay dead and who had played a part in the struggle. The day was drawing to a close when John and Huw made their departure. They had the morrow to make ready for their last task, that of escorting Glyndŵr to his place of refuge.

"When Owain is safely delivered, you and I must have a talk," John said, as they rode through the gathering gloom. "We must decide where we are going to live and how we are going to make our living. I know what your mother will want to do. She has often spoken of her wish to return to Cwmdu and resume her old way of life. You are the master of Argoed by right and the decision must come from you. My own wish is that, no matter what happens, we stay together as a family."

"I must confess that I find it hard to think clearly at the moment," Huw told him. "It is difficult for me to grasp the fact that the war is truly over. I have served as a soldier for more than thirteen years and I am not going to find it easy to suddenly change. However, any new employer would have to be English, and I cannot see me drawing a bow for them. I ask you, John, was it all worth so many lives and such hardship?"

The two separated at the cottages and Huw entered his as quietly as he could. Elinor was already asleep and, loath to waken her, he sat by the hearth and stirred the embers into flames. Although he was tired, he knew that sleep would escape him this night, for his mind kept turning over the prospects for the future.

When he and John arrived early at Glyndŵr's quarters on the given day, they found a small crowd of people gathered around the house, amongst them the commanding figure of Iolo Goch, who came away from the others, so that he could speak with them.

"Owain has told me that you and his secretary, David, are to accompany him to his place of refuge. I do not know where this will be, neither do I want to, for I intend to keep his dreams and hopes alive in the hearts of all Welshmen. Should I fall foul of the King's men, I cannot reveal what I do not know. Wherever the place may be, I pray that you will deliver him safely." He turned to walk back to the people but looked over his shoulder as he did so. "You will find Glyndŵr greatly improved since you last saw him, he seems more relaxed, even happy, now that he has decided to leave us. We must always remember the great burden that he has borne over the past years."

This was apparent to the two mercenaries, when the Prince appeared. Brushing aside helping hands, he mounted his horse unaided and sat upright in the saddle. For a few moments, he looked around at the upturned faces about him, then, raising an arm in salute, he urged his mount forward. With John at his side, he led off down the valley, followed by Huw and David. A mile or so down the track, they found five mounted bowmen waiting for them and, to his surprise, Huw recognised Idwal amongst them. Without a word of greeting, his old comrade unfurled the Dragon standard and, taking his place at the head, rode on, the flag snapping proudly in the breeze. Huw had not seen Idwal for more than a year, the mercenary having chosen to join one of the more active groups further north.

"This life here is that of a farmer," he told Huw. "It is not for me, lad, at least, not for the present."

At vantage places along their route, people had gathered to see their Prince and they watched in silence as he rode past, before returning sadly to their homes.

The tiny cavalcade crossed into Powys and into the hills of Radnor, no longer meeting any waiting groups. Once safely through the almost empty wilderness, they proceeded with caution, the standard furled and Idwal and the other four bowmen riding ahead as scouts. It was noon on the third day when Glyndŵr ordered a halt and sent Huw to bring the scouts to him. Taking the standard from Idwal, he told the five men that this was where they must leave him, and, handing each a small pouch containing coins, thanked them for their service in the past.

"I wish you and your family well, Longshanks," Idwal said to Huw, before riding away. "God alone knows whether we shall meet again. Take good care of John Leggatt for me. I reckon he's earned an easier life for himself."

When the five had ridden out of sight, Glyndŵr took the lead, riding south, then east, and in the evening they came to a wide, tree-clad hollow, a large house in its centre.

"Kentchurch Court," Glyndŵr announced, as they drew near, "and yonder, across the valley, is Grosmont, where we met defeat. It is strange that this place now offers me a safe haven."

He rode up to the house and dismounted, calling a greeting in English to a man who came out of the shadows. "Kindly inform your master that his expected guest has arrived," he told the servant, who hurried indoors.

Within moments he was back, accompanied by a richly dressed figure.

"Welcome, Owain," the man said warmly, though quietly. "Bring your companions into the house. Alice awaits you there. She feels it safest to greet you indoors. Robert will care for your horses."

Inside the house, Glyndŵr was embraced by his daughter, who led him to a chair placed by the hearth, and asked him for news of the family.

"Thomas, would you see to our guests' needs," she said, breaking off her questioning and addressing herself to her husband. "There is food and drink in the kitchen."

John, Huw and David followed a servant to the kitchens, where they were given food. After their meal, they returned to the room where father and daughter sat quietly together, Alice affectionately stroking Glyndŵr's greying hair. Feeling that they were intruding, they pleaded weariness and Thomas Scudamore showed them to their beds.

They awoke at daybreak and found the house already astir. Alice sent for them to come to her.

"I shall feel easier when you have taken your leave," Alice told them, softening her words with a smile. "My father tells me that you are numbered amongst his most loyal friends and I thank you from my heart for your service to him. I only wish it were possible to offer you the hospitality you deserve, though you will appreciate that his safety comes before all else. Should the King's men come here, we have an explanation ready for them. My father will be a cousin of Thomas's, who has returned to his homeland after spending many years in Italy and France. We could not give such a story with regard to you two bowmen. You look what you are and there is no disguising the fact."

"Rest easy, mistress," John told her. "We understand your concern and had not planned to linger here."

Alice saw that they were fed and provisioned for their return journey and Glyndŵr waited for them in the doorway, holding the furled standard. They said an emotional farewell and the prince handed the standard to John.

"Take this with you, old friend," he said. "It would be foolish to keep it here and I cannot bring myself to destroy it. Who knows, someone may be in need of it, some day." Turning to David, he held out a rolled parchment and a small purse. "Your letter, master secretary, as promised. Show it to the one whose name I have told you and he will take care of you. The purse is a small token of my thanks." He stood in silence for a few moments, looking up at the sky, then motioned them out into the open. "Go now and may God be with, you," he said.

Their horses stood ready saddled and mounting up the three rode slowly away from Kentchurch Court. Not until they were leaving the hollow did they look back, only to see that the doorway stood empty.

Chapter 23

Huw leaned back against the smooth rock and closed his eyes. The day was fair and, apart from an occasional bleat from one of the flock, there was scarcely a sound on the hill top. The rock ledge where he sat held a growth of fine moss, a sure sign that it had not been used for a long while. Today was the first occasion since his return to Cwmdu, a year ago, that he'd had to avail himself of the solitude. He made his decision to return here, when riding back from Kentchurch Court; a decision that made John Leggatt beam with pleasure. His mind made up, he wasted no time. With a little of the money from Glyndŵr he bought a cart, on which the Gethins had loaded all their worldly goods.

From far below, the rasping sound made by a wood saw drifted up to him and he pictured the two carpenters heaving away at the great blade. Argoed was almost rebuilt, the craftsmen now finishing a stairway. Within another four weeks, the Gethins hoped to move into their new house, and Emma and Elinor could then transform the interior into a proper home. Huw had been quite content to let his wife have her way in the planning, for she had endured much hardship since leaving Harlech castle. The new Argoed boasted four bed chambers on an upper floor, with two large living rooms and a kitchen below. No longer would the cattle be kept under the same roof as the farm folk; as had been the Welsh custom for generations. Elinor was adamant about this, and a new byre now stood a short distance from the house.

John and Huw had combined their small capital and advised their wives how much they were able to spend on the building, and the cost to date had remained within this figure of almost two hundred pounds, enough to pay masons and carpenters and buy pieces of furniture. A considerable saving had been made when Elinor insisted that the stone from the ruins of Plas Hirnant be used.

It was Emma's wish that the site of the old homestead be turned into a garden, and John and he had slaved over the ground until all traces of the dwelling had disappeared. Flowers already grew in one corner and, on more than one occasion, John had found Emma there, standing alone with her memories. He knew that words would not comfort her. He would put his arm around her shoulders and she would nestle her head in the crook of his arm, drawing comfort from this sturdily built man who loved her so much.

It seemed as if the English had lost interest in finding Glyndŵr. At first, as more and more Welshmen began to take the King's pardon, their patrols had been everywhere but, as the months passed, they became rarer. Now, they were scarcely seen at all. In the company of John, Huw visited Machynlleth on a market day and there, along with others, they signed their allegiance to the King. The men-at-arms who dealt with their pardon asked no questions and seemed friendly enough, speaking with them as soldier to soldier.

"You will know that there are some of your comrades fighting on, up in the mountains," one of the Englishmen said. "Should your paths ever cross, you would be doing them a great kindness if you advise them to give up. They can only survive by turning to robbery and murder. It would be a tragedy for them to end their lives on the gallows, alongside common criminals."

During their journey back to Argoed, Huw mentioned his concern for Idwal.

"I share your feelings," John had answered, "but Idwal knows no other life than that of a mercenary and he has no-one to think about but himself. Were he to find a good woman, things might be different. Anyway, I keep telling myself that he is far too wily for any Englishman to catch him."

Although they had not heard a word of the scar-faced mercenary for many long months, they had occasionally had a visit from David and heard about the new life he had taken up. Armed with Glyndŵr's letter, the secretary had presented himself at the home of one Robert Wynn, a scholar of law, who held office in Shrewsbury. The lawyer had read the letter without commenting on its contents, and had offered David a minor post, which he had accepted. Much of his new employer's business was conducted in Wales and, whenever David was in the vicinity of Cwmdu and could spare the time, he called on the Gethins.

Huw's reverie was broken by Mot, the young hound, who whined with pleasure and, raising himself onto his hind legs, rested his muzzle on Huw's shoulder. Huw was reminded of Pero, who had died of old age some years ago. He had left the old hound in the care of Iolo and Morwen when he took up his duties in Harlech castle and, one morning, they found Pero, lying still by the hearth, his old heart no longer beating. Gently pushing the hound away, Huw got to his feet and walked to the edge of the hill top. The lush green of the meadow land spread out below him and his gaze swept over its richness until they came to rest on the scar where Plas Hirnant had stood. The ditch surrounding the site was still clearly visible, though now choked with a tangle of briars and nettles. A number of cattle, some of which were Argoed's, grazed freely, the other men from Cwmdu having taken advantage of the thick grass for their animals. With the war over, Huw often wondered if Richard Lloyd would suddenly appear, although common sense told him that this was very unlikely. There was little chance that Elinor's brother would find the courage to return here and claim what was rightfully his. In any case, he might be dead, for all the Gethins knew.

Calling Mot to him, he gathered his small flock and drove them down the path to the meadow and on to Argoed, where he penned them in, before crossing to the lean-to shelter, where Mot was kept, and securing the dog. Afterwards, he walked further up the cwm, toward Iolo's holding, where he found the women preparing the main meal of the day. He joined his uncle and John, who were chatting together.

"We need to visit the market in Machynlleth again," John told him. "There are a number of things the women want for their new home. The longer it is taking in the building, the longer grows their list of needs. Will you be using the lean-to tonight?"

Huw said that he would, for he was relishing the prospect of some privacy. He was aware that, without the hospitality of Iolo and Morwen, he and the others would have an uncomfortable existence while waiting for Argoed to be completed, but his uncle's holding was not large enough to accommodate all the family and they seemed to be forever bumping into one another. The lack of space had made him irritable of late and he suspected that he was not alone in his feelings.

The following day he, John and their wives set off early for the market town, arriving there well before noon. The women immediately hurried off in search of some cloth and left the two men to their own devices. It was not long before they entered a tavern, which was already crowded, and the two stood shoulder to shoulder, listening to the talk around them. The main topic of conversation was inevitably the prices of cattle and wool, but they heard one group talking about an army being raised by the King.

"I tell you, lads," one man said, speaking loudly above the hum of voices, "I was in Shrewsbury but two days ago and they were taking on bowmen. They are paying three pennies a day to any man who can handle a bow. They said that Henry has a score to settle with the King of France. Something to do with who rules what over there. I asked a knight if he was hiring Welshmen and he thought this very amusing. He said that the King was anxious to take as many of his old foes with him as he could. That way, he would be able to keep an eye on them."

The two friends finished their ale and ducked through the doorway into the street.

"I've no doubt the King will soon have his share of bowmen," John remarked, as they set off to look for the women. "Wales has more than enough of men like us. I wonder if Idwal has heard this news. He would be one of the first to hire himself out."

They made their way through the vendors' stalls and caught a glimpse of Emma and Elinor.

"Do you not feel an urge to go, Huw?" John Leggatt asked, coming to a sudden stop.

"I do not," came the answer. "I have everything I could wish for at Cwmdu. It is a relief to wake up in the morning and know that there is no more fighting and killing to be done. I have had my fill of both over these past years. There is only one matter which would cause me to draw a bowstring or knife in anger and there is little fear of that ever happening." He was thinking of Richard Lloyd and what he had sworn to do to him, should they meet again.

When the two women completed their purchasing, the four started their return journey, arriving in Cwmdu by dusk. Laden with several bundles of cloth, Huw was the first to enter the holding, and he gave a cry of delight when he saw who was seated at the table. Their visitor smiled broadly, leapt to his feet, called a greeting and slapped Huw on the back.

"What brings you to Cwmdu?" Huw asked the secretary, when the others joined them. "Your new employer must be a very busy man, to keep sending you into these parts."

"He is, indeed," David replied. "However, I have completed my task sooner than expected, so I've called on you, to hear how you are getting on."

They talked long after supper had been eaten, plying each other with questions, then, despite Morwen's protests, her guest insisted on spending the night with Huw and John, under the lean-to at Argoed.

"It will remind me of the old days," he laughed. "We slept in some strange places during our campaigns."

The three walked down to Argoed, where the carpenters were already sleeping soundly in their wagon.

"Make yourself at home," Huw said, waving a hand. "I hope you will not regret your choice of lodgings. It has been a while since you slept outdoors, I'll wager."

He was about to make a joke about the maidens of Shrewsbury when he saw that David was looking very intently at him.

"What's wrong?" he asked bluntly. "Have you got yourself into some trouble?"

David shook his head, looked over at John Leggatt, sighed and returned his gaze to Huw. "I have been praying that I did the right thing in coming here," he said. "The thought of Elinor and your two sons has put my mind into a turmoil these past two days."

He fell silent for a while but kept his eyes fixed on Huw, then, taking a deep breath, he leaned forward. "I have found him, Huw," he said hoarsely. "I have found Richard Lloyd." Huw's stomach muscles tightened into a knot and he felt his mouth turn dry. "Robert Wynn, my employer, was made responsible for recording the names of those who joined the King's army at Shrewsbury. I was helping to write the list of new recruits' names, when Richard appeared in front of us. There was no mistaking him, Huw. He's as fair of head as ever and about your height. He told us that he wished to serve as a man-at arms and showed his horse and armour to the knight who was in charge of recruiting. He was accepted without further question and told to report at the castle."

David sat down and rested his back against one of the lean-to supports, watching Huw keenly in the dim light. What do you want to do about him?" he asked. "Have the years changed your desire for vengeance?"

"They have not," Huw answered. "I shall never know peace of mind until I know that Richard has paid in full for causing my father's and brother's deaths. You have done right in coming here and telling me, David."

"You must seek him out and kill him," John said suddenly, his voice full of loathing. "While he lives, he is a threat to your mother's happiness, lad. I have often wondered whether he might return here, to give his evil plans another try. I shall come with you and help in your mission."

"You will help me more by staying here," Huw told him. "It will make my task the easier if I know that you are caring for Elinor and the family. Besides which, this is a personal matter between Richard and me."

"What of Elinor's feelings?" David asked. "She is his sister."

"She is only too aware of my feelings," Huw answered. "She may disagree with them but she keeps this to herself." He made himself comfortable on a bed of freshly -cut fern, then looked towards the secretary. "We must try to sleep now, old friend. We must be about early and take the road to Shrewsbury in the morning."

It was past noon on the second day when he and David drew rein close by the walls of Shrewsbury. They had ridden hard from Cwmdu, until nightfall forced them to halt. Their roof was one of the great oaks and, for all David cared, they could have been in a princely palace. Tired to the bone, he was asleep the moment his head touched his pillow of leaves. Huw listened to his steady breathing with envy, for, despite the long day, he could not relax. His farewell to Elinor was too fresh in his mind for that. She had not uttered a word when he had told her David's news and, apart from turning pale, she had acted quite normally. Firstly, she had prepared food for the two travellers, then rolled a clean shirt and placed it in Huw's pouch.

Elinor had often thought with dread of this moment,

praying that it would never arrive, and now that it had, everything seemed so unreal. She felt as if she were in a dream and would awaken to normality. Their last embrace had been of the briefest. Huw retained a vivid memory of her standing in the doorway, with their sons on either side. John Leggatt had made one final plea to accompany Huw, but the look on Emma's face had reduced him to silence. Now, as they dismounted and led their horses towards the town's gates, Huw wished that the older man was with him.

"Do you seek to join the King's host?" The speaker was one of a group of soldiers standing guard.

"My friend here desires to do so," David answered, digging Huw in the ribs. "He has been told that he will be well fed and paid regularly."

"Indeed," the speaker snorted. "Tell me, young sir, can he use his bow, or will he run when he hears the drums and trumpets of the King's enemies?"

Stepping clear of his comrades, the man walked over to the two and looked up at Huw, who had understood a few words of the conversation. He was aware that the man who stood before him was one of those soldiers of the King that he had fought for more than thirteen years, and his face must have shown this, for the Englishman stepped back a pace.

"I think he would do well on the field of battle," he said, addressing David Mostyn. "Tell him to hurry, for we march south on the morrow."

The two passed through the town gates, David leading the way up a steep, narrow street. At the top, Huw saw a large, stone block with a wooden beam attached to one end of it.

"The last of the Llewelyns was butchered there, many

years ago," David told him as they passed by. "The English called Dafydd a traitor, just as they did Owain. Yet, how they can call a man that, when all he did was fight for his own country, defeats me."

The street began to go downhill now, and brought them close to the castle walls, where David's employer and two knights were speaking with a man who was obviously an old soldier. They waited until the man's name was entered in a register, then moved up to the table which David's employer was using as his office.

"I have returned, as you can see, sir," David said. "I met this old friend of mine on my travels. He has fought for Glyndŵr in the past and now wishes to join the King's men. He tells me that a number of his comrades, one in particular, have already joined and he wants to accompany them on this campaign."

"Has he taken the pardon?" one of the knights asked, eyeing Huw keenly.

"Indeed he has, my lord," David answered. "His name is Huw Gethin of Argoed and you will find it in the Machynlleth register."

"So be it," the knight replied. "Enter his name, Master Wynn."

David waited until the lawyer had entered Huw's name then spoke quietly to him. "May I speak to you in private?" he said. "It concerns just you and me."

Robert Wynn raised his eyebrows in surprise and stepped away from the table.

"It is of great importance that I accompany my friend, so my name must be entered in the lists, but I cannot pass muster as a bowman; I ask if you would write a short letter, saying that I am to serve as a secretary to somebody who holds a high rank in the army."

His employer looked aghast at the request, peered nervously over his shoulder at the knights, and began to shake his head.

"Owain Glyndŵr would wish you to do me this favour," David urged. "Also, this Huw Gethin was a favourite of his."

"Oh, very well, but do not ask me to take any more risks," the lawyer replied, after a pause. "I am not going to ask why you wish to do this. I fancy it wiser not to know. Go and speak with the knights while I write the letter."

When he had completed his writing, he called David over to him and gave him the rolled-up parchment. "I have put in the letter that you are to serve under the Duke of York. He is second only to the King himself, and no man will question this." He fumbled in his pouch, extracted a small purse and gave David a few coins.

"Your wages in full," he said with a smile. "I have been pleased with your work and, when this business of yours has been completed, I hope that you will return here and serve me further. Stay close to your friend, should danger threaten. He looks more than capable of protecting himself and you. Now, tell him to ask the knights where he has to present himself, and God go with you."

Huw's limited knowledge of English meant that David had to act as an interpreter, and he learned that the latest body of bowmen, which was also the last to be recruited, would form up at the Abbey Gate in the morning.

"Tell your friend that he can get lodgings at the *Three Tuns*; a number of his countrymen will be staying there tonight," one of the knights told him.

"What of the men-at-arms?" David asked casually. "Will they march off on the morrow?"

"That they will not," the knight answered. "They have already set off for Southampton."

His answer completely stunned David for a moment, then he pulled himself together, took Huw by the arm and led him away.

"We have missed him, Huw," he fumed. "Richard has already set off. Do you intend to follow?"

"This is not what we were hoping for, but it would seem that we have little choice," Huw answered.

During their journey to Shrewsbury, the two had decided that Huw's mission would be much easier if he went through the motions of joining the King's army. That way, he would have the freedom to move around the encampment, to seek out Richard Lloyd. He would choose his moment, deal with his enemy and then ride to safety into the hills of Powys. To follow Richard on the morrow meant that every step of the way would take him further from this haven.

"I've waited too long to turn back so soon," Huw told him. "I am going after him and will take my chances, even if it means going to France." He slowed his pace for a moment, while he led his pony through a group of bowmen who were drinking outside a tavern, and came to a stop when he was clear.

"My thanks again for your help, David," he said, looking down at his companion. "I will ask one more favour of you. Get word to Elinor that my absence may be longer than I had thought."

"That could be difficult," David told him. "For, like it or not, I am going with you. Your loved ones want you back and I intend to see that this happens. You may well need to have someone who can think clearly and without passion by your side." He shook his head and, with a grin, thrust the parchment in the air, as Huw began to protest. "I have every right to go and you cannot prevent me," he said triumphantly.

Although his face showed disapproval, inwardly, Huw more than welcomed David's company. In truth, he was already feeling a little lost in Shrewsbury, where few spoke in his native tongue. Shrugging his shoulders, he grunted his agreement.

"Then its the *Three Tuns* for both of us," David beamed, leading the way down a side street. "We need food, ale and sleep. We could have a long march ahead of us."

They tethered their ponies before entering the tavern. "We shall have to find a buyer for these creatures," David said. "We must be prepared to accept less than their value, for we have no time to haggle with a buyer."

Inside, they found the room crowded with men, most of whom held a tankard in one hand and a bow staff in the other. David ordered their ale, then began to talk to the owner of the tavern about securing a bed for the night. Alone for a few moments, Huw stared blankly across the room, his mind on Richard Lloyd.

"By all that's holy! What brings you here, Huw Gethin?" a familiar voice asked. Huw turned to find Idwal standing beside him, his face twisted in a wide smile. "Don't tell me that you have taken up your old way of life again," the mercenary added, pointing at Huw's bow.

"That I have," Huw replied. "Of necessity, however, be assured."

He went on to tell Idwal of his search for Richard Lloyd and how he had joined the King's army and missed his old enemy by a matter of hours. He explained that he would follow Richard Lloyd to France and have his revenge on the man, no matter how far he had to travel to catch up with him.

"A good enough reason to leave your family," Idwal said. "Should I be of use to you, Longshanks, you only need to ask. I'd cheerfully kill him for you, should need arise." He raised his tankard half-way to his lips but stopped when David appeared at Huw's elbow.

"Now, this I find hard to believe," he said. "How do you fare, secretary? Enjoying the peace, I trust. All it needs is John Leggatt to come through the door and it would be just like the old days."

"John remained in Cwmdu," Huw told him. "I could not leave the women without protection and who better than he to provide that. Did you find the innkeeper, David?"

"Aye, and he tells me that we must seek a bed elsewhere," David answered. "He has no space to offer to us."

"To Hell with him; you can share our quarters," Idwal snorted. "We will be sleeping above the stables. You have slept in worse places, often enough."

With that matter settled, the two friends then turned their minds to that of their redundant mounts.

"You can think of today as one of the luckiest in your young lives," Idwal said, with a chuckle. "I could well be able to help you in this, also. Come and meet some of my comrades, they are over in the corner, you may remember some of them."

He led them over to where a group of bowmen sat, talking amongst themselves. Huw recognised several of the faces. The men greeted him warmly, and made room for them to sit down. One man was a small, wiry fellow, whose sharp features reminded Huw of a weasel. He had a pair of intelligent, brown eyes that never seemed to rest on any object for more than the briefest of moments.

"Now then, Bando," Idwal said to him. "I can put a little business your way. My friends here wish to sell their ponies and saddles and I know that you will treat them fairly."

The little man's eyes flitted around the room, ignoring those seated at the table. "There is no call for such animals," he said flatly. "I'm back to Wales on the morrow and there's more than enough of them there already."

Idwal leaned forward and whispered something in his ear which prompted him to rise to his feet and go to the door.

"Treat them fairly, now, Bando," Idwal called after him. "Go with him, Huw, and don't let him talk you down. He is as tricky as he looks."

"What did you say to him?" David asked Idwal, as Huw followed the little man outside. "Whatever it was, it certainly made him change his attitude."

"I told him that I would hand him over to the nearest sergeant-at-arms," Idwal answered, laughing loudly. "Bando is wanted for stealing horses, from here to Chester. Not that I would, mind you. All of us here have found him useful over the past year or so, and who knows, we may have need of him again."

David was about to question the mercenary further, but thought twice about it. He had heard many tales of deeds done by some of Glyndŵr's men of late and knew that he could well be on dangerous ground. Instead, he sat silently, listening to the bowmen's conversation, until Huw returned.

"Well?" Idwal asked.

"Well enough," Huw answered. "He will make a tidy profit out of our deal, but I was in no position to argue for more. Indeed, we can count ourselves lucky, for we could well have had to abandon them."

That night, Huw fell asleep with the sounds of gentle snoring around him and the occasional stamping of a hoof below. He had not lain in a proper bed for at least a year, and the last thing on his mind, as he drifted off, was to wonder now much longer that luxury would be in coming.

Chapter 24

Shortly after daybreak, the Welshmen joined a body of about one hundred other bowmen at the castle's main gate and waited a moment. Almost immediately, several soldiers came through the gate and stood before them. One of these, a strongly built man with a grey beard, took a step forward and looked at the waiting bowmen before taking off his oddly-shaped helmet.

"My name is Thomas Hunt, you will be under my command," he shouted. "I know that most of you here are Welsh and, until recently, you fought against the King. That is now in the past. Those of you who speak English must translate my words for your comrades. The King wishes you to know that all who serve him on this campaign will be treated equally, no matter where you come from. You will be paid the sum of six pence a day and you will be fed daily. Now, mark this and mark it well, lads. There is to be no taking of food or valuables while you are on the march. Any man found looting, no matter who he is, will be hanged straight away."

Next, he ordered the bowmen to form a line. Placing himself at the head, he led them out of the town walls and into the open country. Here, he quickened his pace, striding along for a mile or so, until they came to a well laid out encampment. The place was bustling with activity, as men hurriedly prepared themselves for the march, and they soon formed a column with the new arrivals. Despite the haste, there was no hint of confusion, which told anyone watching that these men were experienced soldiers. Standing amongst Idwal's friends, Huw estimated that about two hundred and fifty bowmen were now drawn up into line and, looking at some of their faces, he saw that they were a rough bunch. When he was satisfied that all were present, Thomas Hunt gave the order to march and led his men south.

After they had gone a few miles, the bowmen had settled themselves; belts were loosened for greater comfort; pouches and bow strings were checked. The weather held fair and the marching feet kicked up a cloud of dust, which drifted up behind the moving column. Huw soon began to feel as if he had never given up his life of soldiering. The old familiar smells of leather and sweat filled his nostrils, and the sounds were those he had heard on scores of marches. As the miles slipped by, the men around him grew familiar, also. There was always the one who talked ceaselessly about matters which interested no man but himself; one who teased any of his comrades who were within earshot; one who made the others laugh with his crude humour; and the one who grumbled at everything, including the weather. These were just like the men he had marched with in the past.

He was suddenly aware that Thomas Hunt was marching at his side, a puzzled look on his face, his eyes fixed on David, who was marching in the middle rank, his short frame almost hidden from view.

"Who have we here?" Thomas asked in a loud voice. "A man with no bow staff, in a company of archers, and not quite built for the task of soldiering either. Step out of the line, my fine fellow, and tell me all. If you think that you can receive six pence a day for simply marching along, you are mistaken."

With a muffled curse in Welsh, David dodged out of the column and looked innocently up at the captain. "I am to serve the Duke of York," he said. "Here is my letter of appointment." He thrust the parchment into Thomas's hand, lengthening his stride to keep up. "I was delayed on my journey to Shrewsbury and joined your men this morning. I had no opportunity to meet with you before we began to march."

Thomas unrolled the parchment, stared at it for a few moments, then handed it back. "Then you are welcome to stay," he said. "My company is also under the Duke's command. Until we reach Southampton, you could be of help by translating my commands. That was a Welsh word you used just now, was it not?"

"Indeed it was," David answered. "I simply gave thanks to the good Lord that you and I had met at last."

Seven days later, the column breasted a low rise in the ground and halted at Thomas's signal. Before them lay the port of Southampton. Scarcely a man gave the town more than a cursory glance, for it was what lay in the calm waters beyond the buildings that caught their attention.

"Hell's fire! Would you look at that?" Idwal cried out. "It is a brave sight indeed. I would wager it is costing young Bolingbroke his treasury and more."

The King's fleet gathered before them was indeed a magnificent sight, a vast array of ships, bright in their new paint and flying their colourful pennants. Around them, a host of smaller craft wove their way up and down, ferrying men and supplies from the beaches. To the left of the watching bowmen, a long pontoon ran out into the water; Huw stiffened when he saw that it was being used to load horses onto a ship. Where there were horses, there would Richard Lloyd be.

Huw looked around, to see what was causing a stir amongst his fellow bowmen. Two lightly armoured knights came riding towards them, and when they reached Thomas Hunt, they reined their horses and spoke briefly with the captain, one of them pointed in the direction of the town, before the two went riding back.

"March on, lads," came the command. "No need for haste. Every ship is full and will be sailing shortly. We are to camp close to the town until they return for us."

He led the bowmen to a recently vacated camp, where he dismissed them with a warning not to wander too far off. Huw immediately strode over to the pontoon, only to find that the last horse had been hoisted aboard and the ship was already moving off, under light sail. Stifling his frustration, he walked along the beach and entered the town. Going to the harbour, he was angered to find the place empty of men, horses and ships, and, with a curse, he returned to the beach. Out on the open water, the fleet was preparing to sail, and the smaller craft were pulling back to the harbour. Huw realised that, if he was to continue with the pursuit of Richard Lloyd, he would have to travel to France.

He was about to return to the camp, when a blare of trumpets came from the fleet. With nothing better to do, he stopped and watched them hoisting their sails, which added to the blaze of colour. It was an impressive sight, when the fleet began to move slowly into deeper water. There were so many ships, that it seemed as if only a miracle prevented one ramming into another. Fascinated by the spectacle, Huw watched in awe as they passed in front of him. Then, to his horror, he saw flames suddenly shoot skywards from the leading ship, setting its sails and rigging alight. The scarlet hull seemed to heel over and, apparently out of control, the ship collided with its closest neighbour. The ship directly behind her sailed head on into the flames, which quickly took hold, and Huw plainly heard the screams of the men aboard, as they jumped into the sea.

A crowd quickly gathered and watched in horror as the three vessels burned furiously, throwing the fleet into confusion. Swinging to the left and right of the burning vessels, the other ships bumped and scraped each other as they sought safety, while an occasional spout of white water told of someone or something being lost overboard. By sheer good fortune and seamanship, the fleet somehow drew clear and, driven by a steady wind, sailed out of sight of those gathered on the beach. Later that night, Huw wondered if Richard had perished in the fire. The thought would not go away and he spent a restless night.

Thomas Hunt and his bowmen waited ten long days before the fleet returned for them, days spent in practising archery, under the captain's watchful gaze. He soon availed himself of David's services, for the secretary was the only man in the company who was fluent in Welsh and English. Thomas accepted that his life as a captain would have been much harder without the help of this young man.

"These men are already skilled in their work," he remarked to David one day. "There is little I can teach them. My only concern is that your countrymen will disagree with my lads from Cheshire and I need to keep them occupied."

"I doubt that you will have trouble," David replied.

"Sixpence a day is a small fortune to most of them and they are not looking to lose it. Besides which, we could well have fought side by side at Shrewsbury."

"So I hear tell," Thomas said with a smile. "But then, you would have been facing me, for I fought for the King that day. It was the warmest contest I've ever been in. Young Henry was lucky to survive that day, for an arrow struck him in the face. I was one of those who helped him from the field. It is strange that events have brought us together once more, and on the same side."

When the fleet again lay at anchor in the port, the bowmen marched down to the harbour with enthusiasm. Their stay outside the town had become boring, then frustrating, as the days had passed, a feeling that Huw had known from the first day. Now, however, they were on the move and soon, they hoped, they would be taking their places aboard the ship allocated to them.

To their disgust, they had to endure the rest of that day and the night at anchor, while the ship was provisioned with fresh water. It was at noon on the following day when the fleet set sail, with a fanfare of trumpets.

"Where are we bound?" David asked a seaman who was busily securing some ropes.

"The port of Harfleur," the man answered. "We landed the other men away from the town and there was no opposition from the French, so all went well. The King has set siege to the place, so I've been told. I fear it will be a difficult place to take. I've never seen walls the like of which protect Harfleur."

The stiff breeze that drove the ships steadily onwards made the sea rough, and their vessel pitched and rolled, as they hit one wave after another. Holding on to the rigging lines, Huw watched with fascination as the ship's bows plunged into the green sea and rose sharply, sending showers of spray flying in the wind. Everywhere there was colour to be seen, from the ever changing sea to the ships themselves, and, for a while, he forgot about France and Richard Lloyd. His enjoyment of the thrilling spectacle was interrupted by some of his fellow bowmen who, oblivious to their surroundings, bumped into him before leaning over the ship's side and spewing away their last meal. The sounds made by these stricken wretches caused him to move, and he lurched unsteadily over the heaving deck to join David and Idwal. Neither of them showed any signs of the awful sickness from which many of the other bowmen were now suffering. Indeed, at Huw's suggestion, they ate some of their rations, taking only a small portion each. With nothing more to do, they settled themselves for the coming night, taking David's advice and resting their backs against a hatch.

"Not even the most experienced of seamen will sleep flat on his back when his ship pitches like this," he said, as if he had spent his whole life at sea.

Huw awoke early on the third morning of their passage, aware that something had changed in his surroundings. It took him a few moments to realise that it was the lack of motion and constant noise; the ship lay at anchor in a wide estuary. Nudging his two companions with his foot, he crossed the deck and looked toward the nearest land. Between it and the ship, a score of small craft were approaching. As he watched, the crew began to lower rope ladders down the ship's side. Thomas Hunt's men were now astir and making ready to disembark. They waited until the small boats came alongside and were secured. The order to board these came almost immediately and the bowmen began to climb down the swaying ladders and were helped aboard. The three friends sat together in a boat and watched their temporary home grow smaller, as the tiny, bobbing craft slid over the calm water. From somewhere in the distance there came a deep rumble, like distant thunder. The sky was clear and a sailor, seeing the bowmen's puzzled looks, shouted across to them.

"The King's cannon bid you welcome," he cried. "Give them a wide birth, lads, for they have killed more of our men than the French."

The boat made good way through the shallows, until it grounded on a wide, flat beach. To the accompanying roar of more cannon fire, Huw and his companions jumped over the boat's side and onto the soil of France.

Chapter 25

It was hot; sweat ran down Huw's face. He peered up through a narrow slit in the latticed screen protecting the trench in which he waited, and saw, less than a hundred paces away, the walls of Harfleur. These massive walls seemed to frown down on the ant-sized figures below, who were attempting to test their strength against them. A cannon boomed loudly and Huw saw its projectile strike the massive gates, which stood slightly to his right. All morning the cannon had pounded them, and still the iron-studded doors held firm. At any moment they would be flung open, to allow the defenders to make a sortie against the cannonade, which was why Huw and the others were positioned in the trench. In the meantime, he leaned back against the earth wall and felt the almost unbearable heat of the sun on his bare chest. He thought wistfully of the cool air in the mountains above Cwmdu, for just one lung full of which he would gladly have traded a day's pay. With a clink of armour, a line of men-at-arms made their way along the trench, brushing the bowmen as they passed. Huw hid his face as they neared him, but his eyes scanned each helmeted head as it drew level with him; there was no-one who resembled Richard Lloyd, and Huw began to doubt that he was in France.

"I don't envy them," Idwal gasped, flapping his shirt.

"With all that armour, they must feel like bread baking in an oven."

Suddenly, a quarrel flashed through the slit and struck the earth, inches from his head. His curse was drowned by a scream of agony, which came from somewhere along the trench when a shower of the deadly bolts fell from the sky. There came a loud crash followed by voices yelling. Risking a quick look through the slit in the trench wall, Huw saw a large body of armoured men rush out through the now open gates of the fortress. From the corner of his eye, he caught a glimpse of movement and he instinctively ducked low as another quarrel thudded into the screen.

"Loose at the gates, you bowmen," Thomas Hunt cried. "Some of you, shoot at the battlements."

To get a clear shot at the oncoming Frenchmen, the bowmen would have to expose themselves to the defenders on the battlements; not one of them made a move.

"Come on, lads," Thomas urged. "Here is where you must earn your pay."

Still the men remained crouched low and, angrily, the captain snatched a bow from the man closest to him, notched an arrow, stood upright, aimed and loosed. Idwal swore and jumped to his feet, to be joined by Huw and a few of the others, their arrows striking home and attracting another hail of bolts, forcing the bowmen to fling themselves flat in the bottom of the trench. Some of the heavy missiles pierced the protective screen and buried themselves in the opposite trench wall. Huw squirmed when one landed inches above his head.

From further up the trench there came the clash of weapons, rising above the din of combat. A bloodied figure appeared around a traverse and staggered towards the prostrate bowmen, apparently oblivious to the fact that he was an easy target. Hearing warning shouts, he came to a halt. He had a head wound, loss of blood from which had partly blinded him. He raised a hand to his brow, to clear his sight, only to be struck in the head by a bolt. The impact knocked him sideways, his knees buckled beneath him and he slumped to the bottom of the trench, already dead. The bowman nearest to him crawled up, inspected the fallen man, and returned to his companions.

Carrying their shields high, to protect their heads, another file of men-at-arms hurried up the trench and joined their comrades fighting around the cannon. Their presence immediately brought another shower of bolts down onto the trench but this time Thomas's men stood as soon as the last one fell to earth. For a few long moments the battlements were devoid of life and the crossbows were loaded once more. At the first signs of movement in the fortress, drawn bowstrings were released. Before the volley had reached the defenders, who dodged back out of sight, the bowmen were again drawing back on the longbow staffs.

Each man sent five arrows away before being forced to desist, to allow the men-at-arms to pass by. Taking cover, they watched the armoured men hurry around the traverse, their battle cries adding to the din of shouts and screams from the wounded. Their arrival seemed to decide the outcome, for the French began to retire back into the town, followed by volleys of hastily loosed arrows from the men in the trench. The great gates slammed together and a hush fell, only to be broken by a defiant roar when the cannon fired once more. There was no further action that day and, when darkness fell, Thomas

Hunt led his bowmen from the earthworks. At his command, Huw and Idwal carried the body of the man-at-arms between them, and left it where some grave diggers were working.

"Least ways, this one went quickly," one of the diggers remarked, as they laid their burden down. "Better that way, say I, than the lingering death of these other poor wretches." He gestured with his spade to where a row of shrouded figures awaited burial. "The fever that is going through the camps is killing more of us than the French are," he said, shaking his head, "and it's getting worse by the day. I reckon that they are using witchcraft to destroy us all."

Huw felt a chill of fear run down his spine and hurriedly he made the sign of the cross.

The man had spoken in Welsh and when Idwal enquired where he hailed from, told them, "I and my friends are from Brecon. We came over on the first ships, with Dafydd Gam, and I don't mind telling you, I wish we had gone back with them. We have buried two of our own already, who died from the sickness."

The following morning, the bowmen were free to do as they pleased. They sought out Thomas Hunt and told him that they were going inland, to look for drinking water. From their first day in France, Idwal had insisted that they drank only from the water drawn from a well.

"'It is as hot here as any place I've known," he said. "We never drank from a stream or river, where ever we found ourselves. John Leggatt saw to that. I don't know the reason, but the heat seems to foul the open water."

The captain agreed but pointed a warning finger at them and said, "Make sure that it's only water you bring back, and not loot, lads. Don't forget the King's warning.

I would hate to lose you to his hangman."

A party of men who had been together at the *Three Tuns* was soon clear of the encampments. The tide was out and had left an expanse of golden sand between the bank and the river, which was being used by mounted men-at-arms to exercise their horses. Huw kept his eye on them as he walked along, still hoping to see Richard Lloyd, but the distance was too great for him to make out the riders' features. By now, the sun was well up in the sky and the bowmen were suffering its heat. There was not a breath of wind in the air and they stripped to the waist, to try and cool themselves.

"God's blood!" Idwal gasped. "I've never known heat such as this, not even in lands far to the south. It's an inferno."

They had walked for about three miles, when they saw a large stone-built farmhouse to their left. It appeared to be devoid of life, but Huw guessed that, from behind the heavily shuttered windows, hidden eyes watched their approach. Apart from a few scrawny hens, which pecked around a large pile of manure, no animal was to be seen. A recently-built well stood near the house. One of the men drew up its wooden pail and they were delighted to discover that the water was cold and clear. After quenching their thirst, they filled some soft leather bags with the precious liquid and closed the necks by means of thongs.

For a while they rested beside the well, but the lack of shade encouraged them to return to camp. Huw and Idwal walked side by side. The mercenary's ugly scar showed vividly against his deeply tanned face and Huw was concerned to notice that his friend was breathing heavily.

"Do you still prefer this way of life to all else, Idwal?"

Huw asked, grinning affectionately at the man. "Surely, you must wish for an easier employment. I could find work enough for you at Argoed."

Idwal stopped and wiped the sweat from his brow. "I'm not ready for the knacker's knife yet, Longshanks," he said. "Though I do find this heat hard to bear. The mountains of home would be a welcome sight right now. However, I'm going to settle for the next best thing and cool off in the river. Are you coming?"

Without waiting for Huw's answer, he walked down to the sands and Huw followed him to the water's edge. Most of the horsemen had returned to camp, leaving one group further upstream. The tide was beginning to come in and, stripping off, the two bowmen lay half in, half out of the slowly moving water, welcoming its coolness. The longer they lay there, the faster the current became; when it began to tug at their bodies, they moved back onto the sand. Huw was pulling on his shirt when the soft thudding of approaching hooves reached him. The men-at-arms swept past at a gallop, most of them now bare-headed. Hardly able to believe his eyes, Huw saw an ash blonde head amongst the foremost riders. The shock of recognition was akin to a physical blow, and made him gasp.

"Hell's fire!" he exclaimed. "It's him, Idwal. It is Richard Lloyd, I swear it."

All the doubts and anxieties vanished in a moment. Richard had not perished in the waters off Southampton, nor been struck down by the fever, as Huw had feared. His hand moved instinctively to the hilt of his heavy, short sword. He was now sure that his journey and its dangers had not been in vain.

Assisted by a page boy, Henry V, king of England, bathed the dried sweat from his body, lightly towelled himself dry, and dressed himself in clean hose and a fine linen shirt, his eyes resting on the gold-plated helmet which stood with his armour in a corner of the tent. This symbol of his authority reminded him that it was his only for as long as he was able to hold on to it. Few kings had been as ruthless as his father, and he had died in his prime, a broken man, with many enemies. A few of these enemies were here in France, come in answer to his summons, and he was well aware that they hoped that he would be defeated.

Leaving his shirt loose at the neck, he quitted the tent and began to wander through the camp. Familiar with this habit, his soldiers greeted him openly, welcoming his presence amongst them. He enjoyed their coarse banter and was more at ease amongst these rough men than in the company of his nobles. At some of the camp fires he was not recognised and he would stop for a while, listening to the conversation before moving on. The men were losing heart as the siege wore on and he could not blame them for that. The cannon had pounded ineffectually at Harfleur for longer than six weeks, yet the walls gave no sign of weakening.

The next day would be Sunday, the twenty-second day of September, the date on which the citizens of the port had agreed to surrender, if no aid came to them from Paris. Mounted patrols had been sent out to seek for approaching French forces and the English troops, to a man, prayed that they would find none. Two thousand men had already died at Harfleur, many from the fever which raged through the encampments. Others were so weakened by sickness that they had to be returned to England. It was late at night when the sentries outside the young King's quarters gave a challenge. Henry was already on his feet when Thomas Erpingham entered.

"Our patrols have returned, my lord," the elderly knight informed him. "They bring you the best of news; they rode the better part of twenty-five miles inland and saw not one French soldier." With a smile, he added, "Harfleur will be yours on the morrow. We can garrison the port, then, God be praised, sail home. We can return with a fresh army next year and march from here to Paris."

The King slowly shook his head. "I have thought deeply about what must be done, now that the town will surrender. To have only Harfleur to show for such a costly enterprise would make me the laughing stock of the French court. It would only serve to encourage them to take my French possessions. I know that we no longer have the strength to march on Paris but if we move quickly, we can make for Calais. It can only do good to show myself to my subjects."

The knight turned away, to hide his concern, then cleared his throat and spoke out boldly. "It would be a risky move, sire. Should we be caught by the French, we would be overwhelmed. We would number six thousand men at the most. It gives us little chance against their armies."

"That is a risk that I have to take," Henry replied. "However, I am sure that, by marching swiftly, we can evade any confrontation. See to it that Gloucester and the others attend me as soon as I have received the keys of Harfleur. We must plan our line of march."

Chapter 26

Huw cleared the dust from his throat and spat on the ground. "A sorry sight," he commented. "It would seem that it is always the innocent who suffer the most in war."

"Never a truer word was spoken," David agreed. "I doubt that there are any who defied the King amongst these poor wretches."

The two were standing close to the road from Harfleur, watching the forced eviction of most of the town's inhabitants, many were elderly and infirm, some of these were being pushed along in handcarts, a number of women carried children in their arms. The fear of what lay ahead of them showed clearly, though a few faces held signs of anger and resentment. A small family group passed by and a young woman called out something in her native tongue.

"She thanks us for sending them out to starve," David said. "She hopes that our loved ones will suffer the same fate."

Huw thought immediately of Elinor and his two sons and, unable to stomach the scene any longer, turned away. "Come, David," he said. "Our presence only adds to their grief. We know that there is not food enough for all these mouths, yet the King's decision to be rid of them is a cruel one."

They began to walk back to the camp, occasionally looking back at the sorry trail of refugees.

"I wonder what King Henry plans to do," David said. "I heard that he intended to make for Paris. That seems unlikely now."

"Don't be too sure," Huw replied. "That young man has the nerve to try anything. Remember what he did to us over the years in Wales."

"How can I forget? Yet he is no fool, Huw. Thomas Hunt reckons that almost half the army have died, or will be returned home, too sick to continue. Henry will not have the numbers to face the French. One thing is sure though, my friend, the decision will not be made by either of us," David said.

They walked on in silence until they were close to the camp. David looked up at his friend and said, "It seems that our hope of encountering Richard Lloyd in a favourable place is fading. The safest place for you to exact your revenge would be on a field of battle. You have to be patient and await the right opportunity. He is not worth swinging for and you have a family to think of. Do not be rash. He will keep a while."

***

The King, having heard his advisers, got to his feet and looked at the anxious faces around him. "Very well, I shall bow to your opinions," he said. "Paris will have to wait until we can return with a new army. However, I must insist that we do not abandon everything and sail for England."

The nobles looked towards their spokesman, the Duke of York, who remained silent.

"We could march swiftly for Calais," Henry suggested. "We have a strong force there, who could meet us part way and add to our strength."

"By your leave, my lord," the Duke said firmly, "I would like to hear whether Sir Thomas Erpingham thinks that we would have a fair chance of success in such a venture. He is the most experienced of us all with regard to soldiering in France. Pray do not misunderstand my meaning, Sire. I will follow you anywhere, yet we must think of those men out there. It would be a criminal act should we lead them to certain death."

Henry motioned to the elderly knight to speak, then seated himself once more, feeling his tension ease.

"Such a move can succeed," Thomas Erpingham said. "The Somme river will be our only natural obstacle, and I know of a ford, Blanche Taque by name, where we can cross with ease in this dry weather. Beyond the river lies a straight road for Calais. Paramount is the need for speed. The longer we tarry, the greater chance there is of meeting the French army."

The Duke of York looked at the assembled knights, who one by one nodded their agreement. "We are willing to take the risk, then" he said. "It will be a bold move, Sire, and we may have the last laugh."

The King thanked his nobles and bade them prepare their men. "I agree with Sir Thomas," he said. "Our swiftness on the march will be of the utmost importance. We shall leave here on the morrow."

Henry's proposal to make for Paris had met with the expected disapproval and, as he had rightly guessed, they had grasped at his suggested compromise. He smiled to himself and was satisfied.

Henry's army of some six thousand, the bulk of which were bowmen, had marched for six hard days. Mercifully, the heat had begun to ease after the first day and they were able to keep up a good pace. Before them lay the Somme and their spirits, already high, rose even higher. Beyond that river, their captains had told them, lay Calais and safety. In good heart, they strode out. Someone began to sing a ditty, which was picked up by those around him. The leading bowmen were almost at the water's edge, when they were suddenly ordered to halt. From up ahead, scouts rode furiously back to the column, their faces grim.

"There's something ill in the air," Idwal commented. "Did you see the way they looked? They might have seen the Devil himself."

In the company of the Dukes of York and Gloucester, Henry questioned the scout who had given the news. "Tell me again, more slowly, I beseech you," he ordered.

"It is true, sire," the scout said. "The French hold Blanche Taque with an army equal to ours. We took a prisoner, probably a deserter, for he was alone and swam to our side of the river."

Henry questioned the frightened prisoner but learnt little more than what the scout had already told him. There was useful item of gossip, that the Frenchman repeated in his endeavour to please his captors. It was rumoured in the French force that the main body of their army would arrive soon at the ford. The man was sent away under escort, to join the other prisoners of war.

"What now? Do we return to Harfleur?" York asked.

"We do not," Henry snapped. "I grant that we are not strong enough to force a passage at Blanche Taque but I am not giving up so easily. Rest the men for a while, then we shall seek another crossing place, upstream."

The bowmen listened in gloomy silence when Thomas Hunt passed on the news.

"I don't know my way around this countryside," one man said, "but if we go further inland, that must surely mean we will be marching further from Calais."

Rested and fed, the army moved into country which was new to Sir Thomas Erpingham, and Henry ordered a party of men-at-arms to ride ahead and seek out the best route. Other mounted men rode to the front of the column, and Huw stepped out of the ranks to see what was taking place up ahead. The nearest horse swerved to avoid him and he moved hastily back. The rider looked down at him from less than three paces away and he instantly recognised the man. Richard Lloyd galloped past and drew rein to glance over his shoulder. Huw pushed his way back through the bowmen to the furthest rank, anxious to hide himself from his hated brother-in-law. Ignoring his companions' curses and puzzled looks, he kept his head down for a while. When he cautiously stood upright, he saw Richard chasing after the other riders. Later that day, when the column were enjoying a brief rest, he told David of the occurrence.

"I hope he recognised you," the secretary said. "Let him stew in the knowledge that he is not safe anywhere."

"What of Thomas Hunt? Does he still believe that the Duke of York agreed that you are to stay with him?" Huw asked.

"That he does," David chuckled. "I think he would be the last man to question it. You know that he is the envy of the other captains, having a translator at his side." He opened his pouch, took out a stale piece of crust and popped it into his mouth.

"I have a feeling in my bowels that your chance to get at Richard will soon present itself," he said, chewing away. "I'd wager the French are not going to allow us to parade through these lands to Calais without a fight."

On the following day the army continued its march, its pace quickening as the miles passed by, and Huw was reminded of the sense of desperation experienced on the march to Shrewsbury, so many years ago. In mid-morning, they passed a corpse swinging from a tree branch, guarded by an English knight in full armour.

"Take heed of the King's command," he called out. "Yonder is one who thought fit to steal from the Holy Church. The same fate awaits any man who steals from a farm or home."

The further inland they marched, growing discontent amongst the men became more evident. Supplies were running low and hunger forced them to think of how to fill their empty bellies. The nobles urged King Henry to relax his ruling on foraging but this he refused to do. Instead, he rode up and down the length of the marching column, cajoling his bowmen, who cheered up at his humour.

On the third day after they turned upstream, a strong body of French knights charged the advance party of men-at-arms. In response to shouted commands, the bowmen strung their bows in readiness but the fighting remained far ahead. To their right the fields had given way to thick woodland.

The King pointed towards the trees and spoke to his captains. "Have your men cut themselves each a stake and sharpen both ends," he told them. "Tell them to keep it to hand wherever they go. Should the French charge us, drive one end into the earth with its point facing the enemy."

When the bowmen caught up with the resting men-at-arms, Thomas Hunt called David to his side. "Stay close to me from now on," he said. "The King has commanded me to protect the mounted men. I want you to ensure that your countrymen understand my orders, for the French would take advantage of any delay on our part." A smile came over the face of the chubby Welshman. "Have I said something amusing?" Hunt asked, in a dry tone.

"Not at all," the secretary answered. "It is just a memory coming into my mind."

"Go tell your friends what we are about," Thomas said. "Make sure that they know what the stakes are for."

Still chuckling to himself, David went amongst the Welsh bowmen and repeated Thomas's words. His amusement became almost uncontrollable when he saw that Huw had jammed a wide-brimmed helmet on his head.

"Richard may not recognise me again, should he ride close," Huw growled. "I've carried the accursed thing all the way from Harfleur, I might as well make use of it. Will you stop that stupid laughter, it cannot be as comical as that."

"It's not your helmet," David chortled, trying desperately to suppress his mirth. "It is the fact you are ordered to protect the very man you have sworn to kill. I find that situation very comical indeed."

After a further march, the army came to a place where the river swung northward, forming a great bend, and Henry commanded his men to march straight on. The French, who shadowed them on the far bank, were forced to follow the longer, outer curve of the bend, and Henry made full use of this advantage. While there was enough daylight left, he urged his tiring army onward; aching legs lengthened their stride. Their route soon became cluttered with unwanted items of clothing and pieces of heavy armour, discarded as exhausted men struggled to keep up with the column. When the order to halt was given, the majority immediately lay down where they were. They were on the move again soon after daybreak, and a watery sun hung low in the grey sky when the Somme barred their way once more. The earth, which had been baked hard during the past summer, now began to soften under their passing feet; when they came to the river's edge, the bowmen were spattered in evil-smelling mud.

The King and several of his nobles dismounted and cast anxious glances at the far bank and the river. The flow of water here was sluggish and Henry called for a volunteer to try his luck in crossing over. Thomas Hunt jumped in and began to wade across, the water, at its deepest, coming up to his chest. As soon as he had reached the far bank, Henry waved the watching bowmen forward and, in twos and threes, they slid into the river, those on the bank helping them. When his turn came, Huw grasped an offered hand, his helmet tipping aside as he lowered himself in. Feeling his feet touch the river bottom, he started to turn away from the bank but the helping hand kept its grip. Rather startled at this, he looked up and stared straight into King Henry's eyes, which held a puzzled look. For a few moments King and bowman looked intently at each other, then Henry released his grip. He watched the tall bowman wade through the river for a little longer, before turning to help the next man. The dark face had touched a vague memory of a stormy night and a crowded north Wales tavern, long ago. With a smile, he put the thought from his mind, for there had been many visits to such taverns in his youth.

God smiled on the young King that morning for he had his army safely across the river by noon, and the road to Calais lay open to him. The elation he felt was soon to be replaced by anger. The army had marched scarcely three miles from the river, when they came to a small village. Hanging boldly from every dwelling were strips of red-dyed cloth. Henry did not need Sir Thomas Erpingham to explain these were there to show defiance in the French manner. His anger was because these people were his lawful subjects; he relaxed his orders about pillaging food from the land. The villagers had prepared themselves for his wrath, hiding their animals in nearby woods, but this proved to be of no avail. The bulk of Henry's army was made up of veterans and they gleefully showed their experience in looting. Leaving David to gather firewood, Huw and Idwal set off in search of a meal, finding it in a barn almost full of hay. Standing silently in the gloomy building, in its depths, they heard a faint rustle and the unmistakable clucking of hens. They dived into the loosely packed hay, causing a flurry of feathers to fly into the air. When they emerged from the barn, they carried a brace of birds apiece. David had lit a fire by the time they returned and the three cleaned the birds, feathered them, then sat waiting for them to roast. Once the meat was sufficiently cooked, the three ate ravenously, leaving not a scrap of the tender, white meat.

By some strange chance, it was Richard Lloyd who found evidence that the King's route to Calais was yet in peril. In the company of some of his fellow men-at-arms, he had ridden ahead of the bowmen, taking advantage of the open ground, which allowed a clear view for at least a mile. As his mount walked along, Richard's thoughts turned to the rich meadow-land at Plas Hirnant, and he knew that his decision to come on this campaign had been the right one. By being here, he could win the King's favour and, once that had been achieved, he would have the protection he needed to enable him to return to his inheritance. The Welsh rebel who had married Elinor would not dare to raise a hand against him, if the Welshman still lived. The thought of the bowman he had glimpsed amongst the column came to mind. The man had looked similar to Huw Gethin but there was small chance that it really had been he. Richard dismissed the thought. His horse came to a halt and brought his thoughts back to the present.

Richard felt a tug of fear course through his bowels when he saw what had made his horse stop. In front of him, the earth had been churned up in a broad band, two hundred paces across, the great scar sweeping on in the direction of Calais. Dismounting, he saw that the churned up soil was still fresh, countless prints of men and horses clearly visible.

"By all that is holy, this is what I had feared," a voice said suddenly at his elbow.

Spinning around, Richard found himself face to face with a dark-complexioned man, who trailed his horse's reins in one hand. "The full might of France has passed this way," Dafydd Gam exclaimed. "I knew in my bones that they would not allow the King a free passage,"

Richard looked wildly at this Welshman who had remained loyal to the King during the recent war.

"Perhaps we can make a detour and slip past them," he suggested.

"I doubt that, my friend," Gam replied. "The French will surely cover every route leading north. What we do is not our decision. We must inform the King."

It was as they remounted and set off back to the army, that they felt the first drops of rain.

Henry listened to their report without showing his feelings. "It seems the game is not yet over, my lords," he said to the gathered noblemen, when the two had finished. "We can try to avoid the French but I have little hope of that. We shall turn west for a day, then resume our march north. Urge the men to make speed while they may. By the look of these gathering clouds, they will not have firm ground under their feet for much longer." Rain pattered on the canvas of his tent.

Their march westward was, indeed, soon slowed by heavy rain, which turned the ground into a quagmire for those at the rear. Anxious to keep their bowstrings dry, some of the men wrapped the twine around their bellies, trusting in their leather jerkins to keep off the rain, others stuffed theirs under their clumsy helmets. After a miserable, sodden night, they turned north, slogging through the thickening mud, their legs aching at the increasing strain. The men were strangely quiet that day, the only sound a muffled curse as someone slipped. Another wet, endless night, after a meal only part-cooked over spluttering fires, was rewarded by yet another day of heavy rain.

At noon of that day, Henry was summoned forward to attend the advanced screen of mounted men. The expressions on their faces forewarned him, but when he saw the sight which lay ahead, he caught his breath.

Drawn up in a dense line between two woods, the army of France awaited his coming. Even to an untrained eye, which Henry's was not, it was clear that this was no hastily gathered body of knights and soldiers. From the number of banners carried in the forefront, it seemed that everyone of rank in France stood to face the King of England. Forcing himself to sit upright in the saddle, Henry brushed the rain from his brow.

"What do you make of this magnificent spectacle?" he asked those around him. "Their numbers must be of some concern."

"We believe that they have ten lines of men and horses," one of the men-at-arms told him. "By our reckoning, there are some thirty thousand Frenchmen in front of us."

The mounted men waited for the king to speak but he remained silent for a long while, frowning in thought.

"Thirty thousand, you say? I calculate that we have five Frenchmen to every Englishman. Good odds, I would say, and scarcely worthy of our prowess. Since we cannot out-march them, we must out-fight them. Stay here and watch for signs of movement on their part. I shall return to the main body of men and draw up my line of battle."

To the sounds of drums and trumpets, the weary bowmen made ready, their eyes continually glancing towards the enemy host so dangerously close. When their battle-lines were in order, they stood in the rain, waiting for their foes to advance, and they were still waiting when darkness descended over the sodden fields.

Few men slept that night, but the rain eased. The majority huddled around smoking fires, talking quietly, or lost in thought.

"I wish it were daylight," one of Huw's comrades said. "I have always found the waiting more frightening than the battle itself. It allows your mind to think of what might happen to you."

"I'd not wish too hard, were I you," another remarked. "There's small chance any of us will live through the morrow."

"My mind is set on one matter," a voice said from the darkness. "I shall not be made prisoner. The French will cut off our fingers. That is their way with bowmen, and I've no wish to live as a beggar."

Such talk disturbed Huw, who walked away and found a place that afforded a clear view of the French camp fires. He was very much aware that his plan to exact vengeance had gone terribly wrong; he was far from Cwmdu and those he loved, with little hope of seeing them again. The words of the unseen speaker came to mind and he shuddered at the thought of losing his fingers. He stood watching the fires for a while longer, then told himself that being alone was worse than listening to idle talk. He returned to his place between Idwal and David.

Shortly afterwards, there was a general stirring amongst the bowmen, and Huw saw the King standing close by. A man-servant held a spluttering torch high, lighting Henry's face, and he began to speak to the bowmen, first addressing himself to Huw and his two constant companions.

"Did you serve the man named Owain Glyndŵr?" he asked, in broken Welsh.

"That we did, sire," David answered boldly. "From the beginning to the end."

The King studied their faces for a while and he smiled at Huw, now certain who he was. "We have travelled a long road since our last meeting," he said. "Though the weather has not changed a jot. My captains tell me that there are many of your countrymen amongst my archers. I pray that you will fight as well for me as you did for Glyndŵr." With these words, the King moved along to the next group of bowmen.

The Welshmen watched him until the torchlight faded from sight, then, as they had done so often in the past, they huddled closer for warmth and waited for the dawn.

Chapter 27

"I do believe the French are scheming to starve us to death," David remarked, as they watched their foe. "It must be past noon by now and they have not moved one step towards us."

"They could be waiting for more men to arrive," Idwal remarked, grinning. "It is likely that they have heard of your presence on the field."

Since daybreak, Henry's small army had stood in line before the awesome power of France, yet their foe seemed content to wait. Indeed, the King was placed in an unbelievable position. Faced by an enemy which heavily outnumbered him, it seemed that he would have to commence the battle.

"Enough of this waiting," he said to Thomas Erpingham. "Order your men forward to within bow's shot. Let us see if we can sting the French into movement. You have been proven right, Thomas, they have learned the lesson of Crécy and will not charge us."

To the blare of trumpets, the three divisions of his army began to move forward, the men's spirits lifting, now that they were at last on the move. They had covered some two hundred paces, when it became clear that the bordering woods came closer at this point, forcing the captains to shorten their lines.

Ten paces ahead of his men, Thomas Hunt called to his neighbouring captain. "We should call a halt here. Their cavalry will be unable to strike at our flanks."

The King, accompanied by the Duke of York, rode forward to find the cause of the halt and they quickly agreed with Hunt's strategy.

"Place some of your men amongst the trees," Henry told him. "They can do deadly work from there. Can your bowmen reach the French from this place?"

Thomas eyed the distance then said, "It is some three hundred paces, sire, we will not pierce their armour but they will have to move one way or another."

Standing in the centre of Thomas's men, Huw looked yet again at the men-at-arms who were positioned to his left. They were now on foot and many, including Richard, had removed their helmets for the moment. The ash blonde hair showed clearly and, satisfied that he could find the man when an opportunity arose, Huw turned his attention to the French. Now that the foe was closer, their numbers were fearful to behold. Rank upon rank of armoured knights, standing shoulder to shoulder, formed an unbreakable wall; behind them stood a mass of foot soldiers.

"Drive your stakes in firmly, lads," Thomas called out. "Then make ready to loose your arrows."

His orders were quickly carried out and the men stood ready, an arrow notched in every bowstring. Thomas Erpingham waited until the Duke of York took up his position in the centre and raised his sword. The Duke glanced to left and right and, seeing that all was ready, brought the blade down in a sweeping arc.

"Loose at will," Thomas shouted, his voice pitched high in excitement.

His order was repeated down the length of the line and, with the noise of a rushing wind, a great shadow of arrows flashed across the sky and fell amongst the closely packed French.

The bowmen repeated the attack and kept a constant hail of deadly shafts upon the French, giving no respite. Shooting as his comrades did, Huw did not bother to take aim but sent one shaft after another into the ranks of his enemy. A growing din of human and animal screams came from the French army as the bowmen continued to shoot, confirmation that many of their arrows were now finding flesh through armour or leather. Sending his last arrow winging away, Huw looked over his shoulder and saw a number of young lads hurrying amongst the bowmen, dropping bundles of arrows within easy reach.

"Now we're for it. Look, yonder," Idwal yelled, snatching a handful of the feathered shafts. "They are making a move at last."

Out of the confused French lines, mounted knights were riding forward, their shields held high. Huw saw them form together in readiness to charge. A trumpet blast rent the air and the heavy horses began to move forward. At first they approached at a trot, but as the distance between bowmen and horses shortened, the knights urged them into a run.

"Aim at the horses," Thomas screamed. "Bring them down, lads, else we are dead men."

The arrows streaked away, no longer arching through the sky, but speeding parallel to the ground. The bowmen now chose their targets, but such was the density of the shafts that no man could see where his arrow went. Horses began to go down in a welter of thrashing hooves, sending their riders crashing to the earth and bringing others down with them. Yet, on the French came, lowering their shields to protect their eyes as they closed on the Henry's soldiers.

Huw quickly drew and loosed, at almost point blank range, at a knight clad in black and gold armour. His arrow struck with such force, that his foe was lifted from the saddle and fell backward into the path of another charger. The animal reared up, skidding wildly on its haunches, and came to a sudden stop when a sharpened stake pierced its soft belly. For a few awful moments, it stood screaming in agony, until a bowman lunged forward and severed a neck artery.

From along the line of bowmen, there came the sound of snapping timber, as the French struck the stakes and horses and riders fell to the ground. Unbelievably, a few knights regained their feet and started towards the men who had tormented them. Immediately to Huw's front, a knight swayed to his feet and lunged forward, gripping a shattered lance in his hands. Leaping nimbly aside, Huw brought his bow down on the helmeted head with all his strength. The blow knocked the Frenchman to his knees and he disappeared under a surge of bowmen with flashing knives.

Gradually the fighting eased and the bowmen leaned on their bow staffs, chests heaving, their damp clothing sending up small clouds of steam. The knights who had managed to remain in the saddle, rode slowly back to their lines, leaving many of their dead and dying comrades behind. However, if any of Henry's men felt like cheering, that mood was quickly stifled. From the French camp, there now came a dense mass of men, moving slowly over the churned up earth. Pikemen, crossbow-men, men-at-arms, all packed tightly together and led by knights on foot, advanced in a seemingly unstoppable tide. Glancing briefly to where he had last seen Richard, Huw saw that he was amongst the men gathered around the Duke of York. At the same moment, he heard that nobleman's command for the bowmen to shoot. Once more the arrows sliced through the air, doing their deadly work, causing dreadful slaughter amongst the more lightly armoured foe. The Frenchmen's courage was beyond belief; despite the carnage, they pressed on, tripping over their fallen comrades. When their front rank reached the mass of dead knights, they unhesitatingly scrambled over the obstruction. Their eagerness to get to grips with the bowmen of England became their undoing, for they became so tightly wedged together, that only a few of their number were able to strike a blow.

Henry's men threw aside their bows and used knives, short swords or swinging captured maces, and flung themselves upon the helpless enemy. A crazy killing lust seemed to take hold as they stabbed and struck blows at the Frenchmen, and the mounds of dead grew higher. Close by, Huw heard someone begin to laugh hysterically; at his shoulder, Idwal made a strange whining sound as he lashed out. He felt himself caught up in this madness and, scrambling over the corpses, he began to swing his heavy knife. By this time, the bodies were covered by liquid mud and, in a few moments, Huw slid helplessly into the French. He was frantically trying to regain his feet when a mailed fist struck him between the eyes and he fell back under the trampling feet.

In blind panic, he lashed out as a surge of men passed over him, threatening to crush him into the mud. He felt the earthy taste in his mouth and found that his nostrils were clogged by blood and breathing was difficult. He knew then that he was going to die, choking in this filthy slime. He tried to think of Elinor but his brain would not function beyond the thought of death and as another crush of men passed over him, he resigned himself to the inevitable. Then, miraculously, a hand grabbed hold of his hair and lifted his head clear of the mud. As though from afar, he heard David's voice call his name, then more hands caught hold and pulled him clear.

"This is not the place to take a nap, Longshanks," Idwal shouted. "Get on your feet and make for the rear."

Summoning all of his remaining strength, Huw stood upright, swaying as though in a drunken stupor. His head was still ringing from the blow and, scarcely aware of the mayhem around him, he wove his way between the bowmen. He had taken no more than a dozen steps before his knees buckled, and he would have fallen if Thomas Hunt had not seen his plight. Grabbing hold of Huw's jerkin, the captain propelled him to where a group of wounded lay at the rear of the melee.

"Stay here awhile," he commanded. "When you regain your senses, rejoin us. You were lucky. Had we lost the ground, you would have been a dead man by now."

Huw sat down in the mud, to ease his trembling legs. He had not understood every word that the captain had spoken, but had got the gist of it. He had indeed been fortunate. Muttering a prayer of thanks, he remained seated for a while, until the ringing in his head ceased. He took stock of his condition. From head to toe he was caked in mud, blood still trickled from his nose and he became aware of an unpleasant, tight feeling over his brow. He was unable to open his eyes fully and, on gingerly touching his brow, he found it badly swollen. There was no doubt that, should he live through this day, he would be sporting a pair of blackened eyes. Despite his fall and the trampling feet, he still held his heavy knife. He drew the blade under his armpit, to clean it.

When he felt better, he carefully got to his feet and began to walk slowly down the line of struggling men, his eyes searching for the men-at-arms. If he was to kill Richard, it would have to be now, before his luck ran out. Ahead of him, the line suddenly swayed backward as a fresh body of Frenchmen flung their weight into the fighting. For a brief moment, a gap appeared and when he stepped into the space, Huw saw a knot of mailed Englishmen, desperately hacking away with their swords. They were being pushed backwards, slowly but surely, by the sheer press of their foes. When Huw raised his knife to protect himself, they split apart.

His helmet gone, his ash blonde hair flattened by sweat and mud, Richard stood before him alone. Huw tried to call his name but his voice was no more than a croak. Turning the knife point upward, he moved forward, his intention obvious. Richard stared in bewilderment, until, suddenly, recognition struck him. Huw saw him mouth some unheard words, raise his sword high and take a step toward him. The next moment, he forgot Richard as a wave of Frenchmen flooded over the heaped bodies and surged forward.

One confrontation with the enemy at close quarters was enough for any man and, frightened out of his wits, Huw turned and ran, heart pounding wildly, feet slithering in the mud. He forced his tired legs to keep moving until he rejoined David and Idwal. By now, all the bowmen were close to exhaustion, barely able to strike a blow with any strength yet, somehow, they fought on as though possessed by demons. How long the killing lasted no man could tell for certain. The French seemed to come at them for ever, giving no respite. The bowmen had almost given up all hope when, imperceptibly at first, their enemy began to melt away. The movement caught hold and soon all the Frenchmen were making for their encampment. Many of them retired in good order, however, keeping their faces turned towards the bowmen in brave defiance. Not a man in Henry's army made a move to follow. Bruised and battered, weary beyond belief, they watched the retreat in silence.

"Well, lads, that's it for me," Idwal gasped, sinking to his knees. "I think that I shall seek my livelihood some other way. A man can get seriously hurt being a soldier. Is your offer of work at Cwmdu still holding, Long-shanks?"

Huw saw the awful grin on Idwal's mud spattered face and nodded. "That it is. Do you know something, Idwal. I've always suspected that there was a little sense somewhere in that head of yours. I am truly glad that you have found it."

"Are you recovered?" David asked, looking up into Huw's face. "God's blood, but you are a frightening sight. You have the worst blackened eyes that I've seen, and I have seen plenty of them." He took hold of Huw's arm and led him away from the other bowmen, "What of Richard Lloyd'?" he asked. "Did you find him when you were sent to the rear?"

Huw told his friend what had happened, including the fact that he had run for his life at the critical moment.

"None can blame you for that," David said. "I cannot think of a worse death than being smothered in this muck. I should know, for it nearly happened to me at Hyddgen, as you may remember."

Exhausted as they were, the bowmen began to search for missing comrades amongst the mounds of bodies, or with the hope of finding a French knight still alive. They kept watch on the French encampment but their foe gave no sign of returning to the field. Indeed, before long, they were told that the King's scouts had reported large numbers of the French on the road back to Paris. The three friends were amongst those ordered to search for the Duke of York, who had been fighting with his men-at-arms. They found the nobleman dead beneath a pile of bodies; close by him lay Richard Lloyd, face down in the mud and with no trace of a wound. The three concluded that he must have suffocated to death. Huw stared down with mixed feelings at the body of the man who had caused him so much grief. The fact that he had not personally caused his death rankled slightly, but it had happened. Richard had suffered a fate far worse than a thrust from Huw's knife. He looked at the corpse once more, then turned and walked away.

On the following morning, Henry's army restarted their march north. A funeral pyre burned fiercely behind them, turning the dead of both armies into ashes, which the winds would later blow over this French field, where some ten thousand had fallen and would lie forever. Huw's gaze followed the grey smoke skyward and he wondered if Morgan and Hywel were watching from somewhere up there. The flames reminded him of the burning of Argoed and Plas Hirnant, and he thought of the new home waiting for him. Saying a silent prayer of thanks for his deliverance, he set his face once more to the north and Elinor.

Titles already published

Aberdyfi: Past and Present – Hugh M Lewis £6.95
Aberdyfi: The Past Recalled – Hugh M Lewis £6.95
Ar Bwys y Ffald – Gwilym Jenkins £7.95
Blodeuwedd – Ogmore Batt £5.95
Black Mountains – David Barnes £6.95
Choose Life! – Phyllis Oostermeijer £5.95
Cwpan y Byd a dramâu eraill – J O Evans £4.95
Dragonrise – David Morgan Williams £4.95
Dysgl Bren a Dysgl Arian – R Elwyn Hughes £9.95
The Fizzing Stone – Liz Whittaker £4.95
The Wonders of Dan yr Ogof – Sarah Symons £6.95
You Don't Speak Welsh – Sandi Thomas £5.95
Clare's Dream – J Gillman Gwynne £4.95
In Garni's Wake – John Rees £7.95
A Dragon To Agincourt – Malcolm Price £6.95
The Dragon Wakes – Jim Wingate £6.95
Stand Up and Sing – Beatrice Smith £4.95

*For more information
about this innovative imprint,
contact Lefi Gruffudd at
lefi@ylolfa.com
or go to www.ylolfa.com/dinas.
A Dinas catalogue
is now being produced.*